"WHO ARE YOU, SINCLAIR?"

Louisa put her hand to her head, which was beginning to ache horridly. "Why do I find you in this moldy place, waiting to torment me with jests and barbs? You are as slippery as an eel. I swear I will dance with glee the day you are gone from my life."

His gaze slammed into hers. His eyes darkened and suddenly lost their guile. When he spoke, his voice sounded distant, utterly removed from the man who possessed it.

"I am the twelfth Baron Sinclair, the last of my line. This castle is mine, and the temple and these ruins and the manor house and the land for as far as you can see. And no one is alive to know it, Miss Peabody, or to rejoice in the fact that the prodigal has returned home at last."

His raw, bitter grin tore a gaping hole in her heart.

"A superior romance brimming with delicious wit, passionate intensity, and stunning originality."
Romantic Times

Other **AVON ROMANCES**

EILEEN PUTMAN

Never Trust A Rake

AVON BOOKS ◆ NEW YORK

AVON BOOKS, INC.
1350 Avenue of the Americas
New York, New York 10019

Copyright © 1999 by Eileen Putman
Published by arrangement with the author
Library of Congress Catalog Card Number: 98-94853
ISBN: 0-380-80289-9
www.avonbooks.com/romance

First Avon Books Printing: July 1999

AVON TRADEMARK REG. U.S. PAT. OFF. AND IN OTHER COUNTRIES, MARCA REGISTRADA, HECHO EN U.S.A.

Printed in the U.S.A.

WCD 10 9 8 7 6 5 4 3 2 1

For Alan

Prologue

London, 1818

He wasn't about to traipse all over England looking for virgins.

Not as long as Our Lady of Mercy convent lay cheek to jowl with the Market Street dock, where his new boat bobbed in waters swollen by high tide. With any luck, he could be on his way before the tide went out.

Like most of the ladies he met, luck danced to his tune. This very night, luck had dealt him a royal flush and the Earl of Sedbury a measly pair of tens, thereby gifting him with the earl's trim little yacht. Luck had not given him the courage to sneak into a convent full of sleeping nuns, but he had found that in the earl's wine.

The gnarled gypsy who had emerged from the midnight shadows as a glum Sedbury was showing him around the boat would have given any man pause. An ageless wisdom inhabited her wrinkled face, and her eyes gleamed with fury.

"Death," she intoned, pointing her bony finger at them. "Death seeks to bring you into his bosom. Bring me a lock of hair from a virgin's head, taken without harm, given without regret. Only then will death loose his grip on your soul."

Sedbury had shooed the woman away. "They haunt the docks," he grumbled. "It's that new penitentiary. Too close by half. Brings the riffraff round." He eyed the yacht wistfully. "Always meant to move her upriver."

They had shared a laugh at the old woman's attempt to scare them off the boat she'd evidently chosen as her bed tonight. Then a strange light had come into Sedbury's eyes, and the wine had flowed anew, and the gypsy's words became a reckless new bet that sent each man reeling drunkenly into the night in search of a lock of hair from a virgin, one of the scarcest commodities in all London.

The gypsy's curse had not bothered Gabriel. He was not afraid of death. In the years since leaving England, he had beaten that black angel more times than he could count. Boredom alone unsettled him, for it left him face to face with a man he did not care to visit long.

Anyway, the gypsy had it wrong. Luck, not death, embraced him tonight. Luck had caused him to wander past this little convent after bidding Sedbury adieu, thereby showing him the means of depriving the earl of his London home, the stake in Sedbury's wager to try to regain his boat. Desperate men made unwise bets. The earl would never find a virgin at this hour, when chaste women slept peacefully in their own beds.

Gabriel suppressed a yawn. What did he need with Sedbury's townhouse, anyway? He did not intend to remain in England, though it might be diverting to sample the life he could have had if fate had dealt him a different hand so many years ago. But a boat was all he really needed. With it, he could bid the past farewell as sweetly as these innocent maidens had said their evening prayers.

Alone in the dark, he stood silently in the stark chamber, studying the women whose heads were presumably filled with chaste dreams. They were young—novitiates, most likely. A veritable bevy of virgins.

Which would he choose? Gabriel studied their sleeping forms, forever removed from the world of men. He imagined them in the secular world, dressed in fine gowns and jewels, their hair piled high atop their heads and secured with combs of finest ivory. They would fan themselves coyly, each daring him to choose her. Would he select the blonde, the chestnut-haired, or the chit with the riot of auburn curls? He could have his pick, for they adored him. Women always did. They were all alike: vain and prideful and needy. Even nuns, he suspected, had their vanity.

He slipped a knife from the slim leather holder he always wore under his waistcoat.

One by one, he inspected them. He slid quickly past the cot of one young woman

whose breathing was shallow and uneven—
too light a sleeper. He passed two others
whose nightcaps obscured their hair. At last he
came to a young woman whose single braid
lay invitingly on the pillow. She snored so
loudly that nothing short of cannon fire would
wake her.

He stared at the knife and wondered
whether he had lost his mind. *A lock of hair
from a virgin's head, taken without harm, given
without regret.* He had not believed in the
gypsy's words, but he did believe in the fate
that masqueraded as luck. For the moment, he
would be its pawn.

Gingerly, he lifted the braid, feeling its
weight, judging its substance. He could certainly take it without harm; he wasn't sure
about the regret part. Then again, the chit
could hardly regret what she didn't yet know.
He shifted the knife to his right hand and bent
over the girl.

"What are you doing?"

He froze. Carefully, he turned toward the
voice. The girl he had pegged as a light sleeper
sat upright, staring at him. "What are you doing to Mary?" she demanded.

She looked just groggy enough to be still
caught in the remnants of sleep. He pitched
his voice low, so as not to wake the others.
"Blessing her, of course." He was surprised to
hear that his words sounded slurred. Perhaps
he should have left the cork in that second bottle.

"But—"

"Keep your voice down." He strove for a note of command, but a whisper had its limitations. "It is forbidden to speak," he improvised.

The girl hesitated. "Who are you?"

"Gabriel." Here, of all places, that name should carry weight.

Apparently, it did. She stared. "The . . . angel?"

"Archangel, actually," he recklessly volunteered. "There is a difference, you know."

"You do not look like an angel."

Insolent chit. "Appearances can be deceiving." He still held the sleeping girl's braid. If his annoyingly persistent questioner would just look the other way . . .

"What is that thing in your hand?" Her gaze was riveted on the knife, though the room was so dark he doubted she could make it out distinctly.

"It's a—er—wand." Did angels carry wands? No, that was fairies. Damnation.

The girl stared at him in stunned silence. Suddenly, her eyes widened in understanding.

"A knife! You've got a knife!"

"Quiet, brat," he growled. That did not sound very angelic. Oh, well. He might as well have something to show for this night's labors. In one swift movement, he sliced off the sleeping Mary's braid. She never even stopped snoring.

"Murderer!" the other girl shrieked.

Even as he dashed down the stairs, Gabriel heard footsteps on the landing.

"Mother Dolores! Help! Come quickly!" The answering screams of the others as they awoke joined in a jarring harmony that would have waked the dead.

When he gained the street, Gabriel looked wildly around. He had not planned for this. Sedbury's carriage, which had brought them to the docks, was long gone. Gabriel had no means of escape except his own two feet, and they were looking strangely blurred at the moment.

Suddenly, his gaze lit on the horse and wagon standing placidly across the way. There was no sign of a driver. Once again, luck had intervened. He sprinted across the street, took a moment to tuck the braid safely into his pocket, and grabbed the reins.

But as he flicked them smartly on the horse's rump, a flock of nightgown-clad young women and one fire-breathing dragon of a Mother Superior in a hideous red nightcap streamed into the street and threw themselves in front of the horse.

"Stop!" shrieked the dragon lady, whom he immediately pegged as Mother Dolores. She clutched a chamber pot and waved it wildly at the horse. Like baby chicks following the mother hen, the novitiates raised their arms, too. And just like that, the street was filled with a mob of flailing, screaming women in flannel nightgowns.

He had a sinking feeling that his luck had turned.

The horse did a nervous sideways dance

and reared. Stupid women, to place themselves in front of a thrashing horse. He ought to mow them down. They would have only themselves to blame for their injuries.

He jerked on the reins, forcing the horse to still or risk slicing its mouth to bits. The horse shuffled backward, trying to ease the pressure of the bit. His tail whipped up and caught the corner of Gabriel's eye and a searing pain shot through him.

"My hair! He cut off my hair!" cried a young woman he took to be Mary, awake at last.

"Quiet, child!" cried Mother Dolores, catching her nightcap as it dipped perilously low over one eye. "You are lucky to escape with your life!" She turned to him. "You shall die for this, sir. They will hang you forthwith, and I shall be among the spectators."

"Now, now," Gabriel warned. His eye hurt like hell, and he was in no mood for vengeful nuns. "You must set a proper example, Mother. Charity and forgiveness and all that."

Mother Dolores stared at him. "What sort of monster *are* you?"

"He claimed he was an angel," said the girl who had first discovered him.

"I see," she said grimly. "Matilde, fetch the Watch."

"That is not necessary," Gabriel quickly assured her. "I will just be on my way." Shielding his injured eye, he jumped down from the seat, squinting as he searched for a path through the sea of women. But their flailing forms pressed against him, forming a human wall.

Imprisoned by a dozen virgins. Was there anything more lowering?

"Ladies, step aside," he ordered in his most sonorous voice. "My work here is done. The—er—heavens demand my return." They looked at him uncertainly. He saw the indecision in their eyes. He almost had them. Then the dragon lady intervened.

"Sit on him, girls!" she commanded.

As one, the young women wrestled him to the cobblestones and planted themselves on him.

"Now, *angel*," she scoffed, waving the chamber pot threateningly. "Let us see you fly away."

"Alas, 'tis the molting season, madam," Gabriel managed, forcing air through his compressed lungs. "My wings have been clipped."

"More than clipped, you heartless villain. Your goose, sir, is cooked!" With that, Mother Dolores brought the chamber pot down on his head.

He should have known—virgins were nothing but trouble. He would never go near one again.

Chapter 1

"**T**he hanging is at noon," said a gruff masculine voice.

"I do hope Miss Wentworth will be brave." Louisa Peabody tied a black scarf over her hair, obscuring flaxen gold so gleaming it could be seen from a distance. She shrugged into a black field jacket several sizes too large. Then she placed a cap over the scarf and checked her appearance in the dingy tack room mirror. "I am afraid that is the best I can do."

The man at her side inspected her dark breeches, boots, and coat. When his gaze reached her head covering, he frowned uncertainly.

"You are remembering the last time." Louisa sighed. "Do not worry, David. I have tied the scarf good and tight. Not a strand of my hair is visible. Besides, I will be inside the carriage."

David Ferguson was a man of few words. And though he did not reply, the tension in his jaw was answer enough. Louisa made one

last effort to assuage his doubts. "Alice Wentworth has no one, David. All she did was steal
a loaf of bread to feed her child. We *must* help
her."

Their gazes met in pain shared and remembered. Then, without a word, David walked
out to the carriage.

"Be careful," warned the only other occu-
pant of the stable, a boy of about twelve. Holding the halter of a big black stallion, he
regarded Louisa with a mixture of determination and doubt. The weight of nascent masculinity sat uncertainly upon his slender
shoulders. "I still say you ought to let me go.
Midnight and I can cut through a crowd like
a knife through butter."

Louisa shook her head. "Midnight is too
high-strung for this mission. Besides," she
added gently, "you are too young, Sam."

"If you got caught . . ." His voice, straddling
the cusp of manhood, wavered.

"We will not."

"The last time—"

"Was unfortunate. But we all learn from our
mistakes. Do not worry. David will take care
of me." She gave him a quick hug, then followed David out to the carriage.

His head was in the noose. Any moment,
now, the executioner would release the lever
on the scaffold and send him on a permanent
trip to the great beyond. He supposed he
should be filled with despair, but in truth he
didn't feel a thing. Only a vast emptiness, far

more desolate than the possibility of death.

The crowd was enormous, no doubt due to Mother Dolores's embellishments at the trial, which had been reported in all the newspapers these past few weeks. "Fallen Angel," the headlines had called him. It wouldn't surprise him if she was out there somewhere, waiting for him to die.

Through his suffocating hood, Gabriel could hear the impatient shouts, the jeers. A great clamoring mass of humanity had gathered outside Newgate to watch the life be jerked out of him in the gruesome satisfaction of justice.

But if there was any justice in the world, those nuns would pay for their lies. Mother Dolores had made him sound like a rapist and murderer. No wonder his trial had taken less than half an hour.

Ah, well. The life of a scoundrel was mercifully short. And the life of a clumsy drunk with the stupidity to invade a convent even shorter.

"Save yerself, angel!" jeered a voice.

"Fly away, angel," ridiculed another. "Fly on to heaven."

A chorus of laughter rose from the crowd. Gabriel felt the executioner check the ropes that bound his hands. Snug and tight. No way out there. He heard the man speak to the magistrate in a low tone. He couldn't make out the words, but his imagination easily supplied them:

All is in readiness, my lord. I'll let him swing

long enough to please the crowds, then hand him over to that surgeon who's been after me to give him something for that anatomy class of his. Did you want him to suffer a bit first, my lord? Those nuns seemed awfully upset.

By all means, executioner, let the bugger suffer. I've seen the way you snap that platform down, and if you do it just right, their necks don't break right away and they hang there reaching with their toes, thinking they can gain a purchase as the air sucks out of them. The crowd loves that.

Well, he was always one to please the crowds. And this was better than that new treadmill invention he had been threatened with, the cylinder of steps that had to be walked until one dropped. Better to die from hanging than to die of boredom.

Gabriel supposed he should say a few words to his Maker, but he doubted anyone up there would hear him. Still, it was worth a shot.

I was looking forward to taking up residence at Sedbury's townhouse, you know. Might have made something of my life, even run for Parliament. Could've turned all those lords against slavery, told them about Jamaica and the plantations and— What's that? Yes, I know it's late to make promises. No, I don't mean a word of them. Hell, the last thing I want is a home.

Abruptly, the floor beneath him shuddered. This was it, then. His time was at hand. Just as well; there was no one up there to hear the ramblings of a doomed man. He swallowed hard, but the noose cinched him, closing his throat. *Afraid? Hardly. It's just that I—*

A cheer went up from the crowd. Blood-thirsty buggers. He had barely formed the thought when his feet left the ground.

Wouldn't have minded one last chance. . . .

Excited shrieks came from somewhere, probably the vicinity of Mother Dolores. The rope cut into his neck, shooting dizzying pain through him. He could not breathe. Instinct sent his hands upward to claw at the thing that was choking the life out of him. But his hands were bound, and it was only in his dreams that he grabbed the rope and flung it off, restoring blessed air to his lungs.

Ah, dreams. He was sliding into the world of dreams that had always lain just beyond his reach. Soon he would slip the knot of his human misery.

Now. It was happening now. He was losing awareness. The cheers of the crowd faded into oblivion. He heard a strange slashing noise. Then the noose at his neck released its hold, and Gabriel floated heavenward to his final reward.

Heaven was deuced uncomfortable, though. Heaven felt like a man's strong arms pulling him through the air, depositing him unceremoniously on his head on the floor of a carriage. Heaven sounded like a man's confused curse and a woman's urgent admonition as a blanket was flung over him and the vehicle lurched through the street with angry shouts in pursuit.

He should have known he would go

straight to hell. How else to describe the sensation of being jostled on the floor of a carriage, blind to his surroundings save for the pain they brought? His neck felt as if it had been seared by the very fires of hell. His air-deprived lungs gasped helplessly for breath. Under the hood, his injured eye burned like the devil.

Every time he tried to right his bruised body, a booted foot pushed firmly on his posterior and a woman's sharp voice cut through his misery. "Stay down!"

Gabriel stayed down. He would not risk the ire of this mistress of hell. But he longed to remove the oppressive hood, to take in enough air to banish the dizziness that threatened to rob him of the thin hold his mind maintained on the events around him.

Heaven or hell? Maybe there was no difference, after all. At last the carriage rolled to a stop, and someone lifted the blanket that had hidden him. Gabriel heard the woman gasp as her trembling hands removed his hood.

"You are not Miss Wentworth!" she cried—rather unnecessarily, he thought. She turned to the Goliath who suddenly appeared outside the carriage door. " 'Tis a *man*, David, a *man!*"

As Gabriel stared at her, dumbfounded, she removed the cap from her head along with a black kerchief that had hidden hair the color of spun gold. But that was not what rendered him speechless. It was those eyes, which regarded him with a mixture of fury and confusion and which were as deep and bottomless and blue as the sea on a cloudless day. And the tiny birthmark that sat between her upper lip and the tip of her lovely nose.

Hair kissed by the sun. Eyes bluer than blue. A small, tantalizing mark above her lip. If heaven had angels like this, he had come to the right place.

"Madam," Gabriel rasped, his voice all but destroyed by the hangman's noose, "will you marry me?" He gave a wild, mirthless laugh as the world around him faded to black.

"A man." Louisa stared at the limp form at her feet. "What in the name of all that is holy am I to do?"

David shrugged. "Take him home, I suppose." He climbed back up to his perch and with a flick of the reins sent the team of horses barreling down the road.

Louisa crossed her arms and stared out the window, trying to look anywhere except at the motionless man on the floor. But outside held only trees and grass and the occasional cow. At her feet was the scourge of her sex.

A man. And from the look and sound of him, an insolent, puffed-up, arrogant, shameless example of the breed. *Madam, will you marry me?* Mad hubris, indeed. Facing death had not even begun to humble him. Louisa had no doubt that he had deserved his death sentence. Flecks of amber in those vibrant green eyes warned of violent, unpredictable passions. He was meant to burn in hell.

And she, of all people, had saved him.

He lay on his side, taking up the floor space between the seats and then some. Louisa curled her legs under her to avoid touching him and then decided that in his current state he would scarcely know that she had used him for a hassock. Gingerly, she let her feet rest on his back.

His hands were still bound. Carefully, she reached out and untied the knots. Free at last, his hands flopped at his sides with the limpness of a rag doll. But there was nothing harmless about their size. They were of a piece with that broad back that stretched the fabric of his shirt taut across a wide expanse of muscle and bone.

The man they had saved was strong, dangerous. A criminal. A killer, possibly worse. Yet even if he had been none of those things, Louisa would have hated him on sight.

Gabriel awoke to find the giant towering over him. The man was six and a half feet, if he was an inch. His face bore deep, irregular scars, as if unskilled hands had chipped his features out of granite. The man studied him from an impossible height with eyes as expressive as stone.

His angel sat in a chair beside a hearth in which a friendly fire was blazing. Her hands were crossed primly in her lap, and she held herself stiffly as she regarded him with a gaze as cold as ice.

"Who are you?" she demanded. Her voice was dry, brittle.

He was lying on the floor. Not the way to meet an angel. It put him at a distinct disadvantage, for though he was not as tall as the giant, he could certainly stand as straight. And a man on his feet thought better than a man on his posterior.

Gabriel tried to rise. He got to his knees and pushed off from his hands and tried to heave himself up. But he was weaker than he thought. Like a babe whose reach exceeds his grasp, he fell backward, toppling helplessly onto the cold, unforgiving floor.

His hands ached, his eye burned, his neck felt as if it had been belted in edged steel. His lungs could not take in enough air. His stomach heaved. He was going to be sick in front of her.

An encroaching blackness came at him, narrowing his sight to a pinpoint of light and pulling him backward into the blessedness of sleep. And though he fought it, his brain felt fuzzy, as if it was packed in cotton wool.

"Name," he murmured. He had to know her name.

"I am Louisa Peabody," she said crisply.

"Lu-we-sa Pe-body." He tried to repeat it, but his tongue kept getting twisted. He wondered if he was hallucinating.

"Who are you?" Her voice was remote, condemning.

"King," he managed. He was losing the battle with sleep.

"King?" He heard the note of puzzlement in her tone. "Mr. King?"

"Not mister," he said thickly. "King—Majesty."

He grinned. It was a little joke—bitter as sin, and too much work to explain now. He thought it would pique her interest, drive that distanced chill from her voice.

"You are a king?"

He nodded, pleased that she understood. Too bad her features kept blurring around the edges. He had the feeling his eyes were crossed, for her nose kept moving around on her face. It would be difficult to rivet her with one of his meaningful stares. Anyway, angels were probably impervious to his charm.

Frowning, he tried to conjure the elusive memory at the edge of his awareness. He vaguely remembered talking to someone—or something—about mending his ways. Where was he now? Among the living or the dead?

"The only king we have is old George," she said dryly. "You do not look a bit like him."

Mad George in heaven, too? He hadn't heard that the king had cocked up his toes, but then Newgate prisoners led a sheltered existence.

"Not George," he murmured in a strange, slurred voice that did not sound like his own. "Gabriel."

"King Gabriel." She rolled the words around on her tongue, experimenting with the sound. "Pray, what are you king of?" she said derisively.

Gabriel looked up from what seemed like a very long way down. She was staring at him, her head tilted to one side, waiting. The firelight caught the lights in her hair and sent their shimmering warmth straight to his gut, a spear of heat that threatened a mortal wound. He could only gape, her speechless slave. He opened his mouth and tried with all his might to say the words that burned in his dizzied brain.

"Take you there," he vowed.

A large booted toe nudged him in the ribs. He had forgotten about the giant. Gabriel ignored the man and smiled at her. Her eyes filled with uncertainty. Good. He had her interest—much better than her contempt. Conquest would be his. Unless she really *was* an angel, and then he would be making an utter fool of himself.

She turned toward the giant. "You had best fetch Dr. Simmons."

No, no doctor. He was better now, much better. He might even be alive.

Gabriel raised his head, tried to speak. "Island. King of island," he managed weakly.

Louisa Peabody eyed him in disgust and left the room. The monster lifted him, carried him up some stairs, and tossed him onto an impossibly soft feather bed. As Gabriel sank gratefully into the covers, letting the darkness take him, the man bent down close to his ear.

"And I," the giant snarled contemptuously, "am Queen Charlotte."

"What happened to Alice Wentworth?" Louisa eyed David worriedly.

" 'Pears they thought this one"—he jerked his thumb skyward, indicating the upstairs where the stranger slept—"needed killing first."

"But . . . how could you have mistaken him for her?"

He shrugged. "Didn't, exactly. Wasn't until I'd driven us into the thick of things that I got a good look at the prisoner. By then, I'd cut the rope and the mongrel was falling into my arms. Nothing for it but to grab him and get out before the crowd closed in."

It wasn't fair to blame David, for he'd had all he could do to control the team, seize the prisoner, and speed them away from the angry mob. Louisa hadn't wanted to take the cumbersome carriage, but after the debacle of Violet's rescue, David had not wanted her to risk exposure again on Midnight. And so she'd sat helpless and protected inside the carriage while the mission went terribly awry. Never again, she vowed, would she abdicate her responsibility.

"Do you think they will proceed with her hanging?"

David shook his head. "Not today. Too much disarray."

Louisa paced the parlor in frustration. "Let us hope she is all right for now. In the meantime, what is to be done with *him?*"

David said nothing. There was no need to. Since the death of her father, no man had ever occupied a bed at Peabody Manor. The fact that a criminal sentenced to death now slept the sleep of the blameless upstairs was almost incomprehensible.

"I can't have a man here, David," she said in a wobbly voice. "You know that."

"Aye," he said softly. His hand came up, hovered over her trembling shoulders for a moment, then fell to his side without touching her. "But he is ill and canna' do ye harm."

David understood her fears, accepted them without question. "I will keep ye safe, lass," he murmured.

Louisa knew he would, as far as it was in his power to do so. But long ago she had learned a bitter lesson: the only certain help for a woman alone in the world was her own two hands—and they were never enough.

Through no fault of their own, women were the weaker sex, dependent on men for their daily bread and the very clothes on their backs. They could not control their money, much less their own fate. They were married off to benefit the family's fortunes, bargained away like chattel, sold on the auction block to the highest bidder.

Her father had given her to a man with a charming smile and a soul as dark as the devil's. She'd despised them both for making her an object to be traded to fill the family coffers. For making her a whore, for that is what it amounted to. But she'd survived. Adversity had made her strong. She had put the past behind her and made her life a positive force for womankind. It all worked splendidly.

As long as there was no one to remind her

that her carefully constructed world might topple in an instant if some clever male decided to apply himself to the task.

The man upstairs had to go. Besides being a criminal, he had the look of trouble. Too charming by half, even fresh from the hangman's noose. A rakish brow bespoke devilish intentions under that flaming halo of unruly red hair. Green eyes glittered with daring and dash and promises that would never be fulfilled. A self-mocking mouth hinted of secrets closely guarded.

Take her to his island, indeed! Nonsense uttered in the heady exultation of escaping a fate he had undoubtedly deserved. Meaningless words flung at a woman cursed with the beauty to provoke such wretched verbosity.

A king, was he?

Aye, king of the thousand hearts he had broken. Louisa's eyes narrowed. She knew the breed well.

Chapter 2

The hand on his brow was cool, soothing. The low murmuring warm, encouraging. Had his angel relented, then, and deigned to favor him with her healing presence?

Sleep still caught at the edges of his awareness, but he moved swiftly, instinctively to capture her hand. Bringing it to his lips, he nibbled lightly on her fingertips. They tasted vaguely of smoke. He frowned.

"My, ye are a bold one."

Gabriel's eyes flew open. The movement pained his injured eye, but he forced himself to bring the images into focus. Above him a lacy white canopy spanned the bed like a thousand dancing snowflakes. Bright yellow and amber framed the perimeter of his vision— the room was awash with colors of sunshine and cheer.

He tried to move, but breathing was an effort. His throat was parched, his neck sore and bruised, as if he had been paraded about on a too-tight leash.

Slowly, he began to remember. The scaffold.

The executioner. And miracle of miracles, being plucked from death's jaws by a heavenly vision.

He turned to the woman whose smoky fingers he nibbled. Streaks of gray fanned through her dark hair, and her ruddy cheeks sagged into heavy jowls. Her gray eyes glinted like steel. A woman to be reckoned with—but most assuredly not his angel.

Instantly, Gabriel released her hand.

The hint of a twinkle appeared in her eyes, then vanished just as quickly. Gabriel tried to sit up, but his body rebelled. His head was still groggy from the deep, unnatural sleep of a man who has faced death and for the moment avoided its relentless jaws.

"Where is—" He broke off, trying to remember. Lu-we-sa. That was it. "Louisa," he rasped. "Louisa Peabody."

The woman merely crossed her arms and regarded him with something akin to a smirk. A movement at the end of the bed caught Gabriel's eye. A boy, his eyes filled with hostility, stepped toward him.

"Who are you?" the lad demanded. "What have you done with Elizabeth's mother?"

"Sam." The voice, soft in its reproof, came from another woman, who had suddenly appeared in his line of vision. She had long, straight brown hair and soft brown eyes that regarded him assessingly.

Gabriel rubbed his aching head. Who the devil was Elizabeth? Where was Louisa Peabody?

"I am Violet," the soft-spoken woman said. "This is Rose." She gestured toward the older woman. "A woman named Alice Wentworth was supposed to hang at Newgate yesterday. You went in her stead. By the time David realized his mistake, the crowd was on him. He threw you into the carriage and fled."

"Men." Rose shook her head in disgust.

Violet's steady gaze did not waver. "We have Alice's baby, Elizabeth," she continued. Her hands curved protectively over the front of her loose-fitting frock. Something registered in Gabriel's brain, but he couldn't complete the thought.

"We will raise the babe as our own if Alice cannot be saved. But we hope you can tell us where the guards have taken her."

Babe. Now he had it. The brown-haired woman was increasing.

"We think they have moved her out of Newgate," Violet said. "Apparently, the disruption of your execution gave the authorities fits."

Now that was a damned shame, he thought grimly.

"You must understand." Violet's voice was low, urgent. "Miss Wentworth's only crime was to steal food for her baby. Louisa would have saved her, had not you taken Miss Wentworth's place. We are very distressed about that."

Her frequent use of the plural was vaguely disquieting. Gabriel struggled to prop himself up on his elbow. "Where am I?" His voice sounded like a piece of rusty metal. "Who are you?"

"There are eleven of us—six women and five children," Violet replied solemnly. "We live here in Louisa's home. She has saved most of us from poverty, sickness, and death at the hands of men. Ours is a community of women."

A community of women. Gabriel tried to imagine six women like these two staring at him with somber, accusing eyes. Those damned nuns must have prayed mightily for revenge, for he had obviously skipped purgatory and tumbled straight into hell. Gabriel stared grimly at the yellow and amber walls—not the colors of sunshine and cheer, but of fire and brimstone.

A fourth figure stepped from the shadows, although how the shadows had contained him was anybody's guess. The giant wore a look of wrathful menace abetted by the deep scars on his face. One large, slashing scar extended downward, disappearing where the folds of his shirt met just below his neck. A nearly fatal wound, that.

But the giant's presence did not make sense here. "If you are a community of women," Gabriel croaked, "what the devil is he—a eunuch?"

The giant froze. Violet gasped. Rose arched one thick eyebrow. And in that moment, another figure condensed from the shadows.

Louisa Peabody. Her brilliant blue gaze, filled with all the anger of the ages, bore down on Gabriel. "Please leave us," she demanded, her voice shot through with rage.

Since he was not in any condition to go anywhere, Gabriel assumed she addressed the others. And, in fact, they did leave, with soft rustlings and padded footsteps. All but the giant. He remained, still frozen in place.

"David," she said softly. "David."

He turned, and in the look that passed between them, Gabriel read the chilling truth.

Sweet Jesus. Six women, five brats, and one enormous eunuch. This was where fate had led him. To hell, where women ruled and men were castrated.

Where he was apparently meant to pay for his crimes—and they were many, in the unforgiving eyes of women scorned.

Pay not with his neck, but with his manhood.

With a wild cry of denial, Gabriel bolted from the bed.

"Help me, David!" Louisa clutched the man's arms, trying with all of her might to stop his reckless flight. Even in his weakened state, the criminal possessed an amazing strength. Moving swiftly, David jerked the man's arms back and pulled him away from her.

But with a deft move, the man dug his heel into David's ankle, throwing him off balance. Then he jumped atop David and snaked his hands around David's throat.

"Stop it!" Louisa dug her fingernails into

the man's back through his filthy shirt. "Stop it, I say!"

David pushed the man off him with a mighty heave that also sent Louisa backward. As she hit the floor, the breath went out of her in a great whoosh of air. Instantly, the criminal jerked her to her feet. One hand went around her ribcage, the other her neck, holding her hostage.

"Don't move!" he growled to David. "If you value her life, stay where you are."

David stilled. Louisa shot him a look filled with misery and apology. She had known the man was a common criminal yet had allowed him to stay the night in her house. Now he had turned on them, displayed his true stripes. Did he mean to murder them all? Or just rape them, as he had those nuns?

No wonder they had pushed his execution ahead of poor Miss Wentworth's. All she had done was steal a loaf of bread. He had assaulted helpless nuns. David had learned the nature of Gabriel Sinclair's crimes just this morning, when he had ridden to town to determine Miss Wentworth's whereabouts.

Why, oh why, had they not left him on that scaffold?

Clutching her to his chest, Sinclair edged her toward the door. Panic filled her. She feared the others would try to intervene, to save her, and be murdered for their trouble. And the children—dear lord, what would he do to them?

"Please do not harm the children," she managed, drawing air into her lungs in one painful breath. "Do anything you want with me, but let the children go."

His hand stilled on the door handle. "What the devil are you talking about?"

She shouldn't have spoken. He hadn't even been thinking about the children, and now she'd given him the idea of using them for his own twisted ends. But it was too late to call back the words. "I beg you, do not hurt them. They haven't done anything and—"

"I have never hurt a child in my life."

Something in his injured tone told Louisa he spoke the truth. No matter, his crimes against the rest of them would more than offset his mercy to the children. "And what of the others? What of those nuns?" she bit out. "Can you say you never harmed them?"

"Look, Miss Peabody, or mistress of hell or whoever you are," he snarled, "I'm no saint, but I've no intention of harming anyone. I just want to get out of this house of bedlam before you turn me into one of *those*."

"Those?"

For an answer, he pointed at David. "You butchered him, didn't you?"

"What?" She stared up at him without comprehension.

"Don't play the innocent," he growled. I'm onto you and your little 'society.' You think to take revenge on every man who has served a female ill. Well, as long as I draw breath, you won't get me."

It took her a moment to understand. A moment to get past the personal insult and indignation, to understand the import of his words. And then, oh wondrous poetic justice, it was clear as a bell.

Her low, hysterical giggle made him draw a sharp breath.

"What is it?" he demanded. "What is so damned funny?"

"You thought we meant to . . ." She could not bring herself to say the words.

"Come now, Miss Peabody, don't be squeamish," he rasped. "Do you deny that you meant to relieve me of my manhood in punishment for whatever you imagine are my crimes against your sex?"

"I do deny it. Whatever manhood you possess," she added disdainfully, "is safe here."

The large hand around her middle tightened with the force of his anger. "If this is a trick," he growled, "I swear I will haunt you from the grave."

" 'Tis no trick." Her breath came in shallow, urgent gasps as she tried to control her fear. "We mean you no harm."

His body shifted slightly, and she felt the tension in the pumping of his heart and the hard, corded muscles that supported her. "Then he is . . . he is whole?"

"As whole as you, mongrel," David snarled.

Sinclair's unnatural stillness told her he was weighing their words, trying to decide the truth. "The scars," he said finally. "How did you get them?"

Only the merest twitch of David's jaw

hinted at any emotion. "The Peninsular War. I was taken prisoner."

"Go on," Sinclair ordered, when he did not continue.

" 'Happens a Scot would rather die than lose his freedom. I did nae show the proper respect. They had to take me down a notch."

"And?" Sinclair demanded.

David shrugged. "Carved me up a bit, but for all that I was one of the lucky ones."

Sinclair's arm went slack. Louisa wanted to go to David, but the look in his eyes kept her away. In some way, Sinclair's assumption had come painfully near the truth, for she had seen in David's eyes the sudden, stunned awareness of a deeply hidden secret. Prison had robbed him of his manhood as surely as any knife, stealing his spirit, his vitality, his sense of worth. For all David's strength and courage, he was a broken man.

"David came to us after the war," Louisa explained. "His sister Molly was a tenant here, but she caught a fever and died. Sam is her son."

She remembered the sadness in David's eyes when he had shown up at her door several years ago in search of the sister he had not seen in years. Sure that his scars would disgust, he could scarcely meet her gaze. For Molly's sake, she had asked him to stay on. He had moved into Molly's old cottage and readily taken on the responsibility of looking after Sam. Louisa had known instinctively that David wasn't a threat to them. His quiet, lonely sorrow had touched her heart. Pain was their common bond, and though there had never been more than that between them, that was everything. In the years Louisa had known him, David had spoken only vaguely of his time in prison. She hated Sinclair for forcing him to relive his torture.

Behind her, she felt Sinclair falter. Louisa turned. The color had drained from his face. It seemed to take all the strength he possessed to remain standing.

"I want—" The words came out a croak, and he tried again. "Bed. Go back to . . . bed." He swayed.

"But you cannot manage it, can you?" Louisa taunted, giving rein to her fury at last. He had ruined her plans, intruded on her world, drawn that awkward revelation from David. "The terror of the convent, king of all you possess—and you cannot walk ten steps to the bed."

His gaze darkened, and Louisa could not suppress a little shudder at the flecks of anger in those green depths. But he could not sustain his rage. He was spent. Somehow he had mustered the strength to flee the knives he imagined were after him, but his ephemeral strength had vanished once panic dissipated.

Whatever this man was, whatever his crimes, at the moment he was as weak as a lamb.

David moved forward, but Louisa shook her head. She put her arm out to support the scoundrel they had so recently reprieved from death. For now, he was helpless.

"Lean on me," she ordered.

His weight was more than she had bargained for, but she refused David's help. She had not touched a man in years, but she wanted this man to feel her strength and know that she was not weak like other members of her sex. He was her enemy, but the battle would be joined another time—when it would be a battle between equals.

Once again, he had made a fool of himself in front of her. Gabriel sank into the mattress, letting sleep pry him from the day's horrors. It was difficult to separate truth from the dreams that had raged as that noose sucked the life out of him. Yet one truth shone clear enough: Louisa Peabody was no dream. She was a nightmare, mad as a midsummer moon.

As best he could figure, she went about rescuing women from dire circumstances with the help of that fellow David, who would have been a match for the giant felled by his Biblical namesake.

The brush with death had befogged his brain. How else to explain why he had seen her as a heavenly vision, the imperfection of that tiny birthmark a harbinger of hope for the truly imperfect like himself? He supposed even fools wanted to believe in something.

He wondered what Louisa Peabody, with her golden hair and fierce azure eyes, believed in. Probably not visions. For all her beauty, she was too grim by half. There was not a whimsical bone in her body.

Her eyes held nothing of the magic he expected from a vision. They were too earnest, too determined. She was the serious sort of female he most detested. For that matter, everyone here was solemn as a judge. Even that lad, who couldn't be more than eleven or twelve, had worried eyes.

What a den of misfits he had stumbled into. And she was the worst of all—for being more than a dream, far less than a vision. For appearing for one interminable moment as a vengeful Judith out for blood on account of his misdeeds against her sex.

And most of all, for making him understand that she would never, ever let him nibble on her fingers.

Chapter 3

"A prison ship?" Louisa was horrified. "Not one of those horrid old river hulks!"

David nodded grimly. "They moved her there yesterday."

Neither of them voiced the thought uppermost in their minds: hanging was the least of Alice Wentworth's worries now. The prison hulks, temporary holding pens for felons awaiting transportation to Botany Bay, were run by corrupt guards who were a law unto themselves. Reformers had complained about the hulks for years, but they remained bastions of misery.

A woman in such a place would be at the mercy of her guards. There was no need to speculate about her fate.

Terrible images filled Louisa's mind, and she shuddered in vicarious horror. "We must get her out of there. There is no time to lose."

"Aye."

At his grim tone, Louisa's heart sank. "It will be difficult, won't it?"

"I know nothing of boats, but I do nae think we can simply walk onto the deck, bold as ye please."

"There has to be another way in," she persisted.

"Even so, we have no notion where they are holding her."

"Gun deck, most likely," said a deep male voice. "Fore if she's lucky. Aft if she's not."

Louisa turned. Gabriel Sinclair stood at the threshold, evidently restored by his night's rest. He wore the same torn breeches and dirty hopsack shirt in which he had prepared to face his Maker, but the similarity between that man and this ended there.

This was no desperate fugitive, fearful of losing his manhood to her vengeance. This was not the man who had lain nearly senseless on the floor of her carriage as they fled the gallows, so dazed that he blurted out that ridiculous marriage proposal.

This man appeared to be in full possession of his senses and, more to the point, fully confident in his masculinity. He stood with his legs slightly apart, taking his weight evenly on both feet in the self-assured manner of a man prepared for anything. His broad shoulders spanned the door frame; his fisted hands rested lightly on his hips.

Masculine confidence radiated from every angular plane and contoured muscle, from the high cheekbones and firm jaw that gave his features a noble arrogance to the expanse of chest exposed by his tattered shirt. A cool alertness held sway in his penetrating green eyes. A mane of unruly red hair framed his face in brilliant fire.

A veritable paragon of male beauty, Louisa thought bitterly. Apollo driving his chariot across the sky, dictating the span of a mere mortal's days and nights with typical masculine arrogance. But Apollo had sworn to tell the truth and flush out evil. Sinclair was a liar, a rapist, and any number of other despicable things besides. Beauty was not the measure of his soul.

He glanced only briefly at David, then fixed her with a measuring gaze.

Lifting her chin, Louisa endured his inspection without revealing her discomfort. So what if he was a paragon of masculinity? She was immune to masculine appeal in the way that a child who has weathered smallpox need never fear its ravages again.

As he was evidently immune to her, for she knew the moment he dismissed her as a woman. His brows arched, and his expression shifted from wary interest to careless indifference as he blinked her image away.

"And what do you know of the matter, sir?" she challenged, stung by his tacit rejection—though it should not have mattered in the slightest what he thought of her.

"Of Miss Wentworth, nothing. Of boats, a thing or two." Sardonic amusement filled his gaze. "It is the best way to get to an island."

Louisa flushed. "I am not stupid, Mr. Sinclair—"

"Delighted to hear it. You have discovered my identity, I see."

"Yes, and your crimes as well."

"Heinous, are they not?"

"You make light of them?"

"It does not matter what I make of them. Do you have a change of clothes? I fear these have outlived their usefulness." He fingered his tattered shirt and regarded David assessingly.

Taken aback by his abrupt change of subject, Louisa glanced helplessly at David, who leveled a gaze at him.

"I do nae think my shirts will fit you."

Sinclair shrugged. "Then I will be on my way. Fugitive from justice and all that." His tone was careless, but the provocative green velvet of his eyes had transformed to hard, purposeful jade. Louisa saw that he did not intend to stay another minute under her roof.

"Wait," she said.

His intent gaze settled on her.

"My father was not so tall as you, but his clothes may serve," Louisa said. "They will be less noticeable than what you are wearing. We are but three hours from London. The authorities will be looking for you and—"

"You are loath to have me risk capture," he finished with a mirthless smile. "How touching."

"I—" Louisa broke off.

"Come, Miss Peabody. You have no interest in seeing my miserable life spared. No doubt you have been reproaching yourself for saving a scoundrel from the execution he so richly deserved."

Louisa stiffened. "Do not put words in my mouth."

"I wouldn't dream of it. Point me in the direction of your father's clothes, and I shall not trouble you further."

"Please." Her voice cracked. Mortified, she took a deep breath to regain her poise. "Please—I must know why you think Miss Wentworth is being held in the . . . gun deck, was it?"

"Simple deduction. They would not leave her in the bowels of the ship, where the rest of the felons can have at her. They would want her more . . . accessible."

Louisa looked away. "Go on."

"Most likely they put her in the carpenter's or boatswain's quarters in the bow. The guards probably occupy the aft cabins."

"So she is separate from the other convicts as well as the guards?"

"If she's lucky. But if the guards wanted her more at hand, shall we say, they would have put her aft with them. And if she was fortunate enough to attract the eye of the captain, she might find herself in an upper cabin."

"With them," Louisa echoed dully. "So that she would be accessible."

"Night and day. Not a moment's rest for her, I imagine. I will take those clothes now, if I may."

Her mouth fell open. "How can you be so

indifferent to another person's suffering?"

"If you take the world's pain on your shoulders, Miss Peabody, you will have a miserable life. It is foolish to mourn what you cannot change. Since I can do nothing about Miss Wentworth's suffering, I choose to disregard it."

With a cry of disbelief, Louisa marched over to him. "I will not allow you to disregard it," she said fiercely.

He merely arched a brow.

His eyes, she noticed, were more intricate than they appeared from a distance. Amber flecks radiated from the dark, intense centers, pinpoints of topaz amid the jade. But there was a coldness in those depths, and she knew Sinclair would never trouble himself over another person's misery.

"It is because of you that Miss Wentworth was moved," she said in an accusing tone.

"No," he said calmly. "It was your doing. You caused all that commotion by interrupting my execution."

"I deeply regret it, you may be sure." She gave him a scathing look. "But the fact remains that Miss Wentworth would have been on that scaffold had it not been for you."

He shrugged. "A twist of fate, no more."

"We would have rescued her," Louisa continued relentlessly, "and she would be sitting here now with her babe at her breast. You have an obligation, Mr. Sinclair, and I mean to see that you discharge it."

"I am obliged to no one, Miss Peabody."

"You are obliged to me, sir, for I saved your life."

"A mistake, as you have acknowledged."

"Mistake or no, you are beholden to us for your miserable existence. And though I am sure you have never done anything of worth in your entire life, you will do so now. You will help us save Alice Wentworth."

Louisa fairly quivered with rage as they stood toe to toe, but he seemed not the least bit moved. He studied her with wry amusement.

"You appeal to the conscience of a criminal? My dear Miss Peabody, you must know that a man who has committed the crimes of which I have been convicted would not let conscience get in the way of self-interest."

He was right, of course. Gabriel Sinclair possessed not a shred of altruism, no sense of obligation. Louisa turned away, hiding the tears that welled in her eyes at the contemplation of Alice Wentworth's fate. They *would* free her. They had pulled off daring acts in the past, and they could now. Just because neither she nor David knew fore from aft didn't mean hope was lost.

Louisa looked at David for confirmation. He nodded slightly, and she knew he would be with her all the way. But she saw uncertainty in his gaze, too. And something else she could not label. He regarded Sinclair, then her, with a curious expression.

"I mistook you for an angel, you know," Sinclair said in a low voice. She whirled, startled to see how close he was. He reached out and gingerly touched the little birthmark above her lip. Louisa took a quick step backward.

"Is that a joke, Mr. Sinclair?" she snapped, to cover her embarrassment.

"Not at all," he replied smoothly. "A man in my situation has no time for jokes. Now, about those clothes . . ." He eyed her expectantly.

Louisa stared at him with loathing. Her mind formed a scathing setdown, but David stepped forward before she could deliver it. "I will fetch the trunks."

Sinclair shot Louisa a beatific smile.

The moths must have loved Miss Peabody's father, for they had positively devoured his clothes. Gabriel found one pair of ankle-length tan pantaloons they had let go with only a nibble, and a linen shirt and waistcoat that were relatively unscathed. The shirt was too small and the style a decade out of fashion, but all in all, the clothes were an improvement over his filthy prison togs.

Miss Peabody was daft as a loon. Neither she nor that giant knew the first thing about sneaking onto a ship. David would never fit through a hawsehole, and Miss Peabody had never shinnied up an anchor cable in her life. Alice Wentworth hadn't a prayer.

Let the devil take the lot of them. The quicker he was away, the better. He had to go home.

What passed for home, anyway. A godforsaken chunk of rock jutting out of the sea southeast of North Foreland, perfectly positioned as friend or foe to the ships that skirted the disastrous sandbars of the Downs. It was a lonely, forgotten place, and he hated it with every fiber of his being. But his father had elected to spend eternity there, looking out over the whitecaps in an endless vigil for the desperate and doomed.

Once, long ago, Gabriel had called another place home—an enormous gray castle in the country, with servants, tutors, and a stable full of prized cattle. It was a happy time, full of vivid but increasingly elusive memories. He remembered St. Thomas's Day, when the whole family would go wassailing. And Christmas, when he helped his father and brother Robert drag in the yule log. Then would come a feast of roasted boar's head and, finally, presents.

All had been right with the world back then—before his mother died of a fever and his brother perished in the attack on the French at Aboukir Bay. Before Gabriel learned that all of his father's hopes and dreams had rested on Robert.

His brother was to have had an illustrious naval career, married a gentle young lady, then given his father plenty of grandchildren to bounce on his knee. His father had intended to have a happy old age, tinkering with his boats and playing games with his various offspring. Instead, he lost his wife and firstborn son and was saddled with a child at a time when he had no taste for childish things.

"Gabriel—a silly name," his father had groused. "Don't know why I let your mother talk me into it. People will expect you to strum a harp."

He had been sent away to school, but he did not stay long. One day his father plucked him from Eton and drove straight to Ramsgate, where he threw Gabriel's meager belongings into a strangely rigged vessel and sailed them east to a spit of land and rocks his father called Sinclair Isle. And like a true lord of the land, his father crowned himself king.

Gabriel had known then that his childhood was irrevocably lost. His father grew as wild and remote as the island, dedicating himself to avenging the son he had lost, ignoring the one who remained. And so the years had passed. Now and again, strangers appeared— men who came and went like clouds slipping across the sky, women with desperate eyes and sad faces who stayed for a while, then vanished as quickly as the days. Children, their eyes too old by far, passing by like the ghost of his own childhood.

Through it all, his father tinkered madly with the thing in the cave, stopping only to lavish attention on the French emigrés whose little boats washed up on Sinclair Isle as they fled Napoleon's tyranny. Gabriel grew tall and strong and forgot about the wassailing that had once brought families together in joyous celebration. He never saw that magical castle again.

When his father died, Gabriel buried him on the island's highest hill, facing east so that he would always look out over the churning seas separating England and France. Then he sailed off in a craft he made himself and discovered something more delightful than wassailing.

Sex.

He'd had no exposure in his youth to brothels or eager village maids. Nor had the wives of his father's friends introduced him to the pleasures of the flesh, as Robert claimed they'd done for him. But though Gabriel had not honed his skills in the conventional way, the ladies liked him, and he was happy to oblige.

He had been an innocent of eighteen when he set a westerly course from Sinclair Isle; a man of seasoned sensuality when he returned to London ten years later. A world had opened to him in those years, and if he had not quite recaptured the joy of his youth, it was something very like.

Gabriel surveyed his image in the reflecting glass. His mother's eyes, his father's hair, and neither of them alive to see the man he had become. What would they think of him now?

Doubtless they, like Miss Peabody, would be unimpressed. Not that he cared what that woman thought. She was another mad fool like his father, risking her neck for every desperate cause. Perhaps, in return for the accident of his rescue, he would give her a few pointers for her foolish attempt on the hulk.

But he was not about to do something as stupid as climbing into that watery prison and rescuing a poor soul Miss Peabody thought a candidate for sainthood.

Deep inside him lay a bleak and barren spot, where his own dreams were as hidden as night. And that suited him just fine, for dreams were for boys, not men. He certainly wanted nothing to do with a woman whose view of life was bleaker than his. Beauty did not disguise the fact that she had lost the joy of her own youth some time ago. He wondered what man had taken it and whether she had enjoyed the experience at the time.

Probably not.

A small kernel of anger welled inside him for the loss of that which could not be replaced. He straightened his waistcoat and shrugged into her father's long jacket with the cutaway front. A man's clothes, not a boy's.

A man learned to put away childish things. And to find joy where he could.

Chapter 4

"**D**aisy, Jasmine, Lily, this is Mr. Sinclair." Louisa turned to Sinclair. "You have already met Rose and Violet, of course."

He bowed politely.

"As you have no doubt become aware," she began as everyone took a seat at the dining room table, "Mr. Sinclair arrived two days ago when we—er—accidentally rescued him instead of Alice Wentworth."

Rose rolled her eyes heavenward. Louisa ignored her. "We have every reason to believe that Alice still lives," she assured them, "though I shall not go into the particulars, for the usual reasons."

"The usual reasons?" Sinclair arched a brow.

" 'Tis for their own protection," she explained. "If David and I were caught, it would be best for everyone here to know as little as possible about our clandestine activities. I should add that our missions are extremely well planned. We rely on the element of surprise and have never been in danger of capture."

Violet cleared her throat. Louisa hesitated. "We did have a close call two months ago, when Violet came to us. But we have rectified the problem."

"What problem was that?" Sinclair fixed her with an interested gaze.

Louisa's face grew warm. "A man in Violet's village—"

"Will. My husband," Violet put in quietly.

"He struck Midnight with his whip. Midnight reared—he is most averse to the whip—and almost threw me. My cap fell off. Everyone got a good look at the horse and my hair. Both are rather distinctive, I'm afraid."

"Indeed." His gaze traveled to her hair, then moved lower, settling in the vicinity of her mouth. Louisa flushed. He was staring at her birthmark, the rude man, trying to embarrass her.

"Since then," she continued, "I have always worn a more reliable head covering if I am going on . . ." Louisa trailed off, realizing she had said far more than was prudent.

"A mission," he finished easily. "By the way, Miss Peabody, how does it happen that everyone here is in bloom, so to speak?"

Titters rippled around the table. Oh, he was clever, this knave, she thought.

"It would not do to let our real names get about," Daisy volunteered cheerfully. "Some of us are still being sought. Violet was accused of murder, you know."

Sinclair eyed the soft-spoken Violet. "I didn't, actually," he said. Violet lowered her eyes.

"Oh, yes," Daisy continued. "Jasmine was condemned as a witch, though everyone knows there is no such thing. Lily stole money from her employer—a wicked man who seduced her."

"I do not think Mr. Sinclair needs as much detail as that," Lily grumbled.

"And Rose killed three husbands," Daisy finished proudly.

"I see," he murmured.

"Deserved it, every one of them," Rose muttered.

Daisy patted Rose's fleshy hand. "They beat her mercilessly. She didn't really murder them, of course. They took sick and died. Consumption or some such, wasn't it, Rose?"

Rose made a noncommittal response and promptly lit a cheroot. Louisa sighed. She had asked Rose not to smoke inside the house, but the woman always went her own way.

Lily coughed loudly, waving her hand at the smoke, but Rose pointedly ignored her.

"By the time the third husband died, people were growing suspicious," Daisy added. "They took to calling her the Black Widow. Her trial was written up in all the papers. Perhaps you read of it?"

"I'm afraid not," Sinclair replied politely. "I have been abroad for a number of years."

Daisy gave him a dazzling smile. "Then you

wouldn't have heard how Louisa spirited her off—"

"Mr. Sinclair cannot wish to hear of such things," Louisa interjected quickly.

"On the contrary," Sinclair drawled. "I am riveted."

"Disguised herself as a barrister, she did, complete with a curly white wig. Walked Rose right out of the Old Bailey after her sentencing."

"She had been convicted, then?" Sinclair arched a brow.

Daisy waved a dismissive hand. "Oh, most of us have been convicted of some crime or other. That's the point, you know. The justice system is weighted toward men. It brings no justice to women."

"He is not interested in our ideology," Louisa said quickly.

"Actually, I find it fascinating." Sinclair crossed his arms and bestowed a wry smile on Daisy. "Please continue."

Daisy beamed. "Louisa has a lovely flower garden. So each of us decided to become one— a flower, that is."

"We took new names because we have new lives," Violet explained quietly.

"The old ones were quite worn out," agreed Daisy. "But do not worry, Mr. Sinclair. We do not expect you to remember our names. There are too many of us."

"You do me a disservice," he said easily. Then, to their utter delight, he proceeded to

call each woman's name as his gaze traveled
around the table.

It was an extraordinary performance, Louisa
thought glumly, watching him charm her
household into admiring submission. Truly he
was a clever rogue, with the looks to match,
even in her father's outdated clothes. He wore
the double-breasted cutaway as if it were
made for him. Just above his waist, where the
front of the jacket stopped, no extra unwanted
flesh protruded or stretched the buttons of his
waistcoat. He had no need for the creaky cor-
sets some men had required to wear such a
revealing style. Nor did the enormous lapels
eclipse the breadth of his chest. His form was
lean, with a hint of hard musculature beneath
the concealing fabric.

Clearly Mr. Sinclair was no stranger to the
demands of hard labor, though she suspected
he had first met its acquaintance at Newgate.
Whatever the cause, his hands looked strong
and capable, in contrast to the soft, coddled
hands she had noted on some gentlemen.

Gabriel Sinclair had not been coddled. And
yet, in his gaze was the willful gleam of a man
accustomed to getting his way. Doubtless
women swooned when he entered a room.
Even the women at the table—and none was
inclined to look favorably on the male gender—studied him from eyes alight with interest and something else Louisa could not
precisely identify.

The man could coax a smile from a fencepost. How she wished they had left him swinging from the gallows.

Especially since he had shown no interest in helping them rescue Alice. Obviously the man knew a great deal about boats. Moreover, he was strong, fit, and clever. Suddenly it occurred to her that she could put the matter to him in business terms. He no doubt had a price, and she possessed ample funds.

Yes, she would make a devil's pact with Sinclair. She would use his skill, his cocky confidence. After all, men had used women since time began. It was only fair that the tables be turned now and again. God would forgive her this unholy alliance, for surely He did not mean Miss Wentworth to die in a floating hellhole, her helpless babe in the care of others. If Satan held the key to her salvation, so be it.

"Trying to ease your conscience?" His voice was low, meant for her alone.

Louisa looked up from her plate. "I beg your pardon?"

"Guilt, Miss Peabody," he said smoothly. "Guilt and discomfort lie within your lovely blue eyes. I must be the cause of it."

"You flatter yourself, sir."

Sinclair merely popped one of Lily's biscuits into his mouth and briefly closed his eyes in an expression of contentment. "Exquisite," he murmured. "Heaven has not seen biscuits like these." His gaze fixed appreciatively on Lily. "My compliments, ma'am."

Lily flushed and passed him the platter, which held one remaining biscuit. Jasmine rose to pour him another glass of wine. Daisy filled his plate with another helping of her dandelion greens. All eyes were riveted on him. Even Rose followed his every move. With no apparent effort, Sinclair held them in thrall.

"Stop it," Louisa snapped.

He eyed her curiously. "Is something amiss?"

"You know very well what is amiss." Louisa tossed her napkin down on the table in disgust.

Sinclair eyed the solitary biscuit he had just plucked from the platter. "Very well," he said with a heavy sigh, placing the biscuit gently in her napkin. "Take the last one, then. I shall console myself with the knowledge that sacrifice imbues the soul with nobility."

Giggles filled the room. A lazy smile flitted over his lips, though his eyes seemed curiously devoid of mirth.

"You, sir, are enamored of your own cleverness," Louisa said scornfully.

"And alas, you are not. Enamored, that is."

"I despise criminals."

He frowned thoughtfully. "Though you are one, of course."

Louisa blinked.

"Snatching prisoners from the jaws of their punishment seems to be something of a habit with you, Miss Peabody. I do not believe the law looks charitably upon the practice."

Did he mean to blackmail her? Surely not, for as a condemned man, Sinclair had a great deal to lose himself. Louisa's gaze flew to David, who sat on a stool near the door, a guarded expression on his face. He did not often take his meals with them, but she had asked him to stay for dinner in the event Sinclair did something rash.

Sinclair did not look at all foolhardy, though. Masculine arrogance sat firmly upon his shoulders, and his demeanor exuded the confidence of a man certain he could seduce any woman in the room.

In *that*, Louisa thought darkly, he was quite wrong.

"So it seems that you and I have something in common," he continued. "We are both criminals. Indeed, you seem utterly without remorse for your crimes. If you do not want that biscuit, by the way, I will take it back."

"I am *not* a criminal," she said frostily. But he spared her not a glance as he reached over and retrieved the biscuit from the folds of her napkin.

As he took a bite, his eyelids slid down—almost, but not quite, veiling his intense pleasure. Louisa studied him uneasily. There was something frankly sensual and wildly inappropriate about Sinclair, something that hinted at rare, unbridled appetites.

"On the contrary, Miss Peabody," he said, picking up the thread of their conversation. "If the authorities knew your identity, you would be sitting in Newgate yourself this very minute. Or perhaps languishing in a rotted prison hulk, playing skittles with the guards, listening to the debauchery below deck, and hoping someone would have the foolishness to come up with a suicidal plan to rescue you."

The room had grown still. The women shifted awkwardly in their chairs.

"We have broken the law," Louisa conceded quietly. "Perhaps, in the eyes of some, we are criminals. But in truth we are victims—"

"Ah. That makes it all right, then." He turned, as if the subject were forgotten. "Miss Lily, I don't suppose you have any more of those biscuits hiding somewhere?"

Wordlessly, Lily rose and went into the kitchen, appearing moments later with a fresh pan of biscuits. Louisa looked around, wondering if anyone else felt her outrage. But the others were looking at her in confusion, as though they did not understand why she was engaged in a bitter battle of wits with such a paragon of masculinity.

"Listen to me." Louisa's gaze moved from one woman to another. "This man is a despicable, irredeemable cad. A rapist. His last victims were nuns."

Ignoring their shocked gasps, Louisa pressed on. "He is a brute, who takes what he wants without a care. Do not look at him as if he were some sort of hero."

"Quite right." Sinclair's voice filled the stunned silence that followed her statement.

Louisa turned, righteous indignation filling her with a buoyant fury. She leveled a fierce gaze at him as her finger pointed straight to his black and poisoned heart.

He regarded her fingertip and smiled, exposing a small dimple in his right cheek and the straight white teeth the Creator had given him. They were all in place, none marred or chipped, testimony to the charmed life he had led. Truly, it was a sin for one man to possess so many natural gifts, especially a horrid man like Sinclair.

Louisa closed her eyes to block out the gold-flecked lashes that narrowed his eyes to amused slits. She wished she had his cool poise. She wished his life of careless greed had ended there on that gallows. She wished above all things that she had not been the one to save him, for the irony was too monstrous. She, who had vowed to live the rest of her life apart from men, had preserved the existence of a snake without conscience or caring.

"Beast," she declared passionately.

The room was silent. And then: "Bravo, Miss Peabody. Bravo."

Her eyes flew open.

Sinclair was smiling. "That is as good a performance as I have seen. Next you will tell me your own heart-wrenching tale of woe. Were you once a nun yourself, perhaps? Did a monster come and snatch you from your self-righteous cocoon and impale you on the staff of his desire? You have only to speak, and I will see that he hangs. But you'd best be sure, because I would hate to hang an innocent man. That is too depressing a thought."

He turned to the others. "Ladies, forgive me for casting a pall on your gathering. Let us change the subject. Shall I tell you about the

West Indies? I have been there and many other places besides. It will be my pleasure to regale you with exotic tales, and I assure you there is not a nun in them anywhere."

Miss Peabody was one of those thoroughly insane spinsters who had made it her life's work to protect womanhood from the evils of men. Gabriel shuddered. He had seen a few of those in his time, though none so embittered as she. Some man had brought her to this pass, he was sure of it. Under other circumstances, he might have been tempted to take up the considerable challenge of bringing a charitable light to her lovely blue eyes. He rarely minded a challenge when it came to women, but Miss Peabody would require more time than he had. Centuries, perhaps.

Anyway, he had to figure out how to get to Sinclair Isle—a difficult task at best. His jailers had removed what little money he'd had on his person, and Sedbury had no doubt gleefully repossessed that sleek little yacht Gabriel had won from him weeks ago. Handbills offering a reward for his capture had probably gone up all over London, so he dared not risk a visit to his father's solicitors yet.

The sooner he left Miss Peabody's bastion of bleakness, the better. The Flowers seemed nice enough, though the notion of outcast females being reborn as garden specimens was a bit too bizarre even for his tastes.

"Mr. Sinclair?"

Gabriel looked over the rim of his glass as

Miss Peabody sailed into the parlor, the giant trailing in her wake. She took a seat at a writing table facing the chair in which he had been enjoying his port—one of the few things about this house he could commend. Certainly not the cuisine, for supper sat in his stomach like lead. Though Lily had produced those excellent biscuits, Daisy had been responsible for the rest of the meal. She seemed proud of her dandelion greens and boiled turnips, but Gabriel had found the dish as appealing as seaweed.

No wonder the giant took his meals elsewhere. He probably had a secret supply of lamb or venison stashed in his cottage. Gabriel regarded the man with undisguised envy.

"I have a business proposition." Miss Peabody sat stiffly in her chair, eyeing him as if he were a spoonful of bitter medicine to be endured. "I am prepared to pay you a great deal of money if you will help us free Miss Wentworth."

Did she think him an idiot? "I am a wanted man," he said dismissively. "I would be a fool to involve myself in anything illicit." He paused. "How much money?"

"Two hundred pounds."

"That would not begin to pay for my services." But it would go a ways toward the purchase of a boat. And it was two hundred pounds more than he had at the moment. But no, he would not play the fool for such a sum.

"Two thousand, then."

Gabriel nearly choked on his port.

"Five thousand?" she ventured.

For five thousand pounds, he could buy half the Royal Navy. Gabriel stared at her in stunned amazement. "How is it that you have access to such a sum?"

"My husband was very rich."

Husband? This man-hating, spinsterish female was somebody's *wife*? Gabriel stared at the giant, perched warily on a sofa much too small for him. David Ferguson was the only other man he had seen in the house, but the giant did not look at her as a husband might. Wait—hadn't she used the past tense? "You were married?" he queried gingerly.

"For six hours. He died on our wedding trip." Her constricted features gave her the look of someone who has bitten into a sour apple. Gabriel tried to imagine Miss Peabody on a wedding trip and failed utterly.

"Then . . . you are *Mrs*. Peabody?"

"Not at all," she replied quickly. "I have chosen to act as if the marriage never existed. Accordingly, I have not taken my husband's name."

"Only his money."

She flushed. "The settlements had been duly prepared and signed. It was my due."

"I see." The mercenary little witch. Had she poisoned the man's wine at their wedding feast? Married and widowed in six hours. A feat, indeed. He would have to remember to watch what he ate during his brief time here.

"I doubt very much that you do, sir, but that is neither here nor there. I am prepared to pay you a great deal of money to bring about Miss Wentworth's release. The sooner, the better. What do you say to my proposition?"

Despite her firm, decisive tone, her lips trembled slightly and her eyes gleamed with unnatural brightness. Clearly, the subject of her marriage distressed her. The notion of making her enticing person part of the bargain briefly entered his head, but he put it aside. Money was what he needed, and he needed it now.

"I would require half the payment in advance," he warned, "half after the job is done."

She put on a pair of spectacles and dipped her pen into the inkwell. She scribbled something on a piece of paper, then handed it to him.

Skeptically, Gabriel eyed the figures on the page. The promises of a woman who dashed about the country causing mayhem were worth little. Now if she were to drop a pile of bank notes in his lap, that would be something else entirely.

"I cannot give you half today, as my trustee will not release my quarterly allowance for a fortnight," she said. "He will balk at such a sum, but I have no doubt that I can bring him around eventually."

Did the woman think him stupid? He was not about to risk his neck for a promise, no matter that it came from a mouth as lovely as any he had seen. With a contemptuous smile, he looked up from the promissory note. "This is all well and good, but—"

"I can give you almost a third now, however. Will that be sufficient?" She thrust something at him.

Gabriel's gaze dropped to the large stack of notes emblazoned with the crest of the Bank of England. With this, he could sail an entire fleet to Sinclair Isle. Come to think of it, he wouldn't need to carry out Miss Wentworth's rescue at all. He could take this tidy little sum and—

"I am trusting you, Mr. Sinclair," she said sternly, evidently reading his mind, "though I know it is unwise. But if Miss Wentworth is to be freed, I have no other choice."

Gabriel plucked the money from her hands and tucked it into his pocket. "Done," he said, and took a bracing sip of port to celebrate his unexpected fortune.

Miss Peabody wore a look of distaste, as if she could scarcely bear to look at him. She settled herself at her desk again and dipped her pen into the inkwell. She eyed him expectantly, her hand poised over a piece of blank paper.

"What is your plan?" she asked solemnly.

The spectacles gave her a studious air and, though they obscured the full beauty of her eyes, seemed consistent with the slight furrow between her brows. Most women did not wear spectacles in company. Miss Peabody seemed perfectly content to do so, though if she did not mend her judgmental ways, she would end up with wrinkles before her time. He wondered whether she ever smiled.

"Mr. Sinclair," she said impatiently, "I asked about your plan."

"Plan?"

"To rescue Miss Wentworth, of course."

Gabriel rather enjoyed her consternation. He took another sip of port. "There are a number of possibilities. Much depends on the type of ship on which Miss Wentworth is incarcerated. Can you tell me about the vessel?"

"No, but . . ." She looked uncertainly at the giant. "That is, David—"

"Cannot tell a warship from a barge, I imagine," Gabriel said. The giant glared at him but offered no denial.

"Surely that cannot be of much importance," she said. "David has at least seen the ship, so he should be able to provide sufficient detail—"

"No doubt." Gabriel eyed the giant. "How many gun ports would you say there are? How big are the hawseholes?"

No one spoke. Miss Peabody looked questioningly at the giant and then at him. "Gun ports—holes from which the guns would fire. Is that what you mean?" she asked brightly.

Gabriel nodded.

"Well, now. That is simple enough." Hopefully, she turned to Ferguson. "Did it have holes, David? You know, little round holes in the side where the guns—"

"Square," Gabriel corrected. "The holes are square."

"Square, then." She frowned. "But I am sure I have seen round holes on ships—"

"Portholes. A ship's windows, if you will. They are small. Smaller than gun ports. Or hawseholes."

"Oh, dear." Miss Peabody looked quite exasperated. "Did the ship have any holes, David? Big or little or round or square or ... hawse-shaped?"

"Hell and damnation!" The giant stood up. "It looked like a blasted big ship, Louisa, and that is all I can say."

Miss Peabody cleared her throat. "Does all of this really matter, Mr. Sinclair?"

Gabriel took another sip of port. He wondered about the relationship between Miss Peabody and David Ferguson. Obviously, they knew each other well. Lovers, he might have said, if Miss Peabody hadn't been the last woman in the world to take a lover. But then, he'd have thought her the last woman in the world to take a husband, too.

The marital union had probably not been consummated—not pleasantly, anyway—for Miss Peabody was not much at ease with her own femininity. Women who had experienced carnal pleasure did not pucker up like a dried prune whenever a man looked at them with desire in his eyes.

"Mr. Sinclair?" she prodded testily. "I asked whether it mattered if the ship had all these holes. Would you quit staring at me as if I'd just said the moon was made of green cheese?"

"How do you know it is not?" No doubt about it, Miss Peabody had the armor of a prickly pear.

"I do nae think we are getting anywhere," the giant groused.

"Nor do I," she snapped. "Come, David. Mr. Sinclair undoubtedly needs time to devise a plan and—"

"Miss Peabody." Gabriel drained his port, set the glass upon the table at his elbow, and rose. He let his shadow fall upon the paper on her desk. "If one intends to sneak onto a ship—or off it, for that matter—one has to find an alternative to the gangway."

She frowned, and he could tell she was beginning to understand at last.

"One must be enterprising, or else walk right into the guards' arms. I should not like to see you behind bars. The experience is entirely too earthy."

"I am not afraid of capture," she said in a steely tone.

"You should be. Do you have any idea what it is like in prison?"

She was silent.

"I thought not. Don't worry—I will not subject you to a litany of complaints. I'm no reformer, but neither am I fool enough to try to breach a ship's security without having a notion as to what sort of craft it is."

Her gaze was troubled. "I'm afraid we will have to do the best we can. Every day Miss Wentworth endures on that awful ship is an abomination. We simply cannot wait. I would like to be more prepared, but . . ." She let her voice trail off, and an ineffable sadness appeared in her eyes.

In that moment, Gabriel knew he would have to see it through. As much as he wanted to take her money and be off, he would stay until the job was done. There wasn't a boat he didn't know inside and out, be it frigate or merchant clipper. Without his help, she'd end up on the wrong side of a prison cell door, looking out with those big blue eyes.

Yes, he would take her money, but damned if he didn't want something else for his trouble, too. She was a strange woman with a prickly spine, not the sort of female he would normally waste his time on, but the knowledge that she could embrace such danger without a care for her own safety aroused him. He lusted—if not for her, precisely, then for the possibility of shaping such resentful clay into raw sensuality. A woman who could face down death could certainly face sex.

Gabriel brought himself up short. It was best not to let his imagination run amok. People couldn't be changed, and Louisa Peabody would have to change dramatically before he would contemplate a liaison with her. Still, a man could be alert for the odd chance.

He felt the giant's eyes on him and slanted a gaze at the man. Ferguson stood with his arms folded across his sizable chest, as if daring Gabriel to touch one hair of Miss Peabody's deranged head. His eyes held a simmering anger, as if he could read Gabriel's very improper thoughts.

Gabriel shrugged. He would not apologize for the images that floated through his mind— images of Miss Peabody lying naked under him, enslaved to the pleasures he could give her. If the giant had never seen her thus, it was his own loss. If he had, then every instinct Gabriel had about women was false—and that was quite impossible.

"Illicit acts are best undertaken under the cloak of darkness," he heard himself say. "We will need a strong rope, a fast skiff, and someone with strong arms."

"Wait." She dipped her pen and began to scribble furiously on her paper.

He stared at her, aghast. "Never say you are taking *notes*."

"But of course." Her brow furrowed. "How else am I to remember?"

"Notes are of no use in the darkness. And there will be no time for reading once the thing has begun."

She flushed. "I realize that. But writing things down makes them easier for me to remember."

"And easier for someone to find out what we are about. Didn't you say you wanted to keep the details from the Flowers?"

"The flowers?" she echoed, puzzled.

"Lily, Violet, Daisy—"

"Oh." She hesitated. "The notes are only for me. I plan all our missions, you see, but I am terrified of leaving something out, some crucial part of the plan that could result in disaster. So I write everything down and look at it from all possible angles just to make sure I have forgotten nothing."

Gabriel sighed. "Then by all means take notes. Commit them to memory tonight, then throw them into the fire. Tomorrow we undertake Miss Wentworth's freedom."

Abruptly, she rose to her feet. Her hands clenched in fists at her sides, and a fierce fervor filled her eyes.

"We shall!" she vowed. The feverish radiance in her gaze seemed to inhabit her entire person, for she positively trembled with excitement. "We shall indeed!"

Gabriel's jaw went slack. He stared into her bespectacled gaze and suddenly realized he was looking at a warrior—one who'd had the misfortune to be born into a decidedly female body at a time when heroism was a wholly masculine sphere.

He glanced at the giant to see how the man was taking this uncommon display. Ferguson's features revealed no shock or surprise. Indeed, his eyes gleamed with respect for her. It was a look a man might give his captain.

Miss Peabody grabbed his hand and shook it violently. "We will pull this off, Mr. Sinclair," she vowed. "I swear it. We will work together, and we will prevail. Justice will be served, and Miss Wentworth will be saved."

Good God. Beneath that spinsterish exterior beat the heart of a bloody revolutionary.

Chapter 5

❦

"Do ye trust him?"

Louisa patted Midnight's nose. She had always loved this big black horse, though he had originally been Richard's. It was a point of pride with Richard that he rode such a dangerous, deadly beast. But where Richard had seen a wild, ungovernable animal only the manliest of gentlemen could tame, Louisa saw a mistreated creature with a valiant, even noble, spirit. It was not a violent nature that had made Midnight difficult to manage but his master's too-frequent application of the whip.

Richard had been amazed and a bit chastened the first time she rode the stallion. He hadn't known what horses had meant to her over the years, how they'd given her a peace otherwise absent from her life. Most young women did not haunt the stables, but Louisa had never wished to be anywhere else. The rhythms of meeting a horse's feeding, grooming, and other needs gave a soothing symmetry to her days.

She'd often wondered what would have

happened if her mother had not died birthing her. Would her father have been less reckless with his money? Would she have learned to abhor the rough calluses that came from mucking out stalls? Would she have gone to London, had a proper come-out, and learned to simper helplessly at eligible bachelors?

Midnight had known from the first carrot she brought him that they were kindred spirits—peaceful, for the most part, but driven to rebellion by tyrants.

Louisa gave the horse an affectionate pat. A thundering good ride was just what she needed to soothe the butterflies in her stomach, but there wasn't time. She sighed. "We have no choice, David."

"Aye." He knelt to inspect the stallion's hooves. "But I do nae like it."

"You have had the dreams again." David was plagued by nightmares. Louisa suspected they stemmed from the atrocities he had suffered in prison. Sometimes the dreams left him with a lingering sense of foreboding she had learned not to dismiss. On the day they had ridden to Newton to rescue Violet, David had had such a premonition.

The memory of Violet's rescue still made Louisa uneasy. Violet had been accused of seducing another woman's husband, then killing him in a jealous rage. Louisa could not imagine anyone believing the mild-mannered Violet capable of such acts. But when Violet's own husband had echoed the accusation, her fate had been sealed.

Pregnant and condemned, Violet had been forced to stand half-naked in the village square for daily floggings, the magistrate having magnanimously deferred her hanging until after the babe's birth. Violet's husband, Will, deemed to have suffered unforgivable injury, administered the floggings. He made a great show of hitting only her back so as to spare the babe, which was assumed to be the dead man's get, but he obviously had no compassion in him.

The case had attracted considerable notoriety and a large number of gawkers who gathered each day to watch Violet's humiliation. Newton was not five miles from Peabody Manor, and when word reached Louisa of such an injustice so close to home, she'd had to act.

There had been little life and no hope in Violet's eyes the day Louisa and David had thundered into the village square. The crowd quickly dispersed, but Violet's husband had viciously lashed out at them with his whip. Louisa would never forget the evil promise in Will's eyes as their gazes met over Midnight's flowing black mane.

"Aye, I dreamed last night," David said, pulling her back to the present. I suspect the mongrel means to leave us in the lurch."

"I am paying him well," Louisa pointed out.

"Money can nae buy everything."

"Sinclair has nothing. He needs what I have."

David rose, his large form dwarfing hers and nearly Midnight's as well. "As to that, I'm thinking ye be right, lass. But there's more than one kind of need."

Louisa frowned. "I don't understand."

"What that man needs no one can give him. Mark my words, he'll be trouble."

The word had never sounded so ominous.

Gabriel strode along the path he had found a few hundred yards from the house. London, she had said, was three hours away. She'd told him nothing else about their location, but that did not matter: he knew this land as well as he knew his own name.

The smells of sawgrass and salt marsh catapulted him back into another time, when the delights of the day had been sufficient for a boy's lifetime, when time itself had no existence beyond the present. Here ancient woodlands gave way to gracious farmland that ran to the sandy river that flowed between bay and sea. An old gray castle conjured images of knights and wizards and wondrous deeds done in the name of honor and valor.

A coastline like none other, meandering from flat meadows to chalky cliffs, from placid lighthouses to stone forts. The very air was evocative of the past, of change. Centuries of invaders had looked out from their ships and coveted this land across the water, and the land had rebuffed their assaults. For this land would not be civilized, and its shifting sands would never be tamed into permanence.

Kent. His home and his curse. It would always reside somewhere inside him, like a bullet lodged near the heart, too close to that frail muscle to be other than a mortal wound.

Inhaling deeply, reluctantly, the salt-tinged air, he followed the path upward to a gently rolling hill. He wondered how the castle had fared and whether the woods had reclaimed it or the sea had breached its stone defenses. He wondered whether the turrets that had protected him and Robert from the dragons of their imaginations had crumbled under the weight of time and broken dreams.

Two months ago, the letter from his father's solicitors had drawn him back to England. He had intended only to make a final pilgrimage to Sinclair Isle, skirting the place that had fired his boyhood imagination with dreams that had turned out to be as illusory as ghosts and as bitter as weeds. Never would he have willingly come to this land or stood at the top of a hill and looked out over the ancient wood at the speck of blue that was the river estuary he knew so well. Never would he have sought this chilling moment of recognition, when the past rushed up and ambushed him like a prodigal son welcomed home at last.

Damn her for plucking him from his fate and bringing him to this place that ran through his blood like a poison. Damn Louisa Peabody to hell and back.

"Oh, here you are," Louisa said brightly as she swept into the parlor. Sinclair was standing at the window, looking out. He did not turn to acknowledge her. Louisa suppressed a surge of irritation and tried to remember that she had purchased only his skills, not his good will.

"David has found a fisherman who will provide us with a rowboat for tonight," she said. "Sam will wait with the carriage just outside Woolwich. Once we have Miss Wentworth, we need only row downriver to him, hide the boat, and be off." She pulled a piece of paper from her pocket. "I believe that covers all the items on the list."

Sinclair turned. He regarded her as if she were a loathsome insect. His lips curled. "You rely on a mere boy to hold a coach and four?"

Louisa forced herself to remember that he held the key to tonight's success or failure. She had to be civil to him for only a few more hours, and then he could crawl back under whatever rock would have him. "Sam is quite capable of managing a team," she replied evenly. "He practically lives in the stable. He knows what to do."

"Do forgive me. For a moment I thought you were relying on an untrained lad to do a man's job." His mirthless smile broadened. "But he is not untrained, is he? You have used him before in your schemes."

"They are not 'schemes,' " Louisa said, bristling. "They are missions to right the terrible wrongs done to women who cannot defend themselves against the men who run our legal system."

"The boy feels as you do, of course."

Louisa hesitated. Sam repeatedly begged to be allowed to help, but his enthusiasm derived from the pull of adventure, not principle.

"Come, now, madam," Sinclair prodded, "you must know what the lad thinks about risking his neck to flout the king's laws." He brushed a piece of lint from the lapel of his coat and stifled a yawn. "With all due regard to your late father, I will not wear this jacket tonight. It is tight about the shoulders and would hamper—"

"Sam is committed to our mission and fully capable of the responsibilities we give him," Louisa declared vehemently. "Moreover, we keep him out of harm's way. All he need do tonight is watch the horses."

"My dear Miss Peabody," he replied, one brow arching in apparent surprise, "I never suggested otherwise."

Louisa stared at him, feeling as if she had entered a hall of mirrors in which every reflection was slightly distorted. Each conversation with Sinclair bent her sense of him into a different image. Try as she might, she could not get a fix on the man.

She would not believe that he cared two figs about Sam or, indeed, about anything. That gaze was too hollow, too empty, too devoid of warmth. His flippant remarks and sardonic humor bespoke a deep contempt for humanity. He would not be helping them tonight without her princely payment, for Sinclair cared for no one but himself. Of compassion and empathy he had none. That practiced smile, that easy wit—they did not fool her. He was a despicable human being, a rake, a scoundrel, a worthless snake, a—

"Finished?"

Louisa nearly jumped. "I—I beg your pardon?"

"I merely wondered whether you had finished woolgathering and were ready to go over the plans for tonight." His face was a careful blank.

Her eyes narrowed. "I am ready."

"Shouldn't you summon the giant? I assume he means to accompany us tonight. I shouldn't like to think of you rowing me and Miss Wentworth all that distance alone."

"David will join us shortly." Louisa plopped into the chair at her writing table. She pretended to study her notes.

To her dismay, Sinclair crossed the room and hovered over her. "What *is* it?" she demanded.

"Ah. Here they are." He retrieved her spectacles, half-hidden by her papers, and held them out to her. "You need these to read, do you not?"

She snatched the spectacles from his hand and put them on her nose. "I know what you are doing, so you might as well give it up."

"Oh?" He wore an expression of wounded innocence. "What nefarious tricks of mine are you onto, Miss Peabody?"

"Every one of them," she ground out. "You mean to lull us into false complacency, to present yourself as the most innocuous of men, when everyone knows you are the proverbial wolf in sheep's clothing.''

''Alas, I am undone,'' he said mournfully. ''Thank the heavens for your perspicacity, else all of the women under your roof would surely become my next victims.''

Louisa glared at him.

''As you have so correctly observed,'' he continued blandly, ''a scoundrel is not bound by the principles of common decency that dictate your behavior. I am not fit to move in your so very righteous universe. Why, the very notion that a handbill might have *your* face on it is unthinkable.'' He stroked his chin in a musing fashion. '' 'Louisa Peabody, Feloness.' Not that it doesn't have an intriguing ring.''

Louisa rose. The top of her head came no higher than his chin, but she was not about to be cowed by his superior height. ''You have the understanding of a flea, Mr. Sinclair, but it does not matter as long as you are fit to guide us tonight. Afterward, you may fall off the face of the earth with my heartfelt blessing. Is that quite clear?''

''Oh, quite,'' he replied easily.

She eyed him suspiciously. ''You will do as you promised—help us free Miss Wentworth to the best of your ability?''

''Insofar as I have any ability for breaking into prison hulks and spiriting away its female denizens, I shall dedicate it to your mission, madam.''

''There!'' she said accusingly. ''You are doing it again. You do not say what you mean, and everything you say is meaningless."

"Surely not everything."

"*Will* you help us, sir, or will you continue with these ridiculous jokes?" To her dismay, her voice broke. "If you are going to leave us in the lurch, I only ask that you not wait until tonight to do so. It is not my fate that concerns me but that of Miss Wentworth. You would not be so cruel as to let us think you are going to help her and then . . . then—" She broke off, mortified to feel a tear running down her cheek. She brushed at it, but he startled her by capturing her hand.

He brought her fingertips to his lips. "Do not be concerned," he said lightly. "Your money has purchased my loyalty. For the night, anyway."

Louisa jerked her hand away from his mouth as though he had sunk his teeth into her flesh. "I did not give you leave to fondle me," she cried angrily.

An arrested expression crossed his features. For a moment Louisa had the distinct impression she was seeing the man himself beneath that cavalier mask. But too quickly, the mask slid into place again.

"Miss Peabody," he said solemnly, "if you believe that to be fondling, someone has given you a rather inferior lesson on the subject."

Her cheeks flushed with embarrassment. "What I believe is not your concern. You need only know that I have no wish to be touched by you or any man, that I find such contact abhorrent, and—dear lord, what are you *do-ing?''*

Louisa stared in horror as he bent his face to hers and kissed her full on the mouth.

It was a gentle kiss, not crude in the way one might have expected of such a man, but feathery-soft and cajoling, so disarming that Louisa stood rooted to the spot while his mouth brushed hers as if it were the most natural thing in the world to do so. Then he lifted his head, regarded her curiously, and let his gaze devour her lips. Louisa gazed at him in stunned amazement.

Then he carefully removed her spectacles—evidently in preparation for another kiss—and she panicked.

Trembling, she tried to push him away, but he merely caught her hands and imprisoned them lightly at her sides. Louisa edged backward, felt the writing table behind her, and knew she was trapped.

The second kiss was much more insistent than the first. His mouth crushed hers into submission, as if he knew that he had her stunned and helpless and must now press his advantage. His tongue flirted shamelessly with hers as he coaxed her lips apart. Louisa tried to break free, but his hands slid around her waist and pulled her firmly against him.

Her breasts sent her a disturbing sensation as they pressed against the solid mountain of muscle that was his chest. Her lower body was supremely aware of his taut, corded thighs and the knee that was wedged ever so slightly between hers. His kiss, urgent now, muffled her gasp of protest, and his tongue seized the opportunity to slip inside her mouth. Then his hands slid slowly up her arms, his thumbs lingering over the sensitive pulse point inside the curve of her elbow. His fingers grazed the outside of her breasts, but they did not linger there and instead moved upward to toy with the neckline of her bodice.

Louisa could not breathe. A terrifying sensation settled in the pit of her stomach. Panic filled her in a great shuddering wave that made her want to scream. Just as the terror peaked, he released her.

For a moment, they just stood there, the silence pregnant with something horrid and strange. Sinclair stared at her with a slight frown. Closing her eyes against his scrutiny, Louisa struggled to calm her uneven breathing. She leaned back against the table, fighting the turbulence inside.

"Please," she murmured. "I feel . . ."

"Overwhelmed?" he suggested lightly. "Swept away beyond your wildest imaginings?"

Her eyes shot open. Sheer masculine confidence radiated from his velvety gaze, along with the amused arrogance of a man who had honed his masculine skills in countless seductions. She took a deep breath, trying to regain her poise, but his nearness conjured unsettling and unwelcome images.

"I think . . ." she began.

"Do not," he commanded, and swept her

into his arms again. A strange dizziness overtook her. "Please," she cried, "please listen. I feel . . ."

"Breathless. Driven. Desperate." He nibbled at her earlobe.

"*Sick.*" Her stomach lurched wildly. "You arrogant man, I am going to be sick!" She pushed herself away from him and put her hands over her face. She swayed, and suddenly he was pulling her to the window and raising the sash and making her inhale the fresh air.

Louisa swallowed long, deep gulps of air as she fought to calm her stomach. She had no idea how long she stood there with her head out the window and his steadying hands at her waist. Eventually the sickening sensation stopped, the pounding in her head relented. She pushed herself back from the window and looked up at him.

He was staring at her as if she had sprouted two heads. "Jesus. You truly are a bedlamite."

"And you are a rapist and scoundrel," she retorted weakly, "so I suppose we are even."

"I have never raped anyone in my life." He handed her glasses to her and regarded her coldly.

"Those nuns—"

"Are as crazed as you. In fact, I'm beginning to believe that every female in England is short a sheet." He shook his head in angry bewilderment, then strode from the room.

Louisa clutched the windowsill and took in another great gulp of air.

Chapter 6

The prison hulk rode high in the water, too high for a gunship. That meant they were in luck—the artillery had been removed, no doubt salvaged for another ship of the line. The empty gun ports would afford easy entry once he had pried the covers loose. Gabriel suppressed a burst of elation—luck was just toying with him, seducing him into thinking they might actually carry off this mad scheme.

As Ferguson rowed them silently toward the hulk, Gabriel wondered whether he had truly lost his mind. Barely three days from the hangman's noose, he was flirting with death as if it were a cherished lover.

All because of a woman as mad as the blazing moon that bathed the whole damned river in its relentless light. Gabriel glared at the thin wafting clouds, willing them toward that shining silver orb. With a woman's coyness, they drifted aimlessly, taking their sweet time.

Watching those insubstantial wisps float airily toward the moon, Gabriel reminded himself of how much he needed the money Miss

Peabody was paying him. He would never have played the hero otherwise. Heroes were fools who paid homage to antiquated notions of glory and honor to mask the selfishness inside. His father had been such a man, and if there was one lesson Gabriel had learned from observing his sire, it was the folly of self-delusion.

Gabriel prided himself on seeing the world as it was, not as some poor fool thought it ought to be. He had no interest in trying to change humanity. As long as a man possessed a heightened sense of the ridiculous, he could float quite well amid the flotsam and jetsam of life.

He was sure Miss Peabody would disapprove of his artful dodging, but she heartily disapproved of him, anyway. Still, he couldn't resist studying her, wishing she was not as crazy as a loon.

She sat motionless on the bench, her hair covered with a dark scarf, her face blackened with coal dust. She wore boys' breeches and looked as much at home in a rough woolen jacket as any seaman. Staring out over the water, her gaze fixed intently on the hulking shadow ahead, she betrayed no hint of nervousness. Determination was etched in every line of her still, quiet silhouette.

What gave her the courage to sail into the teeth of danger, proudly challenging the forces of man and nature? Doubtless it was the same delusional daring that had sent his father into treacherous seas in a metal coffin to challenge Napoleon's fleet.

She did not even know how to kiss, for God's sake.

Gabriel hadn't known whether to be amused or infuriated by her reaction to his lovemaking. Never before had his kisses made a woman ill, yet it was not pride that made him rue that kiss this afternoon. In truth, her reaction troubled him less than his own.

He wanted to kiss her again, to coax that still, stubborn mouth until she cried out in fierce submission.

Hell, that wasn't the half of it. He wanted to do all manner of outlandish things to her person to erase that solemn contempt in her eyes. Like making love to her on the floor of this leaky rowboat as the moonlit river rocked them to the brink of madness.

As Gabriel considered that intriguing image, he looked up and found the giant staring at him. Suspicion darkened the man's eyes. The bastard *knew*, dammit. Knew that she had infected him like the plague.

The clouds picked that moment to cast their flimsy veils over the moon, smothering the treacherous moonlight. Perhaps their luck would hold, after all. Anyway, in an hour it would be over. Miss Peabody would have another wronged woman for her flock, and he would have enough money to sail away in a boat a damned sight better than this one.

Unless they were all at the bottom of the river, riddled with bullet holes. Or clapped in chains and tossed to the fish or keel-hauled or hung on the yardarm or tortured into confessions that would gain them speedy executions.

"My God," she whispered. "It is enormous."

Gabriel ripped his mind from its gloomy contemplation of their fate. The prison hulk loomed not a dozen yards away. And though it was the dead of night and they had blackened their faces and the river had been smooth enough to let them slip through the waters with silent ease, Gabriel saw immediately that they were doomed.

For like a jealous lover, the moon suddenly slipped the flirtatious clouds and unleashed its full, glorious light on the rowboat just as two guards rounded the upper deck of the rotting warship. Unless the men were drunk and blind, they would surely notice the company below.

Instantly, Ferguson stilled the oars, but the current was strong, and the river's steady lapping against the hulk produced little rippling waves that sucked the rowboat closer to disaster. In another moment they would crash into the ship's bow.

Just as they careened into the hulk, Gabriel leaned out and pushed against the ship's stem. His body absorbed the force of the collision, and he muffled the grunt of pain that would have revealed their position to the guards above. Rebounding, the rowboat lurched toward the anchor cable. Gabriel grabbed the thick rope with both hands and, bracing his

feet against the rowboat's bench, forced the little boat to a halt.

They waited, silent and breathless in the
moonlight, to learn whether they were discovered. But the guards' bored chatter never wavered, and the two men ambled away.

Steadying himself against the anchor cable,
Gabriel gauged the distance to the gun deck.
He checked to see that the iron scraper was
securely tied to his waist along with the knife
that he was never without. He'd purloined an
assortment of sewing needles and hooks from
the Flowers, though if Miss Wentworth had
been given free rein in the cabin, they would
be unnecessary. Which was fortunate, since
he'd never actually picked a lock but only witnessed a drunken cutpurse demonstrate the
skill one night in a Jamaican tavern.

"Keep her steady, Ferguson," he said in a
low voice, "but not too close. You want to be
able to row like hell once I've handed over the
woman."

"I am coming with you," Miss Peabody said
quietly.

"We've been over that. You'd only slow me
down."

"But poor Miss Wentworth will be frightened if you simply present yourself and demand that she come with you. The presence
of another woman would—"

"Ruin everything," Gabriel finished. "Look,
Miss Peabody, if I find the sainted Miss Wentworth, I'm going to have my hands full slipping her out without alerting the guards. I

won't have time to worry about you."

"He's right," Ferguson put in.

Satisfied that the giant had the willful Miss Peabody well in hand, Gabriel took a deep breath and began to climb the anchor cable.

It had been a long time since his legs had mastered a piece of rope as big around as a man's thigh or edged over a spit of rake without a breast band to keep him from slipping. As a youth, he had once stowed away on a ship that had put in at Sinclair Isle. The irate captain had given him quite a tongue-lashing before returning him to his father. But the man had also taken pity on him and in the days the ship moored at Sinclair Isle, taught him much about sailing.

Eventually, his father, Aloysius, had put him to work testing his nautical designs. In his ten years on the island, Gabriel sank only a handful of boats. Given his father's radical departure from conventional sailing methods, that was remarkable. Since then, Gabriel had sailed everything from an Irish curragh to a six-masted schooner and had sunk nary a one.

Shinnying up the anchor cable was still child's play, he discovered. His legs were still nimble, his feet sure, his arms strong. He could do this a thousand times.

The rake was a bit trickier. Though his feet edged carefully along the slender spit of wood, they slipped once, and he barely avoided falling into the river. By the time he reached the gun ports, he was breathing hard. The port cover was closed but not nailed. He

wedged it open with his scraper and slipped
inside.

She must have been a fleet little frigate in
her day. He could almost imagine Nelson
here, lying in a cot strung amid the cannons,
making his battle plans to the lapping of the
waves below. But whatever glory the ship had
seen belonged to the past. The gun ports were
barren, the planking dented and rotting. No
one had polished these timbers in years. The
odor of gunpowder had given way to the
stench of bilge water and human waste.
Around him came the hasty scurrying of rats
that had not yet succumbed to their fate.

The hull was thick—three feet or so—and
when the gun port covers were closed, few
sounds penetrated from the outside. But the
ship was by no means silent. As Gabriel stood
motionless in the shadows, letting his eyes ad-
just to the dim light of a solitary lantern that
hung from one of the beams, he heard within
the ship the unmistakable sounds of human
degradation, rage, and debauchery. This dark,
rotted hulk had been given over to human
misery.

Above it all, came a loud, distinctly feminine shriek.

He had been gone half an hour. Louisa felt
utterly useless. Minute after minute passed
without any sign of Sinclair. She sat motionless
on the rowboat's hard, damp bench, her eyes
searching the hulk for any sign of activity.

Only the guards, their discourse laced with

slurred obscenities, jarred the silence as they came round again. But they were either too drunk or too bored to think of looking down to see whether a tiny rowboat waited in the shadows to spirit one of their charges away.

Louisa had known she could not go with Sinclair. The cable he had scaled so easily would have been impossible for her. The little spit of wood on which he had balanced while prying that port cover loose would not have held her nervous feet.

For the good of the mission, it had to be Sinclair alone tonight. How she resented that.

She didn't trust him. Oh, he wouldn't betray them—not yet, anyway, for he needed the money. He had no shred of altruism in him, no interest in the plight of his fellow man. He had no sense of injustice, no burning need to right the wrongs that had been done for centuries. Unlike David, Sinclair had no well of pain and suffering that allowed him to empathize with those less fortunate than he. His past was doubtless as devoid of empathy as his future. He was an empty, hollow man, who cared for no one, who set no principle above his own self-interest. She couldn't trust a man like that to steer by the same moral compass that guided her.

"He is clever, lass," David whispered at one point. "If she can be saved, he will do it."

Louisa would concede that. Sinclair was clever enough to slip through the nooks and crannies of that awful ship, find Miss Wentworth, and free her. Clever enough to kiss a woman who loathed a man's touch and make her sick from confusion and revulsion and god-awful longing.

Yes, he was clever. Clever like a snake.

"There!" came David's sharp whisper.

Louisa's gaze followed David's. Two figures stood silhouetted against the open gun port, one of them unmistakably Sinclair, the other a woman.

Wonder and exultation filled her. He had done it! He'd saved Alice Wentworth from her horrible, unjust fate.

Sinclair slipped onto the tiny ledge that jutted only a few inches out from the port. Louisa saw him speak to Miss Wentworth, who looked to be paralyzed with fear. Then, to Louisa's amazement, the woman started to laugh.

"Dear lord," Louisa whispered as her wild cackling echoed over the water. Fear had obviously made the woman hysterical. Didn't she realize her noise would bring the guards?

Sinclair clapped a hand over the woman's mouth. David strained upward, but even with his great height, Miss Wentworth and Sinclair were an impossible distance above them. David's movement made the rowboat rock. All Louisa could do was hold onto the sides and watch disaster unfold above her head.

When Sinclair removed his hand from Miss Wentworth's mouth, the wild feminine laughter started anew. Louisa heard a muttered oath and caught her breath as Sinclair clamped Miss Wentworth's arms around his neck and leaped out toward the anchor cable. He caught it, and they hung there precariously as the woman's wild laughter turned to shrieks.

"I'm going to die!" she wailed, clawing at Sinclair's head. "Help me! I'm going to die!"

"Shut up!" came his rough command. Louisa suppressed a shriek of her own as Sinclair's grip on the rope slipped. As he fought to hold on, Miss Wentworth gave a bloodcurdling cry.

"Who goes there?" came a sharp voice from above.

"Sinclair!" Louisa whispered fiercely. "Hurry!"

A grunt was the only reply, and she watched in breathless horror as he inched down the cable, Miss Wentworth clinging to his neck from behind and kicking her legs for all she was worth.

A pistol shot rang out. Miss Wentworth shrieked again. Sinclair lost his grip, and they plummeted into the black, swirling waters of the Thames.

David grabbed the oars and began to row toward the spot where they had entered the water. Another pistol report sounded overhead.

"Halt!" came the sharp order.

For one long agonizing moment, Louisa and David could see nothing of Sinclair and Miss Wentworth. Then two heads bobbed up not three feet away. Sinclair heaved Miss Wentworth over the side of the rowboat. As David worked to prevent the boat from being swamped, Louisa tried to pull the woman in. But Miss Wentworth's clawing hands were slippery, so Louisa leaned over to get a better grip on her. In that moment, another shot boomed across the water.

Louisa lost her balance and tumbled overboard.

Cold as death, the river closed over her. Terror swirled around her like the river's greedy, grasping tentacles. Louisa flailed helplessly to no avail. She was sinking. Around her was only black and the deep, relentless darkness of death.

This, then, was how it was meant to end, with nothing to stop her rapid descent to a watery grave.

And then something did.

Sinclair was there. He caught her arms and pulled her up and up until at last her face broke the surface. As she coughed and breathed in great sputtering gasps, Louisa heard him bark an order to David. She watched in horror as the rowboat containing David and Miss Wentworth began to glide swiftly away.

"No need to panic," he said in a low voice as he gripped her waist. "Take a deep breath. We'll swim for it. It's not far to the carriage. If those clouds hold, the guards won't be able to pick us out in the darkness."

Louisa stared up at the thin clouds that had drifted over the moon. Behind her was the prison hulk and a milling group of guards shouting in confusion. Her eyes tried and failed to penetrate the unrelenting blackness where the river and the sky met in an invisible horizon. Her limbs were cold, useless. Her lips trembled. Only Sinclair's arms prevented her from sinking like a stone.

"I'm going to let you go now," Sinclair was saying. "We will swim underwater until we get out of range. Don't worry. I'll be right beside you. Ready?"

He treaded water easily, his legs generating slow, rotary movements that seemed to require no effort at all. He held her lightly under the arms, keeping her afloat while she gathered her senses.

"No!" she cried, her teeth chattering, the rancid taste of fear on her tongue.

More gunshots sounded, and bullets rippled the water precariously close to them. "Come on, woman. This is no time to be hen-hearted." He gave her a little shake. "If they launch a dinghy, we're done for."

"I—I—can't." Cold terror filled her.

"What do you mean, you can't?" he demanded. His eyes, mere inches from hers, were shot through with anger.

"Swim." The word came out a sob.

Incredulous, he stared at her. "You can't swim?"

She shook her head, fighting her own hysteria. Something entered the water at her elbow. A bullet, she thought, wondering why she had not heard the report.

And then she heard a great booming sound. It echoed in her ear and merged with the curse on Sinclair's lips.

Chapter 7

~~~◇◇~~~

It wanted only this.

It was bad enough that the Wentworth woman had sunk her teeth into his hand and then nearly strangled him by grabbing his neck so tightly he could scarcely breathe. Bad enough that the water around him rippled with the plink-plunk of bullets as the rowboat glided away with the object of their misguided adventure shrieking the heavens down. Bad enough that his limbs were numb, his head ached, and he was tired as hell. On top of all that, he was going to have to tow Miss Peabody down the river.

Her eyes were wide with horror, her lips trembling and doubtless blue with cold. Even on a summer night, the river had a bite to it.

"Relax," he told her, trying to stem her rising panic, for panic would send them both to the bottom of the river. "Lean back. Let the water hold you up."

"No. Leave me. It's impossible." Her hands floundered wildly, then closed over his eyes and nose.

"Damn it! You'll drown us both!" Gabriel
pried her fingers away from his face. "Lie
back. No—not like that. Hell."

Her arms went around his neck, cutting off
his air, and then they were both sinking down
and down through the dark waters to their
doom. A strange lightheadedness assailed
him. It was as if a dream beckoned, fraying
the edges of reality, until the water and the
struggling woman receded from his awareness. As the murky river wrapped them in its
embrace, Gabriel felt himself sinking into the
even murkier past.

*"Damn fool! You say the lad doesn't know how
to swim? Where's his father?"*

"Riptide's bad, too. Fetch Aloysius!"

"There's not time!"

Someone had come for him, a stranger, who
braved the riptides and swells for a boy who
had been foolish enough to think he could
build a leaky raft and sail away to a place he
could call home. Finally, his father arrived.

*"Stupid boy! The ocean's no place for a child.
What were you thinking?"*

"Nothing, sir."

*"I've got enough to do without having to watch
you every second. Make yourself useful, boy. And
don't let me catch you pulling such a foolish trick
again."*

"No, Father."

The man who had rescued Gabriel taught
him to swim before he left Sinclair Isle with
the other emigrés. Gabriel practiced in secret
for months until he could swim clear around

the island. His father never knew Gabriel had learned to swim like a fish, never knew that he had vowed to leave Sinclair Isle if it meant swimming to the ends of the earth. Once he had even tried it, swimming a mile or so toward the mainland until a cramp forced him to stop. He'd had to let the current take him, and when it deposited him on the shores of Sinclair Isle, the bitter irony of the sea's betrayal had haunted him for days.

Thus, he was intimately acquainted with treacherous waters. And he was not about to drown in the Thames with a madwoman's hands around his throat.

His lungs burning, Gabriel ripped Miss Peabody's hands from his neck, wrenched her body sideways, and put one arm around her waist. He had no idea how deep they had sunk, but he gave a powerful kick and prayed it would be enough to take them up.

It was. As they broke the surface, the blessed wind whipped against his face. Gabriel took deep, calming breaths and hoped she had the sense to do the same. She sputtered and gagged for a bit, but finally grew quiet. She was doubtless exhausted, but Gabriel could not bring himself to feel sympathy for the woman who had almost drowned them both.

"Lean back," he ordered roughly. To his surprise, she complied. She was too tired to fight him, which was the best thing that had happened all night. With a silent prayer, Gabriel locked his arms around her and let the current take them.

They drifted away from the hulk, away from the bullets, away from the chaos. The carriage waited a mile downriver, and it was a good thing the current was with them, because Gabriel was exhausted, too.

"Let the riptide take you, boy. Don't fight it. She's a good sight stronger than either of us. That's right. When she's ready to let you break free, you'll know."

They weren't far offshore, and the Thames was not the sea, but it was treacherous enough in the dark for a woman who couldn't swim and a man who was nearly done in. The moon was playing them false, had been all night. Gabriel wanted to shake his fist at the capriciousness of the heavens, but it would take more energy than he had. He lost track of time. Like that deadly, long-ago riptide, it swept him through the years, and dropped him somewhere in the Thames with a woman in his arms.

Then he saw the rowboat.

It rested on the bank, pulled up out of harm's way. The carriage was nearby. Three faceless silhouettes stood on the shore, but there was no mistaking Ferguson's great hulking form or that of the woman, whose shrill voice pierced the night like a dagger. He wondered why Ferguson had not shut her up. Surely the man understood the dangers.

"It's them!" It was the boy, excited and thrilled, as if he had just won a game of ninepins. Which was how he should be spending his time, Gabriel thought darkly. The lad was too young to risk his neck like this.

Ferguson waded out toward them. Gabriel's free arm cut smoothly through the water as he propelled them into the giant's waiting arms. Gabriel shoved Miss Peabody at Ferguson, but his legs were wobbly, and he had to crawl out of the river on his hands and knees.

The giant hunched over her, pounding her back until she sat up, coughing and sputtering. Dazed, she looked over at Gabriel.

He didn't spare her a glance. This debacle was her fault, and if she was looking for praise, he was not about to provide it. "We have to go," he snarled. "The guards will be on us."

Ferguson pulled Miss Peabody to her feet, and the boy ran to open the carriage door. But she just stood there, getting her bearings, not moving. With a growl, Gabriel advanced on her, ready to toss her into the carriage himself.

Then he froze.

Her wet hair clung to her head in matted tangles. The coal dust had been washed away, and her face looked unnaturally pale and haunted in the glow of the contrary moon. Her wet breeches clung to her legs, outlining them quite clearly, but the worst of it was that the river had stolen her thick woolen jacket. Her thin muslin shirt revealed a pair of truly spectacular breasts.

Gabriel swallowed hard.

"That's right," wailed a shrill voice, "forget

about Alice. Forget ye ruined my evening. Why, that ruffian over there"—she eyed Gabriel in disdain—"beaned old Tom afore I could give him what the poor man paid for. Now I'll be known as a cheat. Lord save a working girl from the horses' asses in this world!"

Ferguson and Gabriel locked gazes over the top of Miss Peabody's head. Without a word, the giant threw Alice over his shoulder, then walked to the carriage and stuffed her inside.

Yes, it wanted only this.

Miss Wentworth cursed all the way to Kent. Louisa had never heard such language, and she did not understand most of it. Cold and shivering, the two women shared a lap blanket on one side of the carriage. Sinclair sat on the opposite seat, arms crossed over his chest, eyes closed. He might have been asleep, but Louisa suspected he had merely taken that posture to ignore them more easily.

She had to admit that he had done everything expected of him and then some. She owed him her life, and so did Miss Wentworth. It was clear that he did not expect their gratitude, however. Indeed, he looked as if he would rather be anywhere else.

"Mr. Sinclair?" Louisa began, when Miss Wentworth finally lapsed into silence.

His eyelids opened half way, and he regarded her without interest. When he did not speak, Louisa cleared her throat. "I just wanted to thank you for—er—rising to the occasion tonight. We are both"—she broke off and cast an uncertain look at the other woman—"grateful for your perseverance and courage."

"Yes, I can see that Miss Wentworth is bubbling over with gratitude," he drawled.

"Horses' asses," Alice muttered.

Louisa flushed. "She has had a great shock. I am sure she will be herself after a bit."

Sinclair's mouth twisted wryly. "We will all eagerly await that moment."

Alice yanked the blanket up to her neck, uttered another oath, and closed her eyes. In the next minute, she was snoring loudly as the carriage rumbled over the road.

Louisa felt keenly the absence of the blanket. She was soaked and could not stop shivering. What's more, a burning sensation had begun in her shoulder. When she touched the warm spot, her hand encountered a sticky substance. She stared as the moonlight revealed a dark blotch spreading across her muslin shirt.

"I think," she said slowly, not quite able to believe it, "that I may have been shot."

Sinclair reached across the space between the seats and summarily untied the laces of her shirt. He parted the fabric carefully, exposing her bare shoulder and an angry wound at the base of her collarbone. A piece of fabric stuck to her flesh, and she cried out in pain as he gingerly removed it. Blood oozed from the wound.

"It doesn't look deep, but I cannot be sure," he said. "The bleeding must be stopped."

As he reached for the blanket, Alice gave a great snore and wrapped it around her more tightly, settling herself deeper into the seat cushions. Louisa shifted awkwardly. She was wedged between the woman's feet and the corner of the carriage, with her injured shoulder bearing the brunt of the pressure.

"There is something to be said for letting sleeping dogs lie," Sinclair observed darkly, abandoning his effort to obtain the blanket. In one fluid motion, he lifted Louisa from the seat and placed her next to him. Then he tore a piece of fabric from his shirt and pressed it firmly against her wound.

Louisa flinched and tried to draw away.

"Come, now, Miss Peabody. I can scarcely molest you here, even if I felt like it—which I assure you, I do not." He glowered at her. "Pressure is needed to stop the bleeding. If you can't abide my touch, you will have to hold the cloth yourself."

She put her hand over the makeshift bandage, but she was shivering so much that her fingers trembled. Feeling as weak and helpless as a new kitten, she shook her head.

And so they drove to Peabody Manor with Sinclair's hand pressed firmly against the top of her bosom.

The Flowers lined up to greet them. No matter that it was nearly dawn, they were a veritable bouquet of cheer as the groggy Alice stepped from the carriage.

"You will want to see your baby right away, I expect," Violet told Alice.

"She is the cutest thing," Daisy added with a smile. "The precious little angel looks just like you."

"Do not worry about a place to stay," Lily assured her. "Louisa is the soul of generosity. This is your home for as long as you wish it. Should you like to be Petunia? We do not have a Petunia."

Rose studied Alice. "You could be Petunia, I suppose. Though you look a mite more like—"

"Deadly Nightshade," Gabriel muttered.

Alice stared at them in bewilderment. Then she opened her mouth and shrieked for a bottle of rum. The women looked at one another in confusion.

"Miss Wentworth has had a difficult night," Miss Peabody said, brushing away Gabriel's proffered hand as she tried to descend the carriage steps alone. But she swayed slightly and toppled into Gabriel's arms.

"You are hurt!" Jasmine rushed to her side.

"I have sustained a small injury, that is all," she replied faintly as Gabriel carried her up the front steps.

"I'll send Sam for the doctor," Ferguson called after them.

"That's right. Make a big to-do over *her*." Alice whined. "What about me? *I'm* the one what was ripped from a profitable night's work!"

"Toadflax," Gabriel said darkly.

"What?" In his arms, Miss Peabody stared up at him.

"Her new flower name," he drawled. "Toadflax fits her snappish nature, don't you think? Although I suppose a case could be made for Stinging Nettle."

"Stop it."

"Certainly. It would not do to offend Miss Wentworth's delicate sensibilities." Gabriel shifted the soggy burden in his arms as Jasmine held the front door open. Would this night ever end? His clothes were drenched, and his strength shot. "Where is your room?" he demanded.

"Please put me down," she replied. "I can walk on my own."

"You will reopen that wound, and I shall be obliged to put pressure to it once more," he threatened, though that was the last thing he wanted to do at the moment.

Though he had tried not to stare at her in the carriage, Gabriel had discerned well enough that she had perfect breasts, high and round, alabaster smooth and white. The nipples pointed heavenward through the scant protection of her wet muslin shirt, taunting him the entire time his fingers had pressed the bandage only inches away. He had wanted to caress those taut buds, to weigh her breasts in his palms like ripe fruit ready for picking.

Hell. Her life's blood was oozing out of her, and he'd been salivating over her breasts as if they were plump oranges. Well, it had been a long night, what with ripping Alice away from the diligent work she was performing on an ecstatic guard, who was happily and conveniently bound ankle and wrist to a cot. Not to mention swallowing half the Thames to get himself and the mastermind of this scheme to safety. A man had to be forgiven some things.

Besides, her wound wasn't truly life-threatening, though he supposed she could still contract a fever. Sobering, he carried her upstairs to her room and laid her carefully on the canopied bed that occupied the center of her chamber. Several of the Flowers came into the room and busied themselves lighting candles and fluffing her pillow.

"Let me see that wound," Jasmine said. "Do not worry, Mr. Sinclair. I am an experienced midwife."

"Midwife?" Gabriel frowned. "I fail to see how—"

"I am accustomed to blood," Jasmine explained. "You'd be surprised at how many people get sick at the sight of it." Gently, she removed the bandage Gabriel had made from his shirttail. She nodded approvingly. "The bleeding has stopped. That is good."

"At least some good has come of this night," he muttered.

"A great deal of good has come of it," Miss Peabody retorted from the bed, eyes flashing, though her voice lacked its usual vigor. "Miss Wentworth has been restored to her child. A grave injustice has been rectified."

"Now you have only to persuade *her* of that fact," Gabriel shot back.

"Perhaps this discussion can wait," Jasmine suggested, looking from him to Miss Peabody.

"I will grant that Miss Wentworth seems a trifle overwrought," Miss Peabody conceded, "but so are we all tonight."

"Speak for yourself," he snapped. "I, for one, am not overwrought—though when you dragged us to the river bottom, I confess to a small moment of distress." He glared at her. "What possessed you to step into that rowboat when you didn't know how to swim?"

"I never dreamed it would become necessary. I did not mean to be a burden."

"A burden? Oh, you were no burden at all. Whyever should you think such a thing?"

"You have a clever tongue, Mr. Sinclair," she said faintly. "You leave a person very nearly defenseless against it."

Gabriel bent down and was gratified to see her shrink from whatever she saw in his eyes. "*You* defenseless, madam? I think not."

She looked away. Her gaze grew shuttered. "You might be surprised."

"Louisa," Jasmine began, "I must insist that you rest—"

"As it happens, I welcome surprises, madam." His voice dripped with scorn. "But I prefer them delectably packaged, somewhat compliant, and evocatively fragrant—without the scent of a harlot, I might add."

Miss Peabody lifted her chin. "Miss Wentworth is—"

"A whore. Not to put too fine a point on it."

She flushed. "You judge too quickly. It is

obvious that she has not had the benefit of education, and her speech is somewhat coarse, but beneath that rough exterior beats the heart of—"

"A whore, plain and simple." Gabriel leveled a gaze at her. "I am not judging by that foul mouth of hers, by the way, but by the activity in which she was engaged when I found her. If I remember aright—and a man does not easily forget such a scene—the sainted Miss Wentworth was diligently applying a whip to the back of a guard. Did I mention that he was naked and in the throes of pleasure at the time? Ah, well. There is no accounting for tastes. Needless to say, the man was in no condition to deter her hasty departure."

She colored. "You have given me a headache, Mr. Sinclair," she said faintly. "Perhaps you would be good enough to allow me to rest while I wait for the doctor."

"Yes, yes. That is just what you need, dear." Jasmine eyed Gabriel sternly.

He turned to leave. If he never saw this woman again, it would be too soon.

"Sinclair?" Miss Peabody said softly.

"Now what?" he demanded.

"Thank you for saving my life."

"That is not necessary," he said.

"But—"

"You may add a few more guineas to my fee, if that makes you feel better. Good night, madam. Or perhaps I should say good day.

That is the sun through the window, if I am not mistaken."

"Your fee," she echoed dully. "Of course. I had almost forgotten."

"Forgotten? Come, now, Miss Peabody, you cannot believe I would have gone through this night for nothing."

Mutely, she shook her head.

"Now, that would be a fatal mistake indeed." He sauntered out of the room, leaving her to make of that what she could. He did not look back.

Chapter 8

"**P**uny little mite, ain't she?"

Violet smiled down at the sleeping babe in her arms. "She has missed her mother, Miss Wentworth. We knew you would like to see her as soon as you awoke."

In truth, the women had been surprised that Alice showed no interest in seeing baby Elizabeth upon her arrival. They told one another that she had simply been overcome by the rigors of the ordeal she had endured.

"Would you like to hold her?" Violet asked hopefully.

Alice ignored her. Her gaze traveled around the nursery, where three other children were playing happily.

"These yours?" she demanded.

"No. The little girl belongs to Jasmine. Her name is Mary and she is three. The twins, Joshua and Jeremy, are Lily's. They are two. We take turns watching them, and there is a woman from the village, Mrs. Hanford, who comes to help sometimes. As you can see, we are quite accustomed to children here. We have tried to take good care of your baby, but there is no substitute for a mother."

"You're about ready to pop one yerself, if I don't miss my guess."

Violet colored. "My babe is due in a few weeks."

"No husband in sight, I'll wager."

Stunned by the woman's blunt speaking, Violet could only shake her head in response.

Alice laughed. "You see? That's the problem with us women. We always get caught. I'll let you in on a secret, missy." She gave Violet a knowing wink. "There are devices, things that stop a man from planting his seed, if ye get my drift. Wish I'd known about them before." For the first time, her gaze lingered on the babe in Violet's arms. "How did she come to be here?"

"Louisa was shopping in Piccadilly when the commotion began. You had taken a loaf of bread from the bakery window, I believe."

"No harm in that," Alice grumbled. "A girl's got to live."

Violet brightened. "Oh, we quite agree. The baker should not have summoned the Watch for such a petty thing. Louisa was outraged. She had seen you hide your babe under the bakery steps to protect her while you found food."

"Protect her?" Alice scoffed. "Not bloody likely."

Violet eyed Alice uncertainly. "When the Watch bore you away, Louisa took the babe—no one had noticed her little hiding place—

and brought her here until she could win your release. Not knowing the baby's name, we called her Elizabeth. It seems to suit her, but we are most eager to learn her real name." She waited expectantly.

Alice shrugged. "Elizabeth is as good as any, I suppose."

"You . . . have not named her?" Violet stared at her.

"Wasn't necessary." Alice pushed an untidy shock of black hair off her face and yawned. "Is there breakfast? I'm a fair way to starving."

Violet's eyes widened in disbelief. "Why did you not name the child?"

"Ye think I'm not much of a mother, don't ye?"

"I—I would never presume—"

Alice gave a bitter laugh. "Some women are cut out for it, some aren't. Ever try to walk the streets with a babe at yer breast? Not good for business, dearie. Not at all."

Violet gaped at the woman. "Do you mean to say that you left Elizabeth under those steps *intentionally*? You abandoned her?"

Alice gave her a crafty smile. "No harm's been done, has it now? She looks well enough."

"But—"

"I'm too hungry for sermons, dearie. A girl has to eat when she can." Alice brushed passed her into the hall, where she collided with David.

"Forgive me, ma'am," he said quickly. "Are you all right?"

"Oh, yes," Alice replied. "Right as rain." Then, with a broad wink at Violet, she added, "A pair of grand shoulders on this one, dearie. Shouldn't wonder if he'd make ye a good husband. Big in the shoulders, big elsewhere, I always say." With a shrill cackle, she moved on down the hall.

Violet and David stood there, both too mortified to speak. At last he cleared his throat. "Miss Wentworth is nae what we expected."

"No." Sorrowfully, Violet regarded the sleeping baby in her arms. "Perhaps she will come to feel more charitably toward the babe over time."

David stared at the child nestled snugly between Violet's ample breasts and the place where her own child was growing. " 'Tis a shame."

"I—I think I understand some of what Miss Wentworth must have felt," Violet confessed.

"I can nae believe that. You and that woman are as different as night and day."

Her clear brown eyes met his. "I did not want the child I am carrying. My husband did not . . . care for me. He wanted another woman, and—" She broke off, embarrassed that she had said so much. "This babe was not conceived in love."

"I am sorry." He looked down at his shoes. Violet suspected he wanted to be anywhere else but here, listening to such a confession.

She touched his sleeve, trying to make him

understand. "Since coming here, I've realized the future can be different from the past. I've come to want this child more than life itself." Her voice broke, and she gave him an apologetic smile. "A babe is the promise that life starts anew each day, don't you think?"

David looked at her hand on his arm and took a step backward. "I came to take the children outside."

Violet was mortified. She had overstepped her bounds. David had no wish to engage in confidences, he kept to himself more than anyone she'd known. He took most of his meals in that solitary cottage near the woods and came to the house only to confer with Louisa or take the children on outings.

"They would like that." She hesitated. "So would I."

"You should rest," he said quickly. "Getting around can nae be easy when a woman is so—" He broke off, embarrassed.

"Large?" She gave him a rueful smile. "It is all right, David. I know I look like a cow."

"I did nae mean that." His face was scarlet.

"Hippopotamus, then," Violet amended, determined to end the awkwardness between them. "Children," she called brightly, "Uncle David is here to take you outside. Shoes on, everyone."

She thrust the baby into his arms and turning away to hide her tears, began to wrestle little Joshua into his shoes.

David stared down at the baby. Her eyes were open now, and she regarded him solemnly. Her mouth pursed in a round O shape, as if she was surprised to find him looking down at her from such a height. Suddenly, she smiled. Her tiny, delighted grin spread from ear to ear and, despite her size, seemed to him to encompass the world.

All the world that mattered, anyway.

Dr. Simmons had removed the ball and treated the wound with basilicum. Louisa's shoulder still ached, three days later, but it would heal. Wounds of the flesh were nothing compared to the other kind.

Louisa stood in front of the mirror in her room, not liking what she saw. Though she felt well enough to go downstairs for the first time since her injury, she looked terrible. The bodice of the blue morning dress did not entirely cover the thick bandage. Her birthmark stood out against the unnatural pallor of her skin. Her hair was pulled back and fastened at the nape of her neck in a stark, unappealing style. The haunted look in her eyes gave her a fearful air, as if something dark and dangerous stalked her.

Three years ago, she had gazed into this mirror with the same haunted look, pondering her father's words.

"Never asked for a daughter," he had snarled, *deep into his third bottle. "Never wanted one. But by damn, girl, it's time for you to earn your keep."*

She'd kept her father's books, managed his household, supervised his lucrative horse breeding business, studied the new agricultural methods to make the fields more profitable, and tried to keep him from gambling away every penny they had. She could ride any horse in the stable, but for all of that he didn't think she'd earned her keep. Because what she could not do, had never done, was to behave like a young lady schooled from birth in the art of pleasing and catching a man.

"*Damnation, girl! It's time you made yourself useful. Why, Milbrook's chit just snagged herself an earl, and she's not a beauty like you.*"

"*I don't want to marry, Papa.*"

"*I don't want to marry?*" he mimicked. "*Confound it, Louisa. It's your duty. If you had shown the slightest interest in a Season, I might have given you time to choose a mate. But now I'm into Richard Dunworth for twenty thousand pounds. He's a wealthy man in his own right, heir to the Upton fortune on top of that. But he's not about to forgive such a debt. Unless you marry him.*"

Richard Dunworth, she knew, was a reputed rakehell, with notorious tastes for fast women, harsh spirits, and gaming hells. But her father had brushed aside her objections.

"*A debt's a debt, and it must be paid. You're the only currency I possess at the moment. If it's the marriage bed you're worried about, take comfort in the fact that once you give the man his heir, he'll leave you alone.*"

Louisa had listened in shock, wondering why her father cared so little for her that he would consign her to a life of misery with a barbarian.

"What's the matter, Louisa? Are you a coward? 'Tis your duty. You can't shirk it."

In the end, she had done her duty. She'd stood in the village chapel and let her father marry her off to one of the rudest, crudest men she had ever met. Though most women would have considered Richard a catch, Louisa could only stare at his large, cruel hands and wonder what would happen on their wedding night. Soon enough, she found out. From that moment on, she'd vowed to let no man touch her.

No man had. Even David kept his distance, knowing the distress even accidental physical contact caused her.

Yet she'd put her life and her person in Sinclair's hands. She'd never forget the way his strong arms locked around her as they floated downriver or how his fingers stemmed the blood from her wound. She owed her life to a scoundrel who had known her body more intimately than any man save Richard. Some of the touching had been necessary evils of her rescue, but the kiss Sinclair had given her in the parlor yesterday was pure mischief. Richard's kisses had been wet, sloppy, revolting. Sinclair's did strange, unsettling things to her.

Perhaps that accounted for the strained look about her features now, the swirling terror in her eyes. Perhaps the thing that stalked her was her own treacherous heart.

What a clever rogue he was. Doubtless the man had honed his skills over the years so that he could seduce a woman in the blink of an eye. That must be why her body had been so

confused, and why—even as she had fought
that dizzying nausea—part of her had been utterly fascinated.

She must remember that he was a man who
ran roughshod over hearts, who treated
women's bodies as if they were his by right.
She must not let her fascination turn his deeds
into something wonderful and heroic. Money,
not chivalry, had prompted his daring.

Was he still at Peabody Manor? Louisa wondered. Then she remembered: he had not yet
been fully paid.

Louisa gave her fragile reflection a knowing
smile. Sinclair would be downstairs, waiting
for his due.

If he had to endure one more meal with that
woman shrieking in wild laughter, he would
go insane.

"Excuse me, ladies." Gabriel placed his napkin on the table. "Breakfast was delicious, as
usual."

As he strode away from Peabody Manor, he
had half a mind to seek out Ferguson and discover once and for all whether the man had a
secret source of food. Daisy's eggs and onions
sat in his stomach like lead. To think he had
once thought all women knew how to cook.

But Gabriel did not head to Ferguson's cottage. His feet took him to the stable instead.
Three days of waiting for Miss Peabody to recover had given him the fidgets.

Four horses were in the stalls. The black
stallion galloped about in the paddock out-

side, frisky in the morning sun. He was a rare prize, all sleek muscle and peerless bone.

"Easy to see which of you is the early riser," Gabriel chided the mares. He wondered whether anyone would object if he appropriated one of them for a bit.

He found Sam in the tack room, hunched over an open box, concentration etched on his features. Gabriel endured a moment of stark recognition as the boy carefully wound a string around a wooden top as if it were the most important task in the world. He placed the top at one end of the box, yanked the string, and watched as the top twirled madly, only to collapse on its side after only a few seconds. Sam's shoulders slumped in defeat.

"It helps to wind the string from top to bottom," Gabriel offered.

Sam whirled. "Mr. Sinclair!" He beamed with pleasure. "You've played skittles?"

"A time or two." Enough for two lifetimes, Gabriel thought. "I carved a set for myself when I was about your age. It helped the days pass." But not fast enough. "Did you make this set?"

"It was my father's," Sam replied proudly.

Gabriel studied the smoothly polished wood, the intricately carved holes, the deftly turned scoring pins. Time had removed the set's sheen, but obviously not its luster for Sam. " 'Tis handsome. Did he make it himself?"

"I don't know," Sam confessed. "I don't remember him much. He was killed on the Peninsula. My mother always said he was a hero."

Gabriel decided not to notice the boy's faltering tone or the tears that threatened to mortify him by spilling over onto his cheeks. "Wrapping the string from the bottom up makes for an unstable spin."

He knelt and, as though it had not been a decade since he had played the game, wound the string around the top, careful to keep his index finger over the coils to prevent tangling. He threaded the string through the launch slot in the box, then gave it a firm, steady tug.

The top spun through the narrow opening into the field of play, knocking over one pin after the other.

"A hundred points!" Sam exclaimed. "Two hundred!" When the top finally went down, Sam eyed Gabriel with unconcealed admiration.

" 'Tis in the wrapping," Gabriel said gruffly. "It's easy to learn."

They worked on Sam's technique for a quarter-hour. The boy seemed pitifully grateful for the attention, and Gabriel could not help but feel he was staring his own youth in the face. He hoped Ferguson had the sense to stop allowing the boy to participate in Miss Peabody's adventures. The responsibility was too heavy for his thin shoulders, the danger too real. He was entitled to a childhood, for God's sake.

"Look at that!" Sam exclaimed as the top knocked down pin after pin. "Care to go another round?"

Careful, Gabriel told himself. It wouldn't do to let himself get drawn into the boy's concerns. "I'm afraid I don't have time. I thought to go riding."

Sam sprang to his feet. "I know just the mount. Mainstay hasn't had her exercise this morning. You'll find her the eager sort."

"Must be only female around here who is," Gabriel muttered.

"What did you say, sir?" Sam lugged a saddle toward one of the stalls.

"Nothing." Gabriel appraised the roan. A frisky mount, no doubt about it. But she took the bit and saddle without complaint. He mounted her and was on the point of leaving when he chanced to look back at Sam. The lad was regarding him with a hopeful look.

"What is it, boy?" he asked.

"I didn't know if you needed any help, sir. Finding your way about and all. I could go with you if you did." The boy reddened.

"I don't need help."

"Oh." Sam looked crestfallen. "Well, if you change your mind, sir—"

"Since when did I become 'sir'? If I recall aright, you have been anything but thrilled with my presence here."

Sam grinned shyly. "That was before."

"Before?" Gabriel had a sense of foreboding.

"Before you rescued Louisa. And Miss Wentworth, of course," he quickly added. "David told me how you sneaked onto that ship right under the noses of those guards."

So that was the way of things. "Look here,

boy," Gabriel growled, "they were drunk as skunks. They wouldn't have noticed if I'd ignited a keg of gunpowder under them."

"David told me how you dodged those bullets and saved Louisa." Awe filled Sam's wide eyes.

Gabriel shook his head. "Those guards wouldn't have been able to hit the *Victory* broadside if she pulled to within an inch of their guns."

"But—"

"You'll find out soon enough, boy, that there are no heroes in this world—only fools with dumb luck. Keep a knife at your side and your wits about you, and you'll fare better than most. And never make the mistake of relying on anyone other than yourself."

Gabriel flicked Mainstay's reins and rode away. He did not look back, for he did not want to see the disappointment on the boy's face. But the quicker the lad let go of his illusions, the better he would fare in life.

The boy knew his horseflesh, though. Mainstay made short work of the countryside as they headed east from Peabody Manor. Too quickly, Gabriel found himself following the winding lane along the bank of the Medway. Before he was quite ready, the old village lay before him, its thatched roofs and stone cottages unchanged since he had last seen them twenty years ago. Beyond, on the edge of the sandy bay, its crumbling turrets uneven silhouettes against the blazing sun, lay Sinclair Castle.

To the east of everything. Reaching for the light, but not quite finding it.

The horse sensed their destination was at hand. She moved eagerly in response to his command, skirting the village and heading straight toward the pile of stones that had once contained Gabriel's own illusions.

"Easy, girl," he murmured, when Mainstay made for the small freshwater lake that had supplied water to generations of Sinclairs. He dismounted and let the mare drink as he shaded his eyes and looked toward the sun.

He had never thought to see this place again. Now he realized that time had done what his memory could not: erased all trace of his boyhood.

Gabriel stared at the place where his dreams had been born and where, but for fate and his father's madness, they would have been nurtured for a good many more years before evaporating in the bitter dust of disillusionment.

Though Sinclair Castle was not quite in ruins, the years had not been kind. The towers, remnants of a past when invaders were as plentiful as the terns that now nested in the rafters, teetered precariously over the walled courtyard. A small boy would not be able to climb to the top now or stare out to sea imagining himself Sir Francis Drake victoriously sailing home with booty for his queen. The walls on which Gabriel used to balance, pretending to swing the lead line around his head and heave it into the sea, were just crumbling remnants of their past glory.

The outbuildings, many of them constructed by later generations of Sinclairs who sought more comfort than a drafty castle provided, had fared somewhat better. But the manor house that his grandfather had built between the village and the castle gates, the house where Gabriel and his family had lived because it was warm and spacious and the sunshine chased the sea-damp chill, had gaping windows and broken doors. The field where the villagers had gathered with them to celebrate St. Thomas's Day had gone to weeds. The porch where his mother had sat on a summer's night, straining to see her needlework in the waning light, was nothing more than broken boards and fallen railing.

No, there was nothing left of his childhood. And he had known that it would be this way, known from the first time he walked out of Peabody Manor and smelled the sawgrass and salt marshes on the wind that he would have to come to this place he had never expected to see again.

When he was small—too small to know how a boy's dreams could be contained in a tiny, forgotten corner of a man's brain—he had dreamed of restoring the castle of his forebears. Dreamed of setting legions of craftsmen to work on that magnificent pile of stones and giving it back the glory of the time when it had stood against lawless invaders bound for London and the head of a king.

He'd stood on the castle walls and seen his destiny in the ships he watched bringing riches from afar, spreading the news of exotic new worlds. Adventure, daring deeds, spectacular feats—all would be his. And when he grew past the age of daring, he would return to his ancestral home and fill it with children of his own. A family that would bring the past full circle, that would create a host of new memories imbued with the cherished old.

Gabriel turned away from the sight of the castle, as useless and broken as his youth. He wished he had not listened to the ill wind that had called him from Peabody Manor to this most desolate of places in the shadow of dreams.

And then he saw her. Pale and swaying on the enormous black horse, staring at the marble structure an eccentric ancestor had built to face sun and sea, hedging his bets against the whims of fate. Her gaze was riveted on the life-sized statue of a man playing a pipe and wearing only the skin of a wild beast.

"Good morning, Miss Peabody. I see you have discovered the temple." He was glad his voice sounded calm. He did not want to reveal the rage that filled him because she had followed him to his pitiful abandoned castle.

"Temple?" She frowned, obviously trying to place the figure.

"Apollo," he said softly. "God of light, healing, justice, beauty. And of the hunt. Let us not forget the hunt." The hunted and the haunted. Destiny and grace. Mixed up and formless, like one of those bread puddings he and Robert had loved to sample before it was fully set.

She stared at him without understanding. Had he really spoken then? It occurred to him that he might be as mad as his father had been. And then she smiled, a tentative, uncertain curve of her lips that penetrated to the secret place in him that held the past and a bevy of broken dreams.

"Apollo," she repeated. "Yes. That makes sense."

And then she slid to the ground in a formless heap.

Chapter 9

Louisa awoke to find herself lying at Apollo's feet. Sinclair's fiery mane and flashing eyes evoked images of the sun god himself, but his words brought her awake with a cold dash of reality.

"Damnation, woman. If you are bent on killing yourself, must you always involve me?"

Groggily, Louisa sat up—or tried to. Something heavy rested on her shoulder: Sinclair's firm, restraining hand. "Lie still," he ordered. "You've reopened that wound."

His hand pressed against her bandage. He had untied the laces of the loose-fitting shirt she wore over a pair of Sam's breeches, and Louisa was mortified at how much of her was revealed for his inspection.

"I'll thank you to stop envisioning yourself as my guardian angel," she said in a brittle tone. "I can take care of myself."

"About as well as you can swim, I imagine."

Louisa flushed. "I am perfectly capable of riding—"

"You haven't done anything more strenuous than keep to your room for three days, and suddenly you decide to gallop across hill and dale. No wonder you fainted."

Louisa lifted her chin. "I have never fainted in my life. And I did *not* gallop. My pace was quite sedate. We are but a few miles from Peabody Manor, after all."

Sinclair eyed Midnight, munching on clover a few yards from the tree where he'd tied Mainstay. "That's more than you ought to have ridden on that stallion. He's anything but sedate." He made a final adjustment to her bandage. Louisa sat up and brushed his hands away.

"Pray, let me be." Her fingers fumbled to retie the laces. It had been difficult enough to change out of her morning dress when she had spied Sinclair from her window; donning her riding habit, with its fitted bodice and dozens of buttons, had been unthinkable. The shirt had been her father's, and while the laces were simple enough, her fingers had never seemed so clumsy as now, with Sinclair watching. At last she finished and rose to her feet.

"Why did you follow me?" he demanded.

How to explain the sudden urge that had seized her? She had been so certain he languished downstairs, waiting to demand his money, that when she spied him from her window, riding east toward the sea, she had panicked, thinking he was leaving them. Just why that should have sent her scrambling into her riding clothes did not bear examining.

"As you say, I have kept to my room for

three days. It was a fine morning, and when I saw that you had gone riding, I decided the exercise would do me good." Turning away from his scrutiny, Louisa looked around, taking in the crumbling castle, the strange temple, the dilapidated manor house. "What is this place?"

Sinclair did not answer. Instead, he sat down on the temple steps and regarded her thoughtfully. Louisa pretended to study the statue behind him. She couldn't explain her actions, but what irritated her most was that she couldn't explain his.

"I do not understand you, Sinclair," she said at last. "You confound my expectations."

He arched a brow. "I did not know you had expectations of me, Miss Peabody. I am flattered, of course."

She flushed. "One comes to expect that a person will act in a certain way based on his past and the reputation he has acquired—"

"Speak plainly, woman. What in heaven's name have I done now?"

She hesitated. "It is what you have *not* done."

His brow cleared. "Ah. Now I see. I am a known scoundrel, condemned for my heinous crimes, and yet I have not murdered you in your bed or robbed you of all you possess. The lad now thinks I hung the moon, and the Flowers are ever-solicitous. I confess it confounds me also. What do you suppose is the reason I have not run amok?"

"You are making sport of me." Louisa bit her lip.

"Not at all." He shrugged. "You have every reason to expect the worst."

"And yet you rescued Miss Wentworth and saved my life—"

"Only because you are paying me extremely well. When might I expect to see the balance, by the way? No doubt you have been expecting me to demand my due."

He had come painfully close to the truth, and yet something in that insouciant shrug made her wonder. "My trustee has not yet replied to my urgent request, but you shall have the money. I promise you that."

"And your promises are never broken." His mouth twisted into a wry smile. He still sat on the temple steps, whereas she had remained standing, but she felt small and insignificant in the face of his brutal wit. And yet she sensed that his barbs were aimed more at himself than her. A realization struck her.

"You did not rape those nuns." Louisa was suddenly more sure of that fact than of anything in her life.

His lips thinned. "Careful, madam. You cannot replace these devil's horns with a halo."

"I have no intention of doing so," she said. "You didn't commit those crimes, did you?"

"No."

Louisa sighed. "I thought not."

"Is that why you followed me?"

"Yes. No. Dear lord, I don't know. I think I

must be out of my mind." A peculiar light-headedness swept her, and Louisa faltered. "I believe I will sit down for a moment."

Instantly he was on his feet, his hand under her elbow, easing her down to the steps beside him. "Put your head down," he commanded. "That's right. Give it a minute."

Louisa obeyed, and gradually the dizziness dissipated. "I am not usually so weak." Why was she always at her worst with this man?

"You are too hard on yourself. Anyone with such a wound would have difficulty." He patted her back reassuringly.

"There! That is just what I mean." She glared at him. "Now you are being solicitous. It is not at all what I expect."

He did not reply or even look at her. The hand on her back moved in light circles over her shoulder blades. She tensed, but he merely continued to stroke her in that slow, absent fashion as if it were the most normal thing in the world to do so. Gradually, Louisa felt herself relax into his touch. The movements of his hand grew less predictable as it wandered over the curve of her shoulder, down her arm, and up her back again in ever-broadening circles.

Louisa slanted a gaze at him. He stared fixedly at those castle ruins, then his gaze swept the horizon, where the Medway widened to meet the sea. The air was brisk, pungent with salt spray and the sharp cries of seabirds. Sinclair inhaled deeply and closed his eyes, seemingly unaware of her. Carefully, she edged away from him.

"Don't move," he ordered.

She jumped.

"Don't," he said again. There was nothing absent about his expression as he reached for a strand of her hair that had come loose from the clasp at the back of her neck. In a motion as natural as it was familiar, he tucked the stray tendrils behind her ear. His fingers trailed downward, curving around the nape of her neck.

Louisa read purpose in his suddenly focused gaze. Too late, she realized his intent.

His kiss was quick, gentle, gone in an instant. She drew away from him and crossed her arms over her chest.

"You do not like to be touched."

"No."

His gaze narrowed. "Did that husband of yours manage to alienate your affections in the few short hours you were wed?"

"There was nothing short about them." Louisa looked away from that speculative gleam in his eyes. She did not want to talk about Richard or that part of her life.

He tilted his head. "I cannot imagine you allowing yourself to be ill-used."

"It is not your concern."

"Louisa." Soft and resonant, his voice wrapped around her name like an embrace. And she forgot to resist as he pulled her into his arms and kissed her with exquisite gentleness.

His lips coaxed hers apart. His fingers traced the edges of her shirt, lingering over the laces she had just retied. Her pulse raced madly. Dizziness swept her from head to toe. His hands moved to her waist and pressed lightly over the rise of her hip.

Her stomach reeled.

"Take a deep breath," he murmured against her lips.

She inhaled, but the scant space between them was thick with something more than mere air, something heady and sensual.

"Too fast," he cautioned. "Again."

Louisa inhaled slowly, trying to calm the tumult inside. He nodded his approval. She took another breath and eyed him uncertainly.

"Put your hand on my chest," he commanded.

It was a scandalous request—abhorrent, really. She did not want to touch him. But though his eyes held a challenge, it was the plea in them that made her extend her hand hesitantly.

He placed her palm over his heart. Through the fabric of his shirt, she could feel his rapid heartbeat.

"You see?" His lips bore the hint of a smile. "It is racing, just like yours. That is the way of things between men and women, Louisa."

"I am not a child," she said indignantly. "I know perfectly well what it is like between a man and a woman."

"Then perhaps you can explain it to me." His eyes were grave.

"Messy and painful and ugly and degrading."

He arched a brow. "And here I thought you enjoyed my kisses. Too bad. It would have been pleasant to make love to you at Apollo's feet and refute those prejudices of yours."

Louisa bristled. "Arrogant man."

"A trial," he agreed. "Fortunately, you are too smart to be taken in by an unprincipled scapegrace."

"You said you didn't rape those nuns," she said accusingly.

"But I never claimed to be other than a scoundrel."

Louisa put her hand to her head, which was beginning to ache horridly. "Who are you, Sinclair? Why do I find you in this moldy place, waiting to torment me with jests and barbs? You are as slippery as an eel. I vow I will dance with glee on the day you are gone from my life."

His gaze slammed into hers. His eyes darkened and suddenly lost their guile. A hush descended on the temple as the wind, perhaps another tool of his sorcery, stilled. When he spoke, his voice sounded distant, utterly removed from the man who possessed it.

"I am the twelfth Baron Sinclair, the last of my line. This castle is mine and the temple and all these ruins and the manor house and the land for as far as you can see. And no one is alive to know it, Miss Peabody, or rejoice in the fact that the prodigal has returned home at last."

His raw, bitter grin tore a gaping hole in her heart.

"The men in my family have a tendency to madness. It skips generations here and there, but the odds are greatly against any Sinclair's escaping this life with his sanity intact."

Gabriel did not look at her. He did not want to see the revulsion in her eyes. "Legend has it," he continued in a self-mocking tone, "that the very first Sinclair—Peregrine was his name—devised a way to increase the light from the stars to aid nighttime navigation. The king—Richard II, only ten at the time—expressed his pleasure by building Peregrine this castle and giving him a fortune. A favorite bedtime story with subsequent generations of Sinclairs was Peregrine's development of a special adhesive to hold shooting stars in place."

He slanted a gaze at her. She did not speak. Who could blame her?

"It was not Peregrine but Harold Sinclair who started all the trouble," Gabriel continued ruthlessly. "Harold adored everything Greek. He constructed this shrine to Apollo, thinking it would gift him with the ability to see into the future, like the ancient oracle at Delphi. When, after spending a fortune building the temple, he gained no special insight into the future, he decided Apollo's skill at prophecy was less meaningful than the god's renowned passion for justice. In an effort to capture a bit of immortality for himself, Harold became a meddler."

"A meddler?"

"Meddled in people's lives. Got the strange notion that he could right all the wrongs in the world. He was ultimately beheaded for trying to tell Henry VIII he had no right to ruin the lives of all those wives."

She was silent.

"It was the merest stroke of luck that the king did not seize Sinclair land and banish us all," Gabriel added. "I imagine he was caught up in the task of disposing of yet another wife and forgot about us. Sinclairs lived quietly for two hundred years. Then trouble surfaced again in the person of Aloysius Sinclair." He paused. "My father."

It was impossible to tell how she was taking his recitation, but Gabriel told himself he did not care.

"Aloysius was a quiet, unassuming lord with a penchant for inventing things. Once he rigged an elaborate device for feeding chickens. It required the birds to peck at several buttons, which would send a quantity of corn down a chute and into a trough. His intention was that the corn not be wasted but rationed according to the birds' needs."

"So that the chickens were able to feed themselves," she said slowly.

"Yes. When hungry, the chickens would peck and get corn. Otherwise, the corn would remain safely stowed in a large bag rigged at the top of the chute. Unfortunately, he failed to take into account the nature of chickens. It turns out that they are incessant peckers—hungry or no. They have very little else to do."

"Too much feed ended up in the trough?" she ventured.

"Oh, worse than that. When my father came to check on his invention, he found the chickens buried under a mountain of corn. Not a grain remained in the bag or a germ of life in the chickens, I'm afraid. Their pecking had caused a fatal avalanche." He regarded her solemnly.

What might have been the beginnings of a smile flitted around the corners of her mouth. He had never seen her smile. This one looked as though it would be quite breathtaking if she gave it free rein.

"I am sure every inventor has his setbacks," she murmured.

"Indeed." Gabriel took a deep breath. The foibles of past Sinclairs—real and imagined—rolled off his tongue with ease. As a boy, he had loved hearing stories about them. His mother had embraced the strange Sinclair legends with love and humor, and she alone had been able to calm his father when his inventions went awry.

But she had died, Robert had lost his life in Egypt, and Aloysius Sinclair quietly lost his mind. The harmless madness of Gabriel's ancestors was no longer benign whimsy, something to laugh about around the hearth on a winter's eve. His father had escaped into a fantasy world—a living death, had Gabriel but understood it at the time. Doubtless the signs of madness had been there all along, even in that halcyon time of Gabriel's childhood. Sinclair Isle had merely unleashed the lunacy.

"His greatest invention was an underwater boat." His voice held no pride at his father's accomplishment, for Gabriel had hated the thing that took so much of Aloysius's time. He had needed a father then more than he needed a roof over his head or food on the table, but the thing in the cave had robbed him of that.

Her brow furrowed. "I have never heard of such a craft."

"Oh, they have been around in one form or another for centuries," he said. "But no one has been able to figure a way to navigate effectively or stay submerged long enough to deliver a charge against an enemy target. After my mother and brother died, my father threw his inventive energies into perfecting an underwater boat that could be used against the French. He meant to punish them for my brother's death by blowing up the French fleet."

Gabriel forced himself to delve into the memory of that painful time. "He bought an island. It was situated east of Ramsgate, in the path of any French strike. He moved the two of us there and began testing his craft."

Her clear blue eyes held questions, but she remained silent. Gabriel hoped to hell she wasn't pitying him. He couldn't stand pity.

"There was a time," he said, wrenching his gaze from hers, "when Boney was rumored to have dug an underwater channel to England. The War Department was most interested in my father's work. They thought his boat might be used to sabotage Napoleon's efforts. Then Nelson broke the French fleet at Trafalgar, and—"

"The War Department lost interest."

"Yes." Her quickness surprised him. "Alas, my father did not. He devoted the rest of his life to the submersible. He would take it out into the ocean, looking for wayward French warships. Often he took me with him, because my young arms were better than his at turning the crank that propelled the craft. Once he actually found a French frigate and managed to attach a charge, but it failed to explode. He never stopped trying, though. Like Harold, he had pledged himself to seek justice."

"I see."

"No, you do not. You cannot fathom the depth of my father's madness. He envisioned Sinclair Isle as the beginning of a new civilization devoted to avenging the deaths of Englishmen abroad. He set himself up as king, though the only subjects he had were me and the emigrés who occasionally landed on our shores. But they hadn't risked their lives escaping from France to end up as subjects to another mad tyrant. Magnanimous in his madness, my father supplied them with food, shelter, and clothing, which they badly needed, and they left us as soon as they could."

"How old were you when you moved to the island?"

"Eight." Gabriel could feel her pitying eyes on him. "But that was all years ago. It doesn't matter now."

She was silent for so long, he thought she had gone. But when he ripped his gaze from the spot where the sea met the cloudless sky, it was to discover her watching him from eyes as unreadable as that vast horizon.

"King." She regarded him steadily. "That is what you meant that day when you claimed to be king of an island."

He shrugged. " 'Twas a sad joke, no more. My father used to sit and stare out at the sea and talk about how the island would be mine one day. He took his royalty quite seriously."

"He is dead, then?"

Gabriel nodded. "He is buried on the island."

"You have been away a long time."

"Ten years, since his death. It has been longer since I have seen this place." His gaze slid over the castle ruins. "Twenty years, to be precise."

Twenty years. A lifetime. He doubted she had many more years than that on her plate.

"Why did you return?"

Gabriel glared at her. "This is as far as the story goes, Miss Peabody. There isn't any happy ending, like those rescues you are so fond of staging."

"But there must be a reason you came back after all this time," she said.

"My father's will specified that his solicitors

were to sell Sinclair Isle if after ten years I did
not take up residence there. They have recently contracted to sell the island. I returned
to England to see my father's grave for the last
time. That is all. I never intended to come here,
to this place." He gestured toward the castle.

"Why not?"

The woman was like a dog determined to
worry a bone from its hiding place. "Because
this is where it started."

"It?"

"The madness. The lunacy. The end of innocence." Gabriel tried unsuccessfully to keep
the anger from his voice. "The man walked
around in a crown of bayberry leaves. *Bayberry
leaves*, for God's sake."

Fury filled him—and loss. He had never
told a soul about his father. Putting that time
into words somehow brought the full impact
of the past home. Lunacy had stolen his father
away, and the harsh memories would always
be there, never to be replaced by something
softer. No matter how many years or miles
passed, Sinclair Isle and that damnable crown
would always be in the forefront of his mind,
images of his past that could never be erased.

"You have returned to face it, haven't you?"
she asked softly. "To embrace the past—"

"I embrace nothing." Rage roiled his insides, making his words bitter. He rounded on
her. "Must you always see the ridiculous as
sublime?"

Her features were irritatingly calm. "I think

you are afraid of growing mad like your father."

"Afraid?" He eyed her darkly. "Afraid of ending up like Aloysius or Harold or Peregrine? Hardly. Unlike you, I have the sense to know that one human being cannot right all of the earth's wrongs, that meddling with fate is the choice of fools, that the only way to get through life without losing one's mind is to keep away from people like you who think to save the world."

She stiffened. He grasped her arm.

"The world does not want saving," he said in a bitter voice. "It wants to go on spinning as it has done for centuries, without the interference of mindless mortals like you and me. It wants to spin and spin until the past, present, and future are a senseless jumble that mocks our feeble attempts to make sense of it all."

Abruptly, he released her. "The world does not need anyone to stick stars in the skies or build temples to false gods, Miss Peabody. It does not want your heroics or my father's inventions. It is what it is, and we cannot change it. To think anything else is to go stark, raving mad from the enormousness of the task."

Abruptly, Gabriel rose. He strode over to Mainstay and untied the rope he had secured to a nearby tree. His hands were shaking so badly that he barely accomplished the job. His breathing came in shallow gasps.

"Blasted female," he muttered into Mainstay's ear.

The horse gave him a soulful look.

Chapter 10

Apollo. Watching Sinclair untie Mainstay, Louisa decided she must be a little mad herself. For despite her aversion to men, her mind spun a fantasy with Sinclair center stage as that arrogant god.

There was a fire in him. It burned in the flaming red hair and dangerous green eyes that conjured journeys to the ends of the earth and back. It gave his touch the power to make her innards reel with aversion and desire.

Yet the fire warred with something else, which sought to smother those inner flames: apathy.

Despite the fire in his gut, Sinclair cared for nothing. Yet how could a man who burned be cold as ice?

She should have been relieved to learn he was not a rapist or murderer, but the knowledge only made him harder to understand. It was easy to despise a man who had committed heinous crimes, easy to disregard his charm as the wiles of an immoral scoundrel. But Sinclair was not truly evil, at least not in the sense she had come to know evil in men. He was even capable of heroics—albeit for money, not principle.

Louisa could never esteem such a man.

Yet that tale with so much unsaid had tugged at her heart. She saw a young boy, his world collapsing around him, forced to live out his youth on a remote island with no one but a madman for company. She imagined him watching helplessly as his father's brilliance was enslaved by bitterness over the death of a son. She envisioned the loneliness, the neglect, the sorrow Sinclair must have felt, for she had known those things as a child, too.

She thought about David, who had undergone imprisonment and torture and found in his experience an empathy that led him to help the downtrodden. David had a well of compassion in him as deep as the sea.

But Sinclair had gone another way. Suffering had made him shun other sufferers. It had given him an aversion to any emotional involvement. His whimsical nature masked a chilling truth: he was as isolated as any island.

A man who cut himself off from humanity as Sinclair had done would be entirely capable of using other people for his own ends. His kisses would be calculated to seduce. He would be a man to avoid. If a woman tolerated those kisses, even for a moment, she would be in grave jeopardy.

"Ready?"

Startled, Louisa looked up to find him standing before her, Mainstay's reins coiled in his fist. The mare whinnied, and Midnight, who had been grazing near the temple, ambled over to them.

Nothing in those brooding jade eyes suggested Sinclair felt an ounce of compassion for her or anyone. He'd marked her as a meddler, like his long-ago ancestor. There could be no two people with less in common than she and Sinclair.

"I am ready," she replied coolly.

He let go of Mainstay's reins and startled her by lifting her onto Midnight's back. "I will have you know," she said in a frosty tone, "that I have been able to mount my own horse since the age of six."

Sinclair merely gave her a speaking look and swung himself onto Mainstay. Louisa did not look at him as she clicked softly to the stallion. As Midnight started down the path, Sinclair pulled even with them.

He sat the horse superbly, even patted the mare's neck now and again and murmured something low in her ear. Occasionally he looked over at Louisa, apparently assessing whether or not she could manage the ride.

"You need not worry," she said haughtily. "I am perfectly capable of—"

Just then Midnight lunged forward, his sights set on the fox that had just darted across the path. Louisa struggled to control the stallion and might have done so, had she not suddenly felt lightheaded again. Dust motes danced before her eyes, her vision constricted to tiny pinpoints of light. Sensing her acquiescence, Midnight snorted loudly in anticipation of a rousing good chase.

Sinclair pulled her off Midnight just as the horse took off after the fox. Louisa gave a cry of surprise and dismay.

"Put me down!"

Her right shoulder pressed against his chest as he sat her sideways on Mainstay in front of him. The saddle was too small for both of them, and his arms locked around her middle to steady her.

"You are too weak yet. That horse is too spirited."

"Nonsense," she protested, chagrined that his right arm grazed the underpart of her breasts as he worked the reins. "Midnight would never hurt me."

As if to agree, the stallion cantered back to them, snorting loudly, the fox nowhere in sight.

"He is no lady's mount," Sinclair muttered.

"More lady's than man's," Louisa retorted, "especially after the brutal manner in which Richard treated him. Besides, I owe Midnight a great debt."

"Oh?" He sounded bored. Obviously, riding chest to shoulder with her had not affected him in the least, whereas she could barely hold a coherent thought in her head. No doubt he had taken women up with him many times. They had probably gone willingly.

Sinclair's wit and good looks were a devastating combination. Add to that his maddening detachment, and many women would find him an irresistible challenge. To be the one to break through that isolation and touch that hard heart would tempt many a foolish lady.

Fortunately, Louisa could not care less about the splendid wall he had erected around his heart. There was not a romantic bone in her body. Not any more.

"Midnight gave me my freedom," she said quietly. "For that, I shall be ever grateful."

Sardonic humor filled his eyes. "Never say he dashed some knave to pieces while you rescued a fair damsel in distress?"

Louisa smiled thinly. "In a manner of speaking, yes. You see, he killed my husband."

"Easy there, Violet," David said gruffly. " 'Tis one thing for the children to scramble around those rocks, but another for a woman in your condition to—"

"Cavort like a baby elephant. Thank you, but I have had quite enough of your warnings," Violet grumbled. "I am aware of my condition. Indeed, I could not be *more* aware of it."

"I did nae mean—"

"I have not slept comfortably in weeks, so I am quite familiar with my limitations," she added crossly. For the last three days, David had accompanied her and the children on their morning outings. She was grateful for his help, for she could scarcely carry anything these days and was always tired. But pregnant or no, she was not an invalid.

"Ball," Josh said, giggling as he heaved a small red leather sphere at David, who caught it and rolled it back. Immediately, Jeremy jumped into the game and proceeded to fall on the ball. Frowning, Josh tried to wrench it away, and fisticuffs were avoided only when David began tickling both of them.

Violet regretted her show of temper. Playing with the children was one of her dearest pleasures, and she hated to mar it with a quarrel. She loved the way the twins babbled constantly to each other in a language no one had managed to decipher. Little Mary was a dear, always crawling up to sleep in her lap when she was tired, her little fingers curling tightly around Violet's. Lately she had preferred David's lap, and who could blame her? Violet's had disappeared weeks ago.

It was not only lack of sleep that made her so irritable, but also the knowledge that the babe's arrival would bring a new set of problems. She and her child would be alone in the world. A life of subsisting on Louisa's charity was not what she wanted for her babe. One day, perhaps, she would find another mate, someone who valued and respected her. Or perhaps not. Life was not the stuff of fairy tales.

Stifling a yawn, Violet watched David as he let the twins tug on his fingers. He was such a big man, yet excruciatingly gentle. She put her head down on a little pile of leaves the children had kicked up. Her eyelids felt heavy. As they closed, she was dimly aware of a large hand placing one of the children's blankets over her. *David,* she thought groggily.

He would not beat his wife or conspire with

another woman against her. He had been unfailingly polite to her and, indeed, to all of them. He had an especially close relationship with Louisa, but Violet did not think it was of a romantic nature. Besides, Mr. Sinclair seemed bent on stirring the coals of *that* particular fire. Violet did not think Mr. Sinclair had committed those awful crimes; yet there was something unpredictable and dangerous about the man.

She snuggled deeper under the blanket. Men were either dangerous and intriguing or bland and uninteresting. Will had been the former. David, on the other hand, was kind to a fault. It was as if all of the deeper passions had been leached out of him. He kept to himself, never venturing more than careful politeness. Only with the children did he ever let down his guard. And yet those scars bore eloquent witness to the fact that he had not always been thus.

For a moment, Violet allowed herself to imagine David as her husband. Doubtless he would take care of her with all of the kindness he displayed with the children. But Violet did not want to be treated like a child. Nor did she wish to be treated as if she were made of fine porcelain that might break at any moment. David was not for her—not that he would ever entertain such a foolish notion.

As she drifted off to sleep, Violet's eyes welled with tears. She looked like a hippopotamus, clumsy and awkward. No man would ever feel passion for her. She had no right to expect it. And yet there was a wanting in her as deep as loss.

Gabriel decided not to ask. He had no doubt that the huge beast ambling amiably beside them could kill, but he had no desire to hear the tale. The castle, the island, his father, the memories—all of it swirled chaotically inside his brain, sweeping every rational thought into a churning jumble of despair. He did not need to add Louisa's departed husband to the mix.

Nevertheless, as the mare bore them on to Peabody Manor and Louisa held herself stiffly to avoid relaxing against him, thoughts of the unlucky chap who once had the right to claim her intruded.

How the devil did a man get himself killed by his own horse within six hours of his wedding? Doubtless he had been drunk; perhaps he had ridden at breakneck speed over some hurdle or other to impress his bride. Perhaps the stallion balked at a jump and catapulted him to his doom.

Gabriel's eyes narrowed as he assessed Midnight. No, that wasn't it. Bred to the bone, that one. Wouldn't balk at a jump if his life depended upon it. Louisa's husband must have fallen off in a drunken stupor and landed on his head, the fool.

If he, Gabriel Sinclair, had just wed a woman like Louisa Peabody, he would not be spending his first six hours of connubial bliss anywhere near a horse.

He would sweep her away to his chamber—

assuming he had such a place, which, given the state of his finances, was only a dubious possibility—shut the door against whatever merrymaking occupied their wedding guests, and make love to her until the only word on her lips was his name. Over and over she would whisper it—not in that chilly tone she customarily used with him, but in the breathless, uncontrolled cries of a woman so undone she knew naught but her lover's name.

Gabriel. He had heard his name many times from women in the throes of ungovernable passion. It had pleased him to be the cause of their pleasure. But he had found that each woman was like the last, and he had long since outgrown the novelty of discovering that women adored him. He was happy to oblige a lady, but he never invested any of himself in the act. If his partner was not knowledgeable about the French sponges that prevented conception, he was careful to spill his seed in a way that could not result in offspring. He would bring no lonely, fatherless child into the world.

He knew better than to think that this woman who fitted so nicely between his arms—even if she did wince every time the horse's movements sent her hip sliding against his inner thigh—was any different from the others. Yet he couldn't help but notice his growing response to the intimate contact with her hips and the way his arm rode just under her breasts as he held the reins.

What kind of man chose to spend his wedding night straddling a horse instead of her?

"Damn it all," he growled, breaking his silence at last. "What happened?"

Her brow furrowed. "When?"

"On your wedding night. When your husband was killed."

Louisa was silent for so long Gabriel thought she did not mean to tell him.

"After the ceremony," she said finally, "we drove to an inn. Richard rode outside the carriage on Midnight."

"Outside? On his wedding night?" Gabriel was incredulous. A man with any kindness or skill would have tried to build a torrid fire in his shy bride right there in the carriage. Yet her husband had left her sitting all alone watching the scenery go by.

"He never let anyone else ride Midnight, so there was never any choice but that Richard would ride outside." She lifted her chin, but Gabriel was not fooled. She, too, had wondered about her husband's preference for his horse.

"When we got to the inn, Richard settled Midnight in the stable with the other horses. Then he joined me in our room. That is, he tried to." She looked away. "By the time he got there, I had climbed out the window."

Gabriel stared at her.

"I hadn't wanted to marry," she said, looking straight ahead, not at him. "But my father had lost everything to him in a card game, so I had to marry Richard to clear the slate. I never understood why he ruined my father. Richard had acquired a fortune in India. He did not need Peabody Manor or anything we had—"

"Except you," Gabriel said softly. He could well imagine how the man had desired her, not just for her beauty, but for her foolish courage. Then again, Richard did not sound like the sort who liked courageous women. Perhaps it was only her hair he admired or her eyes. Certainly not that tiny birthmark, so emblematic of her wonderfully imperfect charm.

Her chin snapped up. "He did not *need* me," she corrected. "He saw me as a challenge, a conquest. A woman to break to the bit, as he had broken Midnight. In Richard's view, a recalcitrant woman and an unruly horse were exactly the same."

Gabriel studied her. "So you did not mean to keep your end of the bargain."

"On the contrary. It was clear that if I did not grant him his husbandly rights, he would have the marriage annulled, and my father would be ruined." Her lips trembled slightly. "Of course I meant to fulfill my marital duties."

He arched a brow. "That is why you jumped out of the window before the opportunity to do so presented itself."

Suddenly, her defiance was gone. "I was afraid."

Admitting to a lack of courage did not come easily to her, he knew, and he wished he had not pressed her for this accounting. He didn't want to hear about her difficulties. Most especially, he didn't want to feel this outrage on her behalf at the lout who had made her suffer.

"I thought I could submit to him," she said softly, "but I did not realize how impossible it would be to give myself to a man I neither loved nor respected."

"Perhaps we should change the subject."

She looked at him blankly.

"Did you know that Apollo didn't really drive that chariot of fire across the sky?" He gave her an impersonal smile. " 'Twas Helios, a lesser god, who wouldn't be pleased to learn he has been forgotten in favor of the dashing Apollo."

"He caught me in the stable, Sinclair." Her eyes had taken on a glassy look. She was seeing the past, and it was not a pleasant sight— as he knew all too well.

"Ever since Harold, we Sinclairs have regarded ourselves as custodians of Apollo's legend," he continued ruthlessly. "Would you care to hear why he wore a laurel wreath?"

"He tore my clothes. His hands were all over me. He laughed and rutted over me like a pig."

"It has to do with Daphne. A wood nymph who had the misfortune to— Hell, Louisa, I did not mean to put you through this."

"He taunted me with his . . . with his manhood, forced me to . . . take it into my mouth." Her breath caught on a sob. "I begged him to stop, but he would not. I was sick. Right in front of him. *On* him. At first he was revolted, and then he just laughed and said I had plenty of other openings in which he could be happy."

Rage crawled up from Gabriel's gut and threatened to explode. He wanted to staunch the torrent of words that poured from her. If her husband had not already been sent to eternal damnation, Gabriel would have killed him.

"He ripped my skirts and tore at my stockings and tried to push himself into me, and I screamed because he was hurting me," she said softly. "He just laughed. I think he must have been drunk, because I had never seen this side of him."

"Saving it for his wedding night, no doubt." Cold fury filled him.

"I crawled backward, clawing at Midnight's stall. I ripped open the door and threw myself in with the horse. The commotion had frightened him. Midnight was rearing and foaming at the mouth. I did not care. I meant to die then and there rather than submit to the fiend I had married. But Midnight rushed out of his stall and trampled Richard instead." She paused. "The oddest thing was that afterward Midnight was very docile. I've rarely seen him upset by anything since. Only the whip—Richard mistreated him horribly—and maybe a tumultuous storm now and then."

With a preternatural calm, she met his gaze. Her thin, fey smile took his breath away.

"And so you see, Sinclair, I know what you men are up to. The male of our species is a loathsome sort, whose treatment of women makes a mockery of the codes of honor he so righteously trumpets among his fellow men."

"Louisa." He said her name softly, like a prayer, as if it could somehow erase the horror.

"Pray, do *not* take me for an innocent," she said fiercely. "I know your game, Sinclair. You are no different from any other man. Your kisses are carefully orchestrated to seduce, and you lose no opportunity to insinuate yourself with my person in repugnant ways. Even now, your arm presses under the fullness of my bosom as if that were necessary for the purpose of guiding Mainstay—which it is *not*— and your exceedingly intrusive male member is asserting itself rudely against my hip."

Gabriel blinked.

"But it does not matter," she continued lightly, as if she believed it. "Richard's death made me wealthy. I have no further need for men, so what they do is meaningless—just as those six hours of my married life are now meaningless. You may think you are touching me in the most intimate of ways, but I have only to remind myself you are a useless lump of humanity soon to be gone from my life. Meanwhile, I remain a rich and independent woman who has triumphed over base male desire, and who will continue to do so on behalf of myself and all women as long as I draw breath."

Gabriel did not realize he had been holding his own breath until his lungs slowly deflated.

"Good God."

"Just so." She smiled complacently.

Chapter 11

~~~~~~

Frederick Sandingham, Lord Upton, stared at the creature who opened the door in response to his knock. Her bodice dipped rather lower than he was accustomed to seeing among household servants, exposing a great deal of her ample breasts. She was missing a front tooth, and her beady black eyes narrowed in an almost predatory manner.

"Who the devil are you?" she demanded. Her voice was not the respectful, deferential tone one usually heard from members of the lower orders. She reminded him of the sort of female one would encounter in a bawdy house.

This was Peabody Manor, however. The home of Miss Louisa Peabody, his late brother's wife, a lady he fervently wanted to bed.

"Please tell your mistress Lord Upton is here," he told the female coldly.

"Horse's ass."

Lord Upton frowned, whereupon the woman began to cackle like a jackdaw. "Please tell yer mistress that Lord Uppity is here," she mimicked. "And what a grand gent he is, too. Well, *my lord*, Alice Wentworth has no mistress." With that she strolled off down the hall, without another look in his direction.

Frederick stood at the threshold for a long moment. Where, he wondered, was Louisa? And the other servants? If this was the sort of female she kept around the house, he would have to speak sternly to her.

The notion of giving Louisa a talking-to pleased him. He imagined her meek and trembling, accepting his remonstrances like the gently bred young lady she was. Unfortunately, over the course of three years as her trustee, Frederick had come to realize that Louisa had not a meek bone in her body. Pity, for he had at one time even contemplated making her his wife.

To be sure, such a union was prohibited because she was his brother's widow, but Frederick thought the legal difficulties could be got round. Few people knew of the marriage. It had lasted but a few hours. Louisa had never styled herself a widow; she did not even use Richard's surname—something he had considered shocking at the time, but had come to see as most convenient. He'd gone so far as to imagine his own wedding night, sampling all the pleasures that had been denied his younger brother.

Then reality had set in. The more he came to know Louisa, the more he realized that any

man would be daft to want such a meddle-
some and independent woman for a wife. She
would, however, make a perfectly adequate
mistress. From the moment he became her
trustee, Frederick had been planning her seduction.

Progress had not been swift. Louisa treated
him politely enough, especially when he came
to make his quarterly reports on the manage-
ment of her estate. She kept him at a distance,
never granting him any exceptional familiar-
ity, even though Frederick carefully planned
his visits to last for several days. He had
dreamed of clandestine forays down the hall
to her room, of nights spent in passionate
splendor in her bed.

Alas, his hopes remained only that. Despite
the fact that he held the strings of the fat purse
Richard had so unwisely left her, Louisa had
always placed her only brother-in-law in one
of the ancillary buildings, a paltry structure fit
only for a dower house.

Peabody Manor had no room for guests, she
always insisted, since it was occupied by her
dear friends, all females, whose names Frederick could never remember. There were a
great number of such friends. The coarse female who had opened the door just now was
evidently one of them, though she had the air
of the doxies who plied their trade in Covent
Garden. That Louisa allowed such a person
under her roof while she shunted her only rel-
ative off to a dower house was unthinkable.

As he stood in the empty hall listening to

sounds from elsewhere in the house—an infant's cry, children's shrieks, and above it all, that infernal woman's cackling—Frederick decided three years was long enough to wait for the woman he desired. He would give her an ultimatum.

Her request had been unusually urgent. She needed him now, and Frederick intended to make it clear there was only one way she could win his cooperation.

He showed himself into Louisa's parlor, poured out a glass of her sherry, and sat down to wait.

"I prefer to dismount by myself." Louisa scowled at Sinclair's proffered hand. "And I am quite capable of seeing to Midnight's rubdown."

"That's *my* job, Louisa. Remember?" Sam looked downcast at the prospect of being deprived of the privilege.

Louisa suppressed a sigh. "Where is David?"

"He took the children and Violet on a picnic," Sam replied. "But the gig is here, so they must have returned. Did you wish me to fetch him?"

"No," Sinclair answered for her. "Everything is well in hand." His mouth quirked upward as he lifted her off Mainstay and carried her toward the house as if it was the most natural thing in the world to do so.

"Put me down," Louisa cried, furious with him and with herself. He could not know what that impassioned confession about her wedding night had cost her. What had she been thinking to tell Sinclair, of all people, something she had not told a soul? The last thing she wanted now was to remain helplessly in his arms, her face so very near his.

"I am not Richard," he said. "I would not hurt you that way."

Somehow she knew that was so, even though it didn't fit with the bitter knowledge of men that had guided her for the last three years. She felt an unsettling closeness with Sinclair and knew it was a dangerous illusion.

She did not want reason to suspect that something in her merciless creed was wrong. She could not let what she had learned about him soften her. Sinclair was no longer a lonely lad desperate for affection from his embittered father. He was a man who knew how to trick a woman into letting down her guard. For a moment, back at that temple, she had almost done so. She had been trying unsuccessfully to regain her equilibrium ever since.

He held her tightly, as if she was his personal possession. They were in full view of anyone in the house who chanced to look out a window. Kicking and screaming to win her release would only call attention to them. Stoically, Louisa forced herself to endure her ignominious plight.

Then she saw Frederick's carriage on the drive—emblazoned with his elaborate coat of arms, attended by six liveried servants, and accompanied by a baggage coach.

"Put me down," she croaked.

"No," Sinclair said mildly.

Louisa grabbed his lapel. "You do not understand. My trustee is here. He is doubtless bringing the balance of the money you are due. He must not see us or think . . . Dear lord, he must not think that we, that I—"

"Are lovers?" Sinclair's lip curled. "If he knows you at all, madam, I doubt he will think that."

Louisa squirmed in his arms. "He *will*! You do not know Frederick. He has an elevated sense of his own consequence. He will be appalled to see me like this. I have rebuffed his advances, you see, and he will think—well, I do not know what he will think, but this will change his entire view of my character."

"We would not wish to do that, would we?" Sinclair shifted her slightly in his arms, stuck out his boot, and kicked the front door open. It slammed into the wall and announced their presence to all in the house.

"*Please*." She pressed her hands against his chest.

"Please?" he repeated loudly. "But of course, my dear—since you insist. I *so* like to hear you beg."

With that outlandish declaration, uttered in a voice that must have carried all the way to the nursery, Sinclair took her mouth in a hard, bruising kiss.

It was horribly mean-spirited of him, given what she had just told him of her past. For all the indignities she had suffered from the male gender and especially for this, perhaps the cruelest, Louisa wanted to slap his face. Instead, her lashes fluttered shut on her breathless sigh.

Then Sinclair set her down, but her limbs had turned to rubber, and she had to lean on him for support. When she opened her eyes and saw her incredulous brother-in-law standing before her, she gave him a silly smile.

"Louisa!"

"My lord!"

Gabriel had never heard Louisa address anyone as "my lord," and he did not like the sound of it. But then, it had been wicked of him to kiss her like that, knowing that her top-lofty trustee would come running.

Lord Upton did not look as if he could run anywhere, however. His elegant clothing barely contained his ample form, which had been compressed by stays so that he resembled a turnip banded at the middle. His florid features and labored breathing gave him a dangerously unhealthy look.

Upton's gaze shot from Louisa to him. Gabriel gave him a cursory nod. "I see you've got sherry there, Upton. Don't mind a spot myself." He strode past the gaping trustee, poured himself a glass, and settled himself into an overstuffed wing chair as Louisa sank onto a nearby settee.

"Who is this person?" Lord Upton demanded.

Just a man I rescued from the gallows. Gabriel

smiled encouragingly at Louisa and took a sip of sherry.

She glared at him.

A man who has been planning my seduction since he laid eyes on me. She did have excellent sherry. He wondered how she would extricate herself from this pickle.

He has touched me quite intimately, my lord, though not as intimately as he desires. And if I can just get over the wretched illness I feel whenever he so much as looks at me, we might have a night of passion unlike any other.

"Lord Upton," she began, as Gabriel contemplated the amber liquid in his glass.

One night. That was all he wanted. One night to be the man she deserved. Not much to ask, but it might as well be the moon and the stars. Louisa found him eminently resistible, and for that he should feel fortunate. No man in his right mind would involve himself with her.

Gabriel regarded her blandly, hoping she did not see the longing in him.

"This is Mr. Sinclair"—she mustered a polite, frozen smile in Gabriel's direction—"my fiancé."

He nearly choked on his sherry. Upton gaped at them. Close by came the sound of crashing teacups.

"Oh, dear!" Daisy stood at the parlor door, staring at Louisa, ignoring the shattered remains of the tea service she had prepared. "Did you say *fiancé*?"

Louisa jumped up quickly to help mop up

the tea. "Never mind about the tea, Daisy. We are not hungry. In fact, I believe Mr. Sinclair has quite lost his appetite."

Upton finally found his tongue. "What is this nonsense, Louisa? I have not heard a word about your remarrying. I should have been notified at once." He sank into the nearest chair.

"I did not notify you, my lord, for the simple reason that my betrothal has only just occurred. Mr. Sinclair proposed this very day." She fluttered her lashes at Gabriel. " 'Tis *Lord* Sinclair, actually. His family is one of the oldest in Kent."

Upton regarded Gabriel suspiciously. "I know of no Lord Sinclair."

"An old but little-used title," Gabriel supplied, shooting a dark look at Louisa.

She gave him a dazzling smile that did nothing to disguise the answering daggers in her eyes. "We were just celebrating our betrothal, Lord Upton. Your timing is perfect." She paused. "I trust you brought the funds I requested?"

Upton frowned. The man might be a slowtop, but he was no idiot, Gabriel saw. "You have taken me by surprise," the trustee said slowly. "I had planned to stay for several days so that we may discuss your extraordinary request. Perhaps you will be good enough to explain what you intend to do with such a large sum."

"Why, of course," Louisa said calmly. "Lord Sinclair and I are planning our wedding. Significant expense is involved."

"Sinclair is not able to cover it?" Upton eyed him suspiciously.

Gabriel dismissed the question with a vague wave of his hand. "My funds are tied up in investments at the moment."

"Just so." Louisa beamed at him. Gabriel wanted to wring her neck. Did she know what she had started? Upton would have him investigated the moment the man returned to London. Moreover, as soon as the trustee realized she had requested the money a week before the betrothal, he would see through her lie.

Upton pursed his lips. "I should like to discuss the matter of the settlements with Lord Sinclair and his solicitors—"

"Broughton, Welshire, and Stevens," Gabriel supplied in a resigned voice. "St. James's."

"I see." Upton cleared his throat. "If all proves to be in order, I will be happy to advance you the sum, Louisa. I see no need for haste, however."

She hesitated. Gabriel could almost see the workings of her nimble mind. By inventing a betrothal, she had hoped both to explain Gabriel's presence and to send Upton on his way, thirty-five hundred pounds lighter. She must have thought Upton would give her the money once he realized her future was assured. But she had miscalculated. Upton was not the sort to be fobbed off with transparent lies. Moreover, if Gabriel did not miss his guess, the lust in the man's froglike eyes had not vanished upon news of the engagement.

Louisa turned to him, and Gabriel read the plea in her eyes. Ah, well, he was always one to help a lady in distress. He strolled over, took her hand, and brought it to his lips, lingering long enough to be judged most improper.

"We are both men of the world, Upton, so I know you will understand our predicament." Gabriel tucked her hand under his arm. "It's like this: we've anticipated the wedding vows."

Upton blinked.

"At this very moment," Gabriel continued, regarding Louisa with affection, "there may be a little Lord Sinclair bouncing around in my betrothed's lovely—er—person. In short, the die has been cast, so you might as well come across with the blunt."

Daisy, who had stood riveted to the spot since dropping the tea service, gave a little shriek.

"You, sir, are unbearably crude," Upton said, recovering his tongue at last. "I cannot believe that Louisa would—"

"Tell him, my dear," Gabriel interjected smoothly.

Louisa's smile was meant to appear affectionate, he surmised, though her lovely blue eyes held a murderous gleam. "My fiancé is more direct than one might wish." She paused. "But I cannot disagree with his account."

Gabriel grinned. "Sherry, Upton?" He

poured the trustee a glass and held it out magnanimously.

The man drained it.

"Delicious biscuits. And the seaweed is . . . most unusual." Lord Upton had recovered himself sufficiently to partake of dinner, whereas Louisa was nearly in shock.

Daisy had spread the word of her betrothal through the house. Louisa had not been able to take the others aside and tell them the engagement was a sham. She meant to do so as soon as Lord Upton departed, but he had declared himself far too exhausted to return to town tonight. For now, she had to endure their felicitations.

Only David said nothing.

Sinclair accepted the good wishes with aplomb. The man was truly shameless. Louisa could not believe she had let him manipulate her like that—though it was her own fault, of course, for starting the lie. Now she would have to live with the endless embarrassments it brought.

No one mentioned the possibility of a pregnancy, but Louisa could not meet any of their gazes, especially David's. Though she had never revealed the sordid details of her wedding night, he knew enough to understand why she never intended to wed again. He must wonder how Sinclair had managed to overcome her loathing.

Alice had her own ideas. "I saw from the first he had a hankering for ye," she said.

"Wouldn't surprise me if ye'd let him have his way. I'd do the same, if I had the chance." Her peal of laughter rang loud and hollow across the dinner table.

Across the table, Violet gave Louisa an encouraging smile. To Louisa's right sat Sinclair, who was watching her with a mixture of arrogance and—oddly—understanding. Under the tablecloth, safe from prying eyes, his hand covered hers. It felt strong and capable. Louisa looked up and met his gaze.

Alice's laughter faded. David's searching stare drifted from her memory. Even Violet's reassuring smile evaporated in the sudden, swirling current that arced between them.

His eyes, green velvet with flecks of gold, held a mesmerizing softness that slipped past her fears and doubts and connected with something new and strange inside her. It was as if he could see right into her soul, as if the ugly wounds there did not repulse him.

Instinctively, her fingers curled around his. And suddenly, Louisa felt something she had never felt in her entire life.

Safe.

Chapter 12

"**T**hey look like angels, do they not?" Lily tucked blankets over the twins.

Jasmine smiled. "When Mary sleeps with her hands folded under her chin like that, I swear she *is* an angel."

Violet draped a blanket over baby Elizabeth, who slept on her stomach with her feet curled under her. Quiet and still, the nursery seemed a world removed from the noisy, rambunctious place it was in the daytime. The children looked so content in repose, curled up in blissful abandon, trusting that the night would bring no evils that could not be banished by a stuffed animal or tasty thumb.

"It doesn't matter about the circumstances, I suppose," Violet said wistfully. "How they came to be, I mean."

"No, it doesn't. They're precious jewels, every one." Lily's dark, understanding gaze met hers.

Tears sprang to Violet's eyes, as they did so often these days. When Jasmine touched her hand, Violet gave a little sob. "I am sorry," she said, appalled that her feelings ruled her so.

"Mary's father was a thief, a wild and lawless sort, who left the day he found out I was increasing," Jasmine said softly. "Some people thought him the devil himself and marked me as a witch for bedding with him. I was glad he left. 'Tis best that Mary never know a father who is kind one moment and heartless the next. But it has not been easy, Violet. I'll not let you think that."

Lily shook her head. "My boys' father was a hosier. He had more than two dozen frames in the attic of his shop and worked us from dawn to dark—sometimes by candlelight, too. When I wasn't hunched over a frame, I was cooking for those who were.

"One night, when everyone else had gone and his wife was away, he seduced me. The knitting was such tedious work, and I was young and looking for some excitement in my dreary days." She gave them a rueful smile. "Truly, I hadn't strength or will to resist. A few months later, his wife discovered I was increasing and got him to turn me out."

Lily's gaze was pensive. " 'Twas the strangest thing, Violet. Louisa was standing just outside the shop, holding a pair of stockings she had purchased, when I was put out on the street in disgrace. Some things are meant to be, I suppose. Now I wouldn't trade places with the hosier's wife for anything."

Violet gave the women a watery smile. "I have been so unsettled lately."

" 'Tis because your time is near," Jasmine

said. "You cannot go back, but you cannot yet go ahead, either. Have faith, Violet. Life with no man is better than life with a bad one."

Faith. Yes, she would try to find some. But at times she felt so frightened, so worried that she would not be as steady and wise as Jasmine and Lily.

"Good night," she murmured as the other women left. The nursery was her favorite place. She often remained here long into the night, watching the children sleep, trying to absorb the quiet peace.

The knowledge that her babe would soon join them filled her with anticipation and dread. She tried to imagine her babe's face, the eyes that would look to her for every need, the smile that would offer perfect trust.

She could not earn that trust. She could not guarantee that she could keep her babe safe, banishing the evils of poverty or abuse or even those of the night to come. She had no home, no husband, no money. She had only Louisa's generosity, and while that was more than Violet had ever had in her life, she needed something more: a future.

Clouds drifted across the moon as she moved to the window and stared out into the night. The world seemed enormous, endless, far too big to accommodate one frightened woman and a tiny babe. And yet her hopes had once been as big as that round ball in the sky—before Will, before the punishments, before her world shrank to the size of Will's fists. Long ago, it now seemed, she had been a girl on the cusp of womanhood, with dreams and hopes as grand as the night. Then they had vanished.

She had thought them gone forever, but as she gazed upon the moon, feeling her babe stir in its impatience to join her, Violet wondered whether it was possible to get hope back. She was about to bring a child into the world: surely there could be no greater hope than that.

Closing the nursery door softly, she made her way down the hall. She wanted to bask in the glow of that moon while she could still keep her babe safe under her heart. She descended the stairs, careful to hold the banister. A moment later, she opened the front door and stepped out into the night.

A quilt of starlight covered the heavens, its soft radiance bathing her upturned face in glowing gossamer. It was impossible to stare up at that sky and not feel hope. Easing herself down to one of the steps, Violet leaned back against a column and watched the stars.

A dozen yards away, Sam sat in the shadow of the stable, idly scratching figures in the dirt with a stick. He looked up as David approached.

" 'Tis late, boy."

"I couldn't sleep," Sam confessed. "I . . . I keep wondering what's going to happen now that Louisa is to marry Mr. Sinclair."

David's eyes narrowed. "I would nae put too much stock in that."

"You mean they might not wed?" Sam

looked askance at the man who had in a few short years become mother and father to him and everything in between.

"We'll find out soon enough."

"If they do marry, will we still live here?" Sam studied his feet intently.

David put a reassuring hand on Sam's shoulder. "Whatever happens, we'll be together, lad, ye need nae worry about that."

Sam looked up into the steady brown eyes that were the very image of his mother's. "Nothing stays the same, does it?" To his mortification, his voice broke on the last.

"Change is part of life, lad."

"But 'tis not always for the good." Sam's gaze drifted toward the porch. "Look at Miss Violet over there. She seems sad, even though she's going to have a baby. Why would she be sad?"

David looked startled. "How long has she been there?"

"A while." Sam hesitated. "Do you think she's worried about having a baby?"

" 'Tis a big event for a woman."

"Maybe she misses her husband."

"Nae."

Sam eyed him curiously. "You know him?"

David shook his head. "The day we rode into Newton, he was there. Beating her in front of the whole village." He paused, as if considering how much to reveal. " 'Twas clear she was increasing, but he made her bare her back for the whip."

Sam was horrified. "Poor Miss Violet!"

"A real man does not treat his woman like that, boy. Remember that when you get older."

Sam nodded, unable to imagine anyone wanting to hit Miss Violet. She was so gentle and pretty, with soft brown eyes that sparkled now and again.

"Your mother was a pearl." David's voice was thick with emotion. "If she had lived, you would have seen that. As it is, I'm supposed to show you what's what. But I'm nae kind of teacher."

That was nonsense, Sam thought. There wasn't a thing his uncle didn't know about hunting—he'd come home with an enormous buck just yesterday—and fighting and just about anything Sam had ever wanted to learn. But his ready denial died in his throat when he saw David's forlorn expression.

"I'm nae good with women. Never can think what to say to them." He sighed heavily. "You need someone who knows the breed."

"Like Mr. Sinclair?" Sam ventured.

David frowned. "Didn't mean him, exactly." He cleared his throat loudly.

"Who's there?" called a feminine voice.

Sam jumped. "It's Miss Violet," he whispered. "I hope she doesn't think we are spying on her." David muttered something under his breath, then stepped from the shadows into the moonlight.

"Sam and I were taking care of some late chores," he said gruffly.

Violet rose awkwardly, her body heavy and

stiff. "I see," she said brightly. "Good night, then." She turned and slipped into the house.

"I guess I was wrong about Miss Violet's being sad," Sam said after a moment. "Her voice sounded happy."

"No, you were right. She is sad."

Sam eyed him in confusion. "I thought you said you didn't know women."

David ruffled Sam's hair. "Come on, boy, 'tis late."

Lord Upton could not sleep. The meal had not agreed with him. The biscuits were adequate, but the rest of the food made his stomach feel devilish queer. He walked the length of his room several times, glad he had insisted on staying under Louisa's roof tonight. She did not dare to put him in the dower house—not with that Sinclair fellow having the run of the place.

It galled him that she had picked Sinclair, an obviously penniless cad with a worthless title, over him, an earl of noble lineage and some wealth—no thanks due to his younger brother. How Richard had let Louisa's father bamboozle him into drafting a will that left her so much money he could not imagine. Richard must have wanted her badly.

But it was useless to cry over spilt milk. Frederick hadn't wanted to marry Louisa; he'd simply wanted to bed her. And perhaps have a go at her fortune. But there were plenty of other women in this house. Half a dozen, if he had counted right.

One of them would be sure to appreciate his worth.

He stepped into the long hallway. He knew which room was Louisa's, but Sinclair was probably there, sampling the delights of un-wedded bliss with his bride-to-be. The other chambers were this way, if memory served. Although he'd had too much wine—to wash away the taste of that seaweed—Frederick had paid special attention to the direction the women took as they'd bidden one another good night.

Teetering down the hall, Frederick stopped to listen at the various rooms. In one he heard two or three women talking, so he passed that one by. He wasn't up to more than one woman tonight. Another chamber was empty altogether, although the bed looked to have been recently occupied. Finally, he came to a closed door at the end of the hall. He heard no feminine chattering inside, only someone humming tunelessly.

Humming was usually a solitary event. Frederick figured he had found his woman. He pushed the door open, and it swung easily on its hinges.

A woman stood at the window. Her silhou-ette bespoke a well-proportioned and ample figure. Frederick beamed. He had found his bedmate.

She stepped out of the shadows. He paled.

"Hello, ducks," she said with a grin.

*   *   *

Gabriel had not slept a wink. There was too much activity out in the hall. First one door opened, then another. When a third door creaked, he grabbed Louisa's father's dressing gown and slipped into the hall.

There had been no mistaking the speculative gleam in Upton's gaze as it roved over the women at dinner. Upton's chamber was next to his, and, as Gabriel suspected, it was empty. The corpulent trustee had indeed gone wandering. Gabriel made a quick, efficient search of the room, then headed down the hall to Louisa's chamber.

At her door, he stilled, listening for any sound that something was amiss. The quiet within did not reassure him. Upton might have put a pillow over her face so that she could not cry out. Ready to do battle for her virtue, Gabriel pushed the door open. On the threshold, he paused.

To be sure, his motives were not entirely pure. Saving Louisa from a fate worse than death was his primary goal, but the scoundrel in him—or was it the dreamer?—had others. His fertile imagination formed an image of him dashing in to rescue Louisa from her lecherous trustee. Filled with adoration for his heroics, she would open her arms to him with the zeal she gave her most treasured causes.

Almost immediately, he discerned that the real Louisa Peabody, the one who existed apart from his rampant imagination, slept alone. Her thick golden hair fanned out over her pillow like a golden veil. Her breathing was slow, even, peaceful. She had no need of saving tonight.

Disappointment rose in his throat. It was an unpleasant taste, rather like Daisy's dinners.

He knew he ought to leave it at that. He had ascertained that Louisa was safe, which was why he had come. A gentleman would slip away, closing the door behind him.

Gabriel closed the door but did not leave.

Curiosity drew him to the bed to see whether sleep had borne away that guarded expression she always wore. It had. She lay on her back, her features relaxed and untroubled, her lips parted slightly to emit a tiny snore.

He wondered whether she knew she snored. Probably not. It was the sort of thing that only a lover would point out—tactfully, of course.

The little birthmark that so fascinated him was barely visible in the darkness. Her spectacles lay on a table near the bed, along with a large book open to the spot where sleep had overwhelmed her. He glanced at the title. *The Ingenious Gentleman Don Quixote of LaMancha.*

Madmen and windmills. He should have guessed.

One of her arms was flung sideways over the empty space a lover should have occupied. He wondered whether Louisa was a virgin. Her account of her wedding night had left her precise status up in the air, so to speak.

Gabriel yearned to erase that night from her memory. She wouldn't have to exert herself in the slightest. She could just lie there, staring up at him with her brilliant blue eyes, while he showed her how wonderful it could be. If there was one thing he knew, it was how to pleasure a woman.

Except that this woman was different from others. Pluck to the bone, but steeped in bitterness and fear and anger. What had she called him? *A useless lump of humanity.*

So perhaps she wouldn't want the only gift he could give her, the gift of pleasure between a man and a woman that he had taken for granted since the age of nineteen. No, Louisa would want something else entirely.

She would want a man's soul. She would expect him to share her vigilante justice and her wild-eyed schemes. She would want a helpmeet riding alongside that homicidal stallion, sweeping into towns and villages all over England to right the wrongs against women that had occurred since the beginning of civilization, and which would occur long past the time when Louisa was captured and strung up herself. She would want a man to believe in her cause and to be ready to die for it.

She would not care about her own safety, or the question of whether she could swim in the perilous waters of self-righteousness without dragging herself and everyone else down to disaster.

He was not Ferguson. He would not follow a woman blindly into death. No cause was worth living *or* dying for. He ought to turn around now and walk out that door.

Instead, Gabriel walked over and sat down in the chair beside her bed.

He was making too much of this. Really, all he wanted was to watch her sleep for a while. A stolen pleasure, perfectly harmless. She would never know. Besides, he planned to leave on the morrow—he would never see her again.

And he wouldn't care. She hadn't touched him, not really. Aloysius had shown him how important it was not to care. Caring hurt like hell. *Bayberry leaves, for God's sake.*

A sly moonbeam slipped between the curtains to fall across her face, highlighting that tiny imperfection above her lip. He liked that she had that mark, liked that she wore spectacles for reading, that she dressed in breeches and rode astride. She was unlike any woman he'd ever met.

To be sure, she was lovely to look at. Her hair was a rare splendor. She seemed unaware of its beauty and was forever tying it back off her face or stuffing it into one of those caps borrowed from Sam. Gabriel's fingers itched to touch that hair.

Holding his breath, he reached out and smoothed the ends that fanned over the cool muslin pillowcase. It felt like spun silk, gossamer and gold, a king's ransom. He wound a stray tendril around the tip of his finger and marveled at how eagerly it clung to him. Like a woman embracing her lover.

Gabriel felt a surge of satisfaction. Even the dreadful Richard, her lawful husband, had been denied the privilege of watching her sleep, of savoring that glorious hair as it lay on her pillow. Had Richard even kissed her? Gabriel suspected the man hadn't bothered with anything that required finesse.

Louisa—it seemed right to call her Louisa in the privacy of her bedchamber—did not kiss like a woman who had received many kisses. Through inexperience or loathing, she kept her lips clamped shut.

So he was the first, then. The first to kiss her properly, the first to touch her in slumber. Awe filled him—and brought him up short.

A wise man did not get involved with a woman like Louisa. Hanging was too good for a man so stupid as to kiss her and think anything could come of it. But it did no harm to sit here and watch her sleep. Gabriel especially liked her mouth. In sleep her lips parted naturally, without coaxing.

He wondered what she wore. It was impossible to tell, for she had the covers pulled up high. Did she wear a gauzy nightrail, made for a man's pleasure? Or a thick flannel thing that hid every inch of her? No mystery there: Louisa was pure flannel. He didn't need to peek to know that.

But he *would* peek—else what was the reason for sitting here without a soul to know that he had invaded the vestal's sanctum? It was either that or go back to his own room. No contest, really.

Gingerly, Gabriel lifted the coverlet. When she didn't stir, he slipped it down further: Louisa wore thick cotton flannel with a floral design. He smiled. She was a Flower, after all.

He ought to leave. But tomorrow he would be gone for good. He would not get another chance to invade her dreams with a kiss, to coax her awake with the heat of his desire.

Ah, well. Some chances were best not taken. With a wistful glance at his sleeping beauty, Gabriel rose from the chair. Life was too short to live in a fantasy world. Louisa had nothing to give him, and he had nothing to give her, save the desire she would not accept.

But one kiss wouldn't hurt. One tiny kiss, stolen when those lips were unaware. Carefully, he perched on the edge of the bed. And hesitated. A sea of differences stood between them, though she lay but inches away.

Still, it was just one kiss.

Gabriel bent down and brushed his lips against hers. He held his breath, but she did not stir. It hadn't really been a proper kiss. He could do better. Much better.

This time, when he touched her mouth, there was fire.

Sinclair was kissing her. His mouth was on hers, and he was setting her on fire. Louisa struggled to separate dream from reality, for it seemed she had dreamed of this kiss all her life. No, that couldn't be. She had known Sinclair less than a fortnight. She couldn't have dreamed this, couldn't have recognized in his kiss the urgent longing that had haunted her for a lifetime.

As she came awake, Louisa realized it was no dream. Sinclair was here, on her bed, kissing her. He had caught her unawares, which must be why she was kissing him back.

"Yes. That's it," he murmured encouragingly as her lips parted on a startled gasp. One of his hands entwined with hers on the pillow. His other hand rested on her shoulder, his fingers toying with a lock of her hair. Louisa had never experienced such an utter sense of belonging. A strange sensation began in the pit of her stomach, swirled through her like a mighty whirlwind, and threatened to turn her inside out.

She twisted away from him. "Stop it, Sinclair."

Instantly, he stilled. Something rough and altogether breathtaking filled his velvet gaze, inches from her own. "Did I hurt you?"

"No—yes! Dear God. What are you doing?"

"Kissing you. Only that, but I expect you'll want an apology."

Louisa stared at him. Her heart was racing. Her breathing came shallow and fast. Yet the instant she looked into his eyes, the fear melted like ice tossed into the fatal heat of a blazing fire. Confusion filled her. "I feel so—"

"Overwhelmed?" The ragged voice belied his self-mocking smile. "Swept away beyond your wildest imaginings?"

Louisa sat up. She saw immediately that her coverlet had slipped off. Her thick flannel nightgown was far less revealing than the ball gowns most ladies wore nowadays, but she felt exposed and vulnerable nevertheless.

Crossing her arms protectively over her chest, she glared at him.

"What are you doing in my room?"

He sat back on the edge of the bed and slanted a gaze at her. "I don't suppose you'd believe I'm an inveterate sleepwalker?"

In spite of herself, Louisa smiled.

"You want to be careful. I might take that smile for an invitation." His sardonic tone did not surprise her—Sinclair never said anything without a twist to it. Yet his eyes told another story. They held something naked, unadorned, breathtaking. His gaze dropped to her mouth, and she wondered if he meant to kiss her again.

Scooting back against the headboard, she reached for the coverlet and yanked it up to her chin.

"Don't," he murmured. "Flannel suits you." Strangely, his voice was devoid of sarcasm.

Each time she encountered this man, he was someone different. Each time he kissed her, she grew more confused. "Please leave," she ordered in a chilly tone.

"Yes. I should have left some time ago." But he did not move. "You see, I heard noises—though you won't want to believe that—and suspected your trusty trustee had gone wandering, possibly into your room to settle accounts."

"Lord Upton? He would never do such a thing."

"He would. Don't tell me you haven't seen that in his eyes." Sinclair's gaze raked her. "I came to check on you, only to discover you were safe and sound. I've been sitting in that chair, watching you, for some time now. Did you know that you snore?"

"Dreadful man!" But Louisa could not summon the anger she ought to have felt. She shook her head. "You are mad, Sinclair."

"Gabriel," he said softly. "My name is Gabriel."

"Like the angel." She tried to smile, but her mouth did not cooperate. Instead, her lips parted slightly, almost with a will of their own. She stared at him, mesmerized by the magnetic force between them.

"Watching you was almost enough. Almost, but not quite." He put his fingertip under her chin. "Do you still feel ill?"

He might as well have spoken in a foreign language. All she heard was the low, mesmerizing timbre of his voice.

"It's a strange feeling, isn't it?" he continued. His thumb touched her lower lip. "Like it's going to take you over, turn you into someone else."

His fingers grazed her cheek. "You sense yourself losing control. At first, you're afraid because you don't know how it will end. But you go with it just the same."

Their gazes locked. "First you dare," he said softly, "and then you soar."

"S-soar?" Louisa stammered. Dear lord, what was he doing to her? Her heart was thundering in her chest.

"You really don't know, do you? That man did everything he could to ruin it. I want to touch you, Louisa."

He reached for the coverlet. She held her breath as he pulled it away and put his hands on her shoulders. His hands felt solid, strong, strangely gentle. She sat there, scarcely daring to breathe, knowing somehow that he would not hurt her. But when he closed the distance between them, her stomach lurched wildly.

"Stay with it," he murmured into her ear.

"I—I don't know what you mean."

"Follow it down. Face the fear, Louisa. You're a strong woman. You can do it."

Louisa closed her eyes and tried to concentrate on taming the reeling inside her, but when Sinclair's fingers trailed over the tiny buttons of her gown, the swirling sensation only escalated. She shook her head. "It's *you*, Sinclair. You're the cause. You're only making it worse."

"I know." His breath warmed her cheek. "It gets worse," he whispered as his mouth covered hers, "and then it gets better."

For his arrogant daring, for his easy assumption that he could kiss her whenever he wished, Louisa wanted to hate him. Instead, she let him kiss her.

She sat motionless and pliant as his mouth coaxed her into the dizziness and beyond. She whimpered as his hand grazed her breast. She heard his low growl of satisfaction as his other hand dropped to her waist.

But when his tongue pushed past her teeth,

Louisa jerked away from him. He wouldn't be so cruel, not after what she had told him of Richard's coarseness. She tried to pull away, but Sinclair's arms held her fast. And then he was stroking her hair, comforting her, as she buried her face in his shoulder.

"Leave me alone, Sinclair," she said shakily.

"Gabriel," he corrected. He made no effort to kiss her again. Instead he simply caressed her back in gentle, concentric circles that felt comforting and wise.

She understood then that Sinclair was the most dangerous man she had known. More dangerous than Richard, because Sinclair made her feel as if beneath the wry facade, he cared just a little. Only he didn't care. He merely knew how to mask the coarseness long enough to allow her defenses to fall.

"Stop it, Sinclair," she said fiercely. "I know what you are up to. I won't be a pawn to your animal urges."

His hands fell away from her. Silently, he studied her. "Very well, Louisa," he said at last. "I won't touch you. But you may touch me, if you wish."

Louisa gaped at him. "Why should I want to do such a thing?"

"Put your hand on my chest. Here." He indicated the area over his heart. "As you did before."

"No!"

"Yes." Amusement filled his eyes. "I won't bite."

Yes, you will, her mind screamed. "I . . . I

don't want to," she stammered. But her willful hand touched the lapel of his dressing gown.

"Not there. I can't feel a thing." To her shock, he parted the edges of the dressing gown so that a small wedge of his chest was exposed. He caught her hand and placed it over his heart. "Yes. That is better."

Her hand curved over the firm, smooth musculature. Her fingers curled around the short, wiry hairs. Under her palm, she felt his heart pounding rapidly. Too rapidly for a man who appeared so calm and self-possessed. Her eyes met his, questioning.

"Animal urges, acting up again." He gave her a pained smile. "Disregard them. I am a master of control." He eyed her curiously. "Haven't you ever wanted to touch a man, Louisa?"

"No. Men are—"

"Coarse. Like those little hairs of mine you have wrapped around your fingers." Suddenly, his voice sounded strained.

Louisa hesitated. "Richard was coarse. You are not that, exactly—"

"Smooth, then. Like those muscles you are caressing so delightfully."

Louisa jerked her fingers away. "I was *not* caressing them."

He caught her hand and returned it to his chest. "Now that"—he touched her finger to one of his nipples—"is hard. See the way it perks up when you address it? 'Tis because I like it when you touch me there. You have power, Louisa. A vast power you do not even know exists. When you touch me, I feel that same reeling inside that you do."

Louisa stared at him. "You do?"

"Yes. But what I feel is the other side."

"The other side?" Seemingly of its own accord, her hand moved lower, to his rib cage. She was curious about those chest hairs. How far down did they go?

A muscle moved in Sinclair's jaw. "The other side of fear is desire," he said after a moment. "Polar opposites, but the feeling is the same. Your innards constrict, then the waves come shooting up inside, and the only thing to do is let them take you."

Louisa liked the feel of Sinclair's chest. He was built so differently from her, and yet there were similarities. She traced the contour of his muscles around to the other nipple and stared in fascination as it, too, puckered up. Instantly, he removed her hand.

She frowned. "Did I do something wrong?"

"No. But you are stirring up the waves too much." He took a deep breath.

"Do you feel sick, then?"

His shaky laugh held no mirth. "In a manner of speaking." His eyes held the heat of banked fires about to blaze anew. *"Louisa."*

No one had ever said her name in such a way, violent and gentle together. She stared at him, as if seeing him for the first time. As if seeing a *man* for the first time.

What she saw did not repulse her. Not in the least. On the contrary . . . dear lord, it could not be. She couldn't care for a man as aimless as the wind, as empty as a sigh. She could *not*. But even as she held that thought, she returned her hand to his chest and felt the violent shuddering in him. And she knew that he ached for her, and a part of her rejoiced in it.

Yes, she had power over him—but even as she grasped that truth, she knew her power was nothing to the power he wielded over her. She prayed he would kiss her before she went out of her mind.

Sinclair crushed her to his chest and took her mouth in a hard, bruising kiss. Under the thick flannel that separated her skin from his, her breasts ached for him. The queasiness welled up inside her, but his kiss spun it into something terrifyingly wonderful.

When Sinclair laid her back on the pillow and loomed over her, she thought she'd die of longing. For what, she didn't exactly know, but it was there in his kiss and in the wild reeling that spun them out of control.

He touched her breast, not gently, through the fabric of her gown. He fumbled impatiently with the tiny buttons, and when they didn't accede to his wishes, he ripped the thick flannel as if it was the most fragile of silks. One of his legs pushed its way between hers, and suddenly her world was spinning fast, too fast.

Her breathing came in short gasps, but Sinclair did not relent. Trailing kisses down her neck, he nibbled a path downward to the rise of her breasts. When he took one of her nipples in his mouth, a cry of pleasure escaped her.

His hands slid over her hips, then slipped lower, under her gown.

"Stop, Sinclair," she moaned. " 'Tis too much."

He stilled. For a moment he did not move. His hand rested on her bare thigh, and Louisa felt the pulse point at his wrist fluttering wildly against her skin. The air between them was thick with need. At last, he rolled away from her, propped himself on an elbow, and gave her a brooding look.

"I should have known. My own damn fault."

"*Your* fault? That I did not wish you to maul me?" Louisa covered her confusion by retreating into anger. "Why, you arrogant man!"

"My fault for not guessing the humbling lesson fate had in store for me." His eyes searched hers.

"I'm sure I don't know what you mean." She reached for the coverlet and brought it up to her chin.

His mouth curved into a rueful smile. "I thought I knew everything about desire. I was wrong."

Louisa stared at him, wondering why his self-mocking smile was so at odds with the simmering heat in his eyes. Before she could reply, a loud, terrifying shriek pierced the night.

"Merciful heavens! What has happened?" Louisa scrambled out of bed, only to discover that her torn gown gaped scandalously. She grabbed her robe and wrapped it around her.

Sinclair was still in her bed, propped on one elbow. He regarded her through hooded eyes.

"Perhaps Lord Upton has finally met his match," he said lightly. "It happens to the best of us."

Chapter 13

Gabriel studied the interesting pattern Lord Upton's blood made on the carpet in the trustee's chamber.

"Dear lord, Alice! Have you killed him?" Louisa knelt over the senseless Upton, inspecting the lump on his head.

Alice shrugged. "Not hardly, though he deserved it. A gel doesn't give herself to just *anyone*."

Louisa eyed her in horror. "Never say Lord Upton forced himself on you!"

"Tricked me, he did," Alice grumbled. "Lured me to his chamber and turned on me like a snake."

"And you had to defend yourself with those candlesticks." Louisa looked stricken. "Oh, Alice. I am so sorry. In my own house, too! I had no idea Upton was capable of this." She turned to Jasmine, who was gingerly wiping the blood from Upton's forehead. "Is his wound bad?"

"I cannot tell yet. There is much blood, but

head injuries bleed a great deal, even when the wound is not grave."

As Jasmine worked over Lord Upton's balding pate, Gabriel decided the charade had gone far enough. Louisa and the others wore blinders when it came to the sainted Alice.

"Not a farthing anywhere to be found, eh, Miss Wentworth?"

Alice shook her head. "Him with his grand clothes and airs—promised me a fortune, he did. Fifty pounds!"

"He couldn't lay his hands on the money?" Gabriel prodded sympathetically.

"Not a bit of it." Alice scowled at the man lying senseless on the floor. "I should have known better. A gel doesn't come across with the goods until she has the blunt. But he looked good for it, so I let him have his way. Then he brought me to his room and made a great show of searching for the money. But he had nothing—not a farthing!"

"Perfectly dreadful," Gabriel agreed.

Alice bent closer. "Do you know how much he claimed to have in this very room?"

"About thirty-five hundred pounds?"

She stared at him. "That is it exactly!"

Louisa, who had been following the conversation with a pained expression, slanted a suspicious gaze at Gabriel.

"How is it that you are able to pinpoint the sum so exactly?"

"A lucky guess." He shrugged. "I tried to imagine what sum might command Miss

Wentworth's undivided attention, and the number simply came to me."

Alice beamed. "Would that every gent had your understanding of a gel's needs. I don't suppose *you're* interested in—"

"Unfortunately," he put in quickly, "I have much to do to prepare for my departure. Packing and the like." He beat a hasty retreat from Lord Upton's room.

He hadn't gone two steps toward his chamber before he heard Louisa behind him in the hall.

"A moment, Sinclair."

Gabriel turned and smiled politely, as if they were not both standing in their dressing gowns, as if he did not know that beneath hers that flannel gown was ripped almost to the waist.

"Yes, Miss Peabody?"

Their gazes met. Hers, suspicious and knowing, his, undisciplined and restless as it roamed over her, recklessly rekindling his desire.

"How did you know Lord Upton was traveling with such a sum?" she demanded.

A mere four feet separated them. Not beyond his reach, certainly, but the frosty look in her eyes put her miles away. "I assumed, as you did earlier, that he was bringing the money you had requested," he replied lightly. "You do recall that you owe me thirty-five hundred pounds?"

"I am aware of my debt." Her gaze narrowed. "You stole that money from his room."

"Foul, madam. A man cannot steal what is rightfully his. Besides, when I entered Upton's room to check on his nocturnal pursuits, the purse was in plain view on his bedside table."

"That was *my* money." She glared at him. "Why couldn't you wait until Lord Upton gave it to me? I would have paid you forthwith."

Gabriel gave her a pitying look. "Such an innocent you are, Louisa. You assume Upton intended to hand over the money. On the contrary, our betrothal gave him the excuse he needed to withhold it until he could have me investigated."

"Oh, dear." Louisa put her hand to her mouth in horror. "I had forgotten! Lord Upton thinks we are to be wed. And that we are possibly to have a . . . a child."

"I doubt he cares much about that at the moment. I expect he will take himself off at first light, assuming Alice's skill with the candlesticks did not kill him."

"But he will still think that we are engaged."

"It will give him something to do. He has the name of my father's solicitors. They will not have heard that they are supposed to be negotiating a marriage settlement. That will confuse Upton and delight his greedy heart. I imagine he will lie low for a while, hoping that our putative betrothal vanishes and he can continue to handle your money. In a few weeks, he will be pleased to receive your note informing him you have decided we do not suit. Which we do not."

"No," she quickly agreed.

"Abominable combination," he muttered. "But I doubt you will have difficulty with Upton in the future. Especially if Alice decides to join the Flowers."

Louisa looked troubled. "Alice has shown no sign of taking to little Elizabeth. She doesn't seem to fit in here, but Elizabeth needs her mother."

"She needs *a* mother. I seriously doubt she needs that one," Gabriel said grimly. "You would do well to be wary around her."

She frowned. "Are you saying we are in danger?"

"You must have guessed that she did not receive her death sentence merely for stealing a loaf of bread," he said quietly. "The reformers have made some inroads, after all. 'Tis likely that she would have been imprisoned for only a short while."

"But stealing bread *was* her only crime," Louisa protested. "I saw her myself that day in Piccadilly."

"You saw what you wanted to see, Louisa." Gabriel decided that he liked the sound of her name. Deliberately, he said it again. "What you saw, my dear Louisa, was the arrest of a woman who had likely been sought for some time. Alice is a thief and a whore and many more things besides. She will never care for that babe, and she will stay only until she finds something better. Tonight she had the chance to pluck a fine pigeon. Her failure to do so must only have whetted her appetite. She knows her future is not here, but in town, where wealthy pigeons are plentiful."

"Aye, listen to him, dearie." A piercing cackle reverberated in the hall. "He's a clever one, and not bad to look at, neither."

"Alice!" Louisa turned, aghast. "We did not mean to insult you."

"No offense taken, ducks. What he says is no more than the truth." Alice regarded Gabriel through narrowed eyes. "A gel likes to be paid for her labors."

He returned her a level gaze. "You want to watch out for that greed, Miss Wentworth. Please do not take offense, but I have difficulty imagining that your going rate is anywhere near fifty pounds."

"How would you know?" Alice tossed her head. "You probably get yer gels for free."

"Alice!" Louisa looked horrified.

Suppressing a sigh, Gabriel reached into his dressing gown and pulled out some bank notes. *Upton's* bank notes, to be precise—or Louisa's, the chain of ownership was a bit murky now. "I could be wrong," he acknowledged. "There is always a first time for everything."

Alice's gaze was riveted on the bills. "Must be about a hundred pounds there, eh, ducks?" she asked slyly.

"All yours, Miss Wentworth—if you catch my drift." Gabriel's gaze bored into hers until he was satisfied she understood.

With a loud cackle, Alice danced off down the hall to her own room. "Come and see me, ducks," she called flirtatiously. "It won't cost you a thing."

Louisa's expression changed from bewilderment to disgust. "I'll leave you to your pleasures, sir." She stomped off toward Upton's chamber, presumably to see to the unfortunate trustee.

Pleasures. The word echoed in his brain, along with some foolish others. *First you dare, and then you soar.* Gabriel shook his head ruefully. *And then you fall on your face.*

"Where are you going?" Louisa stared at Alice, who was carrying a bandbox and wearing a bonnet she must have obtained from one of the other women.

Lord Upton had left at dawn, just as Sinclair had predicted, and now Alice stood on the threshold of Peabody Manor, looking as if she were about to embark on a grand adventure.

"Don't think I'm ungrateful, dearie," Alice said. "But country life's not for me. I'm a city gel; always have been."

Violet had come into the foyer. "What about Elizabeth?" she asked, bewildered.

Alice shook her head. "No place for a babe where I'm going. Shouldn't wonder if ye think that's harsh, me being her natural mother and all, but the fact is she's better off here."

Violet and Louisa exchanged glances. Baby Elizabeth *was* better off here—and if it seemed harsh to separate mother and child, it was harsher still to keep them together.

"We will take good care of her," Louisa promised. "You need never worry for her welfare."

Alice chuckled. "Worry is something I never do. Why, even when they threw me onto that prison ship, I did just fine. The guards were happy to have a willing woman instead of those screaming ninnies who fight them all the time. With me it was an even trade. I let them do what they wanted, and got a nice cabin and blunt besides. The other gels hadn't a clue how to better themselves."

Violet stared at Alice as if she could not believe her ears.

Louisa did not move a muscle. "There are *other* females on the prison ship?"

"Oh, yes." Alice straightened her bonnet. "Where is that nice Mr. Sinclair? He promised to escort me as far as the village."

"How many?"

"What?"

Louisa spoke slowly, enunciating every word. "How many other women are on the prison ship?"

But Alice was not listening. "He said he'd be here at nine, and an ungodly hour it is, too." She frowned. "That's one thing about men, ducks. They're not dependable unless you make it worth their while."

"*Alice*," Louisa demanded in an awful voice, "how many other women are on that ship?"

"Don't get uppity, dearie. Let me think. About five. No, that was before Sarah died.

She was a frail sort. Didn't get along with the guards, so they put her down with the male prisoners. Me, I had a nice cabin above and a breeze at night. Pity the other gels never learned how to manage. Oh, here's Mr. Sinclair now. I'll be leaving. Don't think I'm ungrateful, but a gel has to go with the main chance."

Sinclair sat atop Mainstay, his features expressionless, as Alice flounced down the steps. David waited in the gig. Louisa couldn't imagine why it took two men to escort Alice to the mail coach. Then she remembered: Sinclair had declared his intention of leaving today.

Dry and empty as dust, his gaze was devoid of the liquid fire she had seen last night. "I will return the mare after I make my purchases in town," he said.

"You are going to London?" she asked, surprised.

"I need a horse, a boat, a crew, supplies. After I return Mainstay, I'll be bound for Sinclair Isle."

London. Where his name and likeness were probably on handbills all over town. An ominous chill shot through her. "But—"

"Enough talk, ducks." Alice stood in front of Sinclair, waiting expectantly. Bank notes passed from Sinclair to Alice's nimble fingers. Then Alice settled herself in the gig. Louisa suddenly realized she had woefully misunderstood that mysterious conversation in the hall last night. Sinclair had purchased Alice's departure, not her favors.

Foolishly, Louisa had been awake half the night imagining the two of them together, certain that Sinclair was comparing her unfavorably with Alice. After all, Alice was an expert in sexual matters, whereas Louisa's only experience had been that degrading night with Richard.

She had not felt degraded last night. Sinclair had made her feel special, almost . . . cherished. But she mustn't read anything into that. He'd had dozens of women. He would know how to make each one feel treasured.

Louisa had heard that some women actually enjoyed intimate relations. Jasmine had spoken of the eagerness of some new mothers to recover quickly from the ordeal of childbirth so they could lie with their husband again. Louisa had never imagined such a thing, any more than she had imagined herself as a mother. The prospect of raising baby Elizabeth frightened her. What if she dropped her? Or fed her the wrong food? What in the world did babies eat?

"That was clever of Mr. Sinclair." Violet's soft voice broke into her tumultuous thoughts. "Alice didn't want to be here, and now she is gone. How nice it must be to have a choice." Her voice quavered.

Louisa had forgotten Violet's presence. "Now is not the time to think about choices and changes, Violet," she said gently. "Your babe will soon need all of your time and energy. Later, you can think about the future."

"The future is all I *can* think about." Violet's

lips trembled. "You have been very generous, Louisa, but I cannot live on your generosity forever."

"Your child will have playmates here. We are your friends. It's not a bad life, is it?"

Violet sighed. "I feel ashamed for wanting more. But somehow I must make a home for myself."

"Is it your husband? Do you miss him?"

Violet gave a bitter laugh. "Not hardly."

"Did you love him once?" A foolish question, Louisa knew. Love was but an illusion fostered by poets and young women who had no better sense than to moon over the latest crop of bachelors while their fathers negotiated settlements to bind them to a man for life. At least Louisa had never deluded herself that love had anything to do with her marriage to Richard.

"Yes." Violet was staring at the horizon. "That was before he began to beat me. The drink turned him into a monster. I tried to tell myself that Will was still inside that monster, but finally I stopped believing it. That was the worst—that I had to stop believing."

"I am sorry," Louisa murmured.

"My heart is so full of wonder that I will soon see my babe." Violet smiled through her tears. "But there's sadness, too. Surely it is not too much to hope for a man who can share this joy."

Louisa enveloped her friend in her arms. Violet hoped for too much—no woman should pin her happiness on something as ephemeral as love.

And yet there seemed to be within the female breast, perhaps even in Louisa's, the seeds of a woman's undoing: a tiny and fatal hope that the poets were right.

Her mind gave her images of Sinclair holding her palm to his chest, letting her feel his heart racing.

Face the fear. The other side of fear is desire.

He had shown her desire, and it had not repulsed her. She had wanted to trust him, to give him whatever it was he sought.

But she would never be tricked into believing in love. She knew better than to let her guard down for something as fleeting and illusory as desire. Beyond desire lay disappointment, disillusionment, degradation.

Sinclair had been wrong about fear. Fear kept her whole. Fear prevented her from falling prey to his devastating eyes and wicked wit even as she touched his bare chest and trembled before his masculine splendor. Fear stepped in when that strange, spiraling desire threatened to topple her defenses and her heart threatened to burst from yearning for his touch.

Fear had saved her. But maybe only just.

Thank goodness that she was a strong, contented woman who had no use for men. And that Gabriel Sinclair was gone from her life.

Gabriel couldn't remember when he had made love to a woman so ineptly. Perhaps

long ago, when he had been awkward and unskilled. But even then, he'd had more finesse
than to rip a woman's nightrail in two.

Why did Louisa Peabody have to be the one
woman on earth to make him lose control? He
would count himself lucky if he never set eyes
on her again. Resolutely, Gabriel forced his attention to the horses for sale.

"Fast goers they be, sir. You couldn't do better than these bays. Perfectly matched,
too. . . ."

"Good bottom, that gray. Usually go for
geldings myself, but the mare is something
special. Look at those haunches. She'll take
you to the brink and back, milord. . . ."

"The chestnut's an excellent leader. Won't
pull or shy off the bit. Good for more than a
dozen years of hard driving. . . ."

A man in a hurry could do no better than
Tattersall's yard for excellent horseflesh. And
though Gabriel had not seen any handbills
that bore his likeness, the quicker he left London, the better. Carefully, he studied the
horses paraded before him.

Perfectly matched. To the brink and back.
Hard driving. He thought of Louisa.

Ah, the agonies of unrequited desire. He
wouldn't call it love, whose power he had always thought floridly overstated. But desire—
now that was something else. Desire could
move mountains and turn men into fools.

Even the gods were not exempt. Apollo had
chased Daphne until she had herself turned
into a laurel tree. Gabriel had always thought

that if Apollo had been so stupid as to desire the one woman who despised him, he deserved all the pain he got. Now he was inclined to look more charitably on the poor devil.

He wanted Louisa more than any woman he had known, but it was not in him to feel the tender emotions that so inspired the poets. He was relentlessly unfettered, and he meant to keep it that way. If anyone had asked after his emotional state, he'd have summed it up in one word: numb.

But Louisa unleashed in him unsettling desires beyond the sensual appetites that had always kept boredom at bay. She was courageous and damaged, and she intrigued him beyond reason. Thank the gods she found him immensely resistible, because this sort of desire was dangerous.

Oh, he'd survive. He'd get himself far away from her. And if the fates decreed that he was to be filled with longing for a woman as aloof as that laurel tree, so be it. He could deal with longing. He'd had a lifetime of it.

He had always wanted what some people had: a connection that transcended life's twists and turns, something that endured. Faith, maybe. But more solid than that. He wouldn't call it trust, because a man couldn't rely on anyone but himself. He wouldn't call it love, because love didn't last. It wasn't a soul, either, because he thought he had that—though it was doubtless an empty and rootless specimen.

Gabriel had the strangest feeling Louisa could provide whatever it was he yearned for. Which was why he had run like hell from Peabody Manor. Because if he had stayed, he would have been tempted to take too many chances. As it was, he had a feeling he was hovering on the brink of something.

He surveyed the horses once more. One had speed and beauty, another steadiness and reliability. The third, that dappled gray mare, had bottom. To the brink and back, its owner had said.

Ah, well. How could a man resist?

How fitting that Louisa should inspire his choice of horseflesh. Gabriel patted the gray on the nose. "I'm afraid I must have you," he murmured apologetically. "Shall we charge to the brink together?"

Chapter 14

"**G**et the tail. Hurry, lad! Mind the hooves—ye don't want to get trampled."

Violet, who had come to summon Sam to dinner, stood at the entrance to the breeding shed and watched in fascination as Sam and David facilitated the mating between Midnight and the mare. David stood at the mare's head, holding her halter and lead rope, as she whinnied loudly. Sam had the simple but tricky job of pulling the mare's tail aside at the right moment.

Nostrils flaring, the stallion kicked out wildly as he tried to get at the other horse. The mare switched her tail and stepped nervously from side to side. Dodging the stallion's flailing hooves, Sam pulled the mare's tail out of the way just as Midnight mounted her. The act was completed in less time than it took the boy to breathe a huge sigh of relief.

Afterward, Midnight condescended to take a carrot from Sam and to be led away. Lingering in the shadows, Violet stared at the stallion as he pranced away without sparing the mare so much as a glance. *Arrogant male*, she thought uncharitably.

David moved his hands over the mare, checking for injuries, then offered her a carrot.

"How complacent she looks," Violet observed. "You'd think that after such a violent joining she would be furious. Out of sorts, at the very least."

Startled, David turned. "Starfire's accustomed to the stallion," he said after a moment. "He has given her six foals."

Violet drew near the mare, who was munching contentedly on the carrot. "Am I to assume, then, that she considers herself lucky?"

David reddened. "I'm sorry you witnessed the joining. 'Tis nae for a gently bred female."

"I am not gently bred. I have seen it all before," she said softly. "And then some."

Only Starfire's chewing disrupted the prolonged silence that followed her statement. David checked the mare's halter, then checked it again. When Sam dashed into the shed, David's relief was evident.

"That was something!" Sam enthused. "Did you see the way Midnight came at her? Thought I was going to get poked myself." The boy laughed. "Being buggered by a horse—now that would be a bit of odd fish!"

"Sam." David cleared his throat.

The boy looked around, saw Violet, and turned crimson. "Sorry, Miss Violet. I didn't know you were here."

"It is all right, Sam. I am quite familiar with the process of procreation."

The boy's glance went to her protruding abdomen before he recalled himself, then looked as if he wanted to sink into a hole. Violet took pity on him. "Lily sent me to call you for dinner. She's made biscuits."

The lad brightened. "I'll go along, then." His eyes threw a desperate plea at David, who nodded his assent. Sam raced out of the shed.

Sam was at that awkward age when sexual matters were a source of constant fascination, bewilderment, and embarrassment. Violet hoped he would not grow into a man who treated women as Midnight treated his mares. And yet Starfire did not look displeased.

"Perhaps animals have the right of it," Violet said, half to herself. "They do not take offense or persist in foolish expectations."

" 'Tis no wonder you've taken a dislike to my sex. Like Louisa, you've been treated badly."

Startled, Violet looked over at him. David was inspecting Starfire's halter as if he found it intensely interesting. " 'Tis only one man I detest," she said. "Though many would fault me for that. They believe 'tis a husband's right to do as he wishes with his wife."

"Nay." His normally placid gaze filled with anger. "I've seen death and more besides, Violet, but I've never seen a woman treated as you were that day at the hands of that mongrel ye married."

Hot tears sprang to her eyes. She lowered

her lashes, but David had already seen. "I should nae have spoken." He looked stricken. "Forgive me."

"I cannot get it out of my mind," she said.

He hesitated. "The floggings?"

"The stallion. He didn't care who she was. Or if he hurt her."

"She did nae mind, I'm thinking." David patted Starfire's nose. The mare nuzzled his pockets, looking for another snack. He took out a second carrot and gave it to her. Starfire munched away on his offering, apparently perfectly content.

Violet gave the mare an affectionate pat. "Traitor," she murmured.

"Do ye pine for him?" David asked abruptly.

She looked up in surprise. "Will? How could I? He's a monster."

"Ye must have cared for him some." He stared fixedly at the mare, watching her consume the carrot. "Ye are having his babe."

She stilled.

"Ye must have gotten along sometimes. Otherwise, ye wouldn't have—" David broke off, his face scarlet.

He had not asked out of prurient interest, Violet knew. David was a man of few words, but she had always sensed an inner torment under that sturdy chest.

"I welcome this babe," she said evenly. "I will hold it to my breast and love it as much as any woman has ever loved her child. But I did not consent to the conception."

David stared at her.

"I had discovered that Will and my friend Helen were lovers." The words came out in a rush. "When I confronted him, he lost his temper."

"He beat you."

Violet nodded. "Then he mounted me like an animal, pinned my arms back, and rammed himself into me like that stallion covering that mare."

She heard David's sharp intake of breath, but she could not stop the flow of words. Somehow it seemed right to tell this big, taciturn man who had helped her to freedom.

"That was how he liked it—the beatings and the takings together. Once I ran away, but he found me at a neighbor's cottage. When he dragged me home, no one stopped him. It was his right as my husband." Violet took a ragged breath. "It is not men I despise, David. Only one man."

"He deserves to die." His low voice shook with rage.

Violet shook her head. " 'Tis in the past. He cannot hurt me now."

"No one is beyond reach of the past." David's jaw clenched as he looked down at her from his great height. How had she not seen that raw pain in him until now? It was etched in his features like that jagged scar.

"David," she said softly.

"It was nae until prison that I realized my strength was a gift." He looked away. "I swore that if I survived, I'd use my gift for good. When I met Louisa, I learned she felt the same. We became partners."

"Partners," Violet echoed. She could not help wishing she had such a man as her champion. "Louisa is fortunate."

"Nay, 'tis I. She gave me a purpose when I had none. Without her and Sam, I'd have been lost. Now I've a family."

A family. Yes, that was it. She wanted someone to love, someone to lie with her at night and share the wonder of the babe's kicks. Simple pleasures. Solid and good.

"I—I had best go in for dinner," Violet said.

He did not reply. Perhaps he thought he had said too much already. He stood staring straight ahead, scarcely moving. Violet wondered how she had ever thought him uninteresting.

She walked to the house as quickly as she could, given the fact that she possessed the girth of a cow.

It was only later that she began to mull over what he had said. *He deserves to die.* But more violence was not the answer. Only one thing could vanquish the terrible past.

Love. And she hadn't a prayer of finding it.

Louisa could not forget Alice's words. Four other women were imprisoned on that ship. Four others, no matter what their crimes, forced to submit to the guards' depravity or be tossed in with the dregs of humanity. Though Alice had bartered her way to more comfortable conditions, Louisa suspected the other female inmates did not share Alice's instinct for survival.

"Don't you think so, Louisa?"

Louisa looked up. It was Lily who had spoken, but the others also eyed her expectantly. "I'm afraid I was not attending," Louisa apologized. "What did you say?"

"We are agreed that we should help that nice Mr. Sinclair." The women nodded, except for Violet, who seemed lost in a world of her own. Sam had finished his dinner in a gulp and had gone to help David with evening chores. It was the time of evening when the women lingered over the remnants of the meal to exchange confidences or merely gossip, depending on the mood.

"Help Sinclair? Whatever do you mean?"

"The poor man is quite adrift," Rose explained. "Surely you noticed."

Louisa had noticed nothing of the kind. "We have not seen him for three days. How can you say that he is—"

"Adrift," Rose repeated firmly. "And here he has helped us so much, too. We know that he pretended to be your fiancé just to get rid of that nasty Lord Upton. I am sorry, Louisa, for I know he is your trustee, but I could not like the man."

"Alice taught him proper, didn't she?" Daisy trilled. The others laughed.

"Yes, but Mr. Sinclair had a hand in it," Rose reminded them. "Remember who was responsible for Alice's rescue. He saved her *and* Louisa. The fact that Alice elected not to remain here—and we must thank the saints for that—does not detract from Mr. Sinclair's heroics."

Louisa stared at them, amazed that even absent, Sinclair worked his strange magic on women. "Sinclair played the hero because he was paid to do so," she said in a clipped voice. "That is the long and short of it."

Rose glanced at the others. "With all due respect, Louisa, we think you are biased in the matter."

"What?" Louisa blinked.

"I am sorry if it hurts to hear this, dear," Rose said. "You must know that we hold you in the highest esteem. Most of us owe you our lives. But in this one matter, you are not to be trusted. You took Mr. Sinclair in dislike from the very first." She paused. "Though lately, we have been gratified to see progress."

"Whatever are you talking about?"

Around the table, eyes met meaningfully.

"Lily and Jasmine saw him enter your chamber the night Alice settled her—er—account with Lord Upton." Rose reached for her cheroot and rolled it between her fingers. "It is wonderful that you are lovers, dear. I would have gone after him myself, had I been younger."

Louisa made a strangled sound.

"We have been worried about you," Rose continued, oblivious to Louisa's apoplectic features. "Though you have never confided in us about your own past, it is clear that some man has made you suffer terribly. Otherwise, you would not have embarked on this quest—"

"Quest?" Louisa said stiffly. "What quest?"

"To emasculate the opposite sex," Lily said gently.

Louisa's fork clattered to the floor. "I never—"

"Perhaps you did not set out to do so," Rose conceded. "But we have known you for quite a while, dear. I myself have watched you fume and rage each time you heard of an injustice against our sex. Your courage is commendable, of course—so little is done to help the plight of cast-out females. We are most grateful."

Lily nodded. "I would have starved had you not been there to buy those stockings that day."

"I might have been burned as a witch," Jasmine added.

"I would have perished in debtors' prison, all because of my spendthrift brother," Daisy averred tearfully. "We owe you our lives, Louisa. But while it is true that these evils were forced upon us by men—"

"Not all men are cut from the same cloth," Rose finished. She lit her cheroot from one of the candles on the table.

"We think Mr. Sinclair is cut from another bolt altogether," Daisy added.

"That is why we wish to help him," said Jasmine.

Louisa rose shakily to her feet. Of all the

possible rebuttals, only one came to mind. "Sinclair is *not* my lover."

There was a long silence.

"That is too bad," Rose said at last. "We were hoping you had finally found a man you could like."

"He was in my chamber that night to make sure I was safe from Lord Upton," Louisa insisted.

Lily tittered. "It certainly took him a long time to do so."

"If you haven't taken him as your lover, you should," Rose interjected, despite Louisa's stormy countenance. "He is witty, handsome, gallant, strong, and from the way he fills out those breeches, wonderfully proportioned—"

"Rose!" warned Daisy. "Be kind enough to remember that some of us are maiden ladies."

Rose arched a brow. "Just who would that be, I'm wondering?"

The Flowers looked at each other and tittered.

"No one to make the claim outright, I see," Rose observed. "As I was saying, all one has to do is look at Sinclair, and the mind fills in the rest. If you have any sense, Louisa, you will take him as your lover."

"It would be the making of you, dear," Jasmine added.

Louisa gritted her teeth as Rose's smoke ring wafted over the table. They had turned against her, and it was Sinclair's fault.

"Since you know him best," said Rose, "perhaps you can tell us why he is so lonely."

"Lonely?" Louisa was taken aback. She had not thought of Sinclair as lonely, but perhaps they were right. His jokes held little real mirth. His biting wit kept every feeling at bay. If he'd held any tender emotions, any empathy for his fellow man, they had been buried long ago.

"No doubt about it. That man needs the right woman," Rose said. "We think it is you."

Louisa stared at them. "Me?" she repeated, aghast.

Only a fool would try to breach that wall around Sinclair's heart. Even so, he'd almost made her want to see what was on the other side of her fear. Thank goodness he had left when he did. She might have made an utter fool of herself. Louisa closed her eyes in a silent prayer of thanksgiving.

"Good evening, ladies. I see I am just in time for dinner. May I join you?"

Louisa's eyes shot open. Sinclair's velvet gaze slammed into hers. And like a fool, she smiled at him.

Chapter 15

Damn. She wasn't supposed to smile. Gabriel plucked one of Lily's biscuits from the platter. A quick meal, a brief farewell to the Flowers—that was all he had intended when he'd stopped to return Mainstay and allowed himself to be lured in by the aroma of fresh, hot biscuits.

All right. Perhaps he'd wanted to see *her*, too.

Gabriel had braced himself for her brittle, disapproving gaze. But wonder of wonders, Louisa had actually smiled at him. It wasn't *that* kind of smile, but desire had stabbed him in the gut, anyway.

She hadn't meant to smile, of course. She looked quickly away, so no one would notice. But the Flowers had seen, and they were positively beaming.

"We have *all* missed you, Mr. Sinclair," said Lily, with a meaningful glance at Louisa.

"Louisa has not been herself since you left." Daisy set a glass of water on the table in front of him.

217

Studying them warily, Gabriel sipped his water. Something was not right.

"Too subtle, dears." Jasmine shot him a knowing look. "The fact of the matter is that Louisa hasn't slept a wink since you left her bed."

The water slid down Gabriel's windpipe and sent him into a coughing fit.

"Hush!" Rose scowled at Jasmine. "You may know a thing or two about birthings, but you are positively cow-handed at stirring the caldron of romance."

The caldron of romance. How poetic, Gabriel thought darkly, as Jasmine pounded on his back until it no longer appeared that he would choke to death.

"Thank you," he managed.

Jasmine smiled. In fact, all of the Flowers wore mysterious smiles. A vague sense of dread filled him. Rose soon enlightened him.

"We have been discussing your visit to Louisa's chamber the night Alice thrashed Lord Upton," Rose said.

Gabriel's gaze shot to Louisa, whose face was pink with embarrassment. Did they mean to suggest that he had compromised her? Did they want to push him into marriage?

"Don't worry, Sinclair." Louisa's wobbly voice belied the steel in her eyes. "I wouldn't have you."

Now *that* was a relief. He managed a weak smile.

"We don't meant to embarrass you, Mr. Sinclair," Rose assured him. "But you must see that you and Louisa are made for each other."

Gabriel cleared his throat. Everyone eyed him expectantly. It was time he made a statement. "I—"

"What Sinclair means to say is that he's not the marrying sort," Louisa said quickly. "And neither am I. Besides, we do not suit."

There. She had said it outright, let him off the hook. Gabriel knew he should be forever grateful that she didn't expect him to do the honorable thing and marry her. Marriage to Louisa would be a living hell.

"Oh, dear." Daisy eyed him mournfully. "Is that true, Mr. Sinclair? You are not the marrying sort?"

"I'm afraid not." Gabriel tried to sound suitably apologetic.

The dining room fell silent.

"Perhaps," Lily said tactfully, "we should speak of something else. Pray, what are your plans, Mr. Sinclair?"

Plans. Yes, one must have them. Otherwise, life was bound to be chaotic—unlike *his* life, of course. "I have purchased a boat that I plan to sail to the island where my father is buried. The island has been sold, so I suppose this is a farewell journey. A pilgrimage of sorts." Gabriel felt awkward confessing such a thing, but the women nodded encouragingly.

"Where is the boat now?" Louisa asked, a thoughtful look in her eyes that Gabriel found rather alarming.

"I hired a crew to stock her with provisions and sail her to the harbor near Sinclair Castle.

From there, I will take her to Sinclair Isle."

Daisy's eyes widened. "You own a castle?"

"Not much of one," he replied. "It has long since crumbled, along with most of the other buildings on the property. The only remotely habitable structure is the manor house, and it has not been lived in for two decades."

"I see." Daisy's eyes bore a dreamy look. "You have returned from your travels to reclaim your past."

"I beg your pardon?"

"The restless wanderer, weary of his travels, at last returns to restore his ancestral home." Daisy sighed wistfully. "Only then can he take a bride and start a family of his own."

"Daisy," Rose warned.

Daisy shot him a misty smile. "Forgive us, Mr. Sinclair. Of course you are not ready to marry Louisa. You must make your peace with the past. Only then can you put down roots—"

"You have been reading too many of those Minerva novels," Louisa snapped.

Again Gabriel cleared his throat. "I have no plans to restore the property."

"Oh, but you must!" Daisy protested. "You cannot let a perfectly good castle go to waste."

"I am in England only to finalize the island's sale with my father's solicitors," he said. "That was where I was bound weeks ago, before I had the bad judgment to undertake a drunken bet that landed me on the gallows. So you see, ladies, the sooner I leave England the better."

"A drunken bet." Louisa eyed him contemptuously. "Was that how you ended up in that convent?"

Gabriel returned her a bland gaze. "Yes. That night I'd won Lord Sedbury's yacht in a card game—commerce, I think it was—but the poor man couldn't bear to be parted from her. Sympathetic fellow that I am, I agreed to give him a chance to recoup the loss: his townhouse against the boat. Whoever could secure a lock of hair from a virgin's head would carry the day."

"How clever!" Lily clapped her hands.

"Clever?" Louisa frowned. "I fail to see—"

"The *convent*." Lily could hardly contain her laughter. " 'Tis perfect."

"Virgins, Louisa," put in Rose. "Quite a lot of them in a convent, I should imagine." She turned to him. "Did you get what you wanted?"

"I think it is accurate to say that the experience brought rather more than I anticipated," Gabriel said.

Rose and the others erupted in laughter. Louisa gave him a thin smile and looked away, as if a man who risked his neck on an absurd, drunken bet was not worthy to sit at the same table with her.

"The yacht is gone, I suppose," Rose said.

"Quite," Gabriel replied. "But the sloop I've purchased is quite adequate for my needs."

"But with your estate in ruins," Lily said thoughtfully, "you have nothing truly . . . permanent."

"Permanent?" He frowned.

"Except the island," she added, "and it has been sold."

"Such are the fortunes of a felon," he said lightly.

"Perhaps," said Daisy, "we can help you restore your home."

Gabriel prayed he had not heard aright.

"What a wonderful notion!" Rose nodded. "I know a bit about such things. My late husband—the first one, may he burn in hell—was a carpenter. We can draw up the plans, then hire workers to complete the job."

"And after that," Daisy put in happily, "you and Louisa will be free to marry."

This discussion had gone on long enough. "I do not wish to seem ungrateful, ladies, but restoring that old pile of stones is the furthest thing from my mind." Gabriel rose. "Please excuse me. I must be on my way."

"It is too late to dash off now," Rose declared. "You will stay the night, at least. Do not worry," she added at Gabriel's dubious expression. "In the morning we will let you go. Isn't that right, Louisa?"

"Yes," she responded grimly. "We certainly will."

When the Flowers waxed eloquent about a match between her and Sinclair, Louisa had realized an alarming truth. She and Sinclair had become symbols of their dreams.

Daisy had hopes. And Violet. Jasmine, Lily, even Rose. None had given up on the dream of finding a man to love. For all the abuse they had suffered, for all that they were infinitely better off now, for all that they thrived in one another's company, they still yearned for romance. Perhaps they reasoned that if such an unlikely pair as she and Sinclair could find happiness together, there was hope for them, too.

Louisa did not want to carry the burden of their hopes and dreams. It was easier to plot a daring rescue than to contemplate a union between her and Sinclair. Besides, any interest he had in her stemmed wholly from lust.

For tonight, that was quite perfect.

She strode purposefully toward the stable. She had not seen Sinclair since dinner. He was probably avoiding them, and who could blame him? Daisy's head was filled with nonsense, and the usually practical Rose had taken leave of her senses. Why did women lose their bearings around him? A subject to be pondered another time—for now, she had more pressing concerns.

The plan had come to her as Sinclair spoke of his boat. He was sure to be difficult, but she thought his cooperation could be bought. And if money failed to sway him, she had something else to barter.

Night had settled over Peabody Manor, spreading a star-dusted curtain of silent beauty. The animals had quieted, and the familiar smells of hay and horse wafted from the stable. Louisa hesitated for a moment, then slipped inside.

Sinclair was tending a big gray. Midnight pawed nervously in his stall and eyed the mare wildly. The stallion was gentler by far than he'd been under Richard's heavy handling, but a newcomer to the stable could still provoke him. Only a single lantern burned on the wall, but Louisa saw well enough that the gray was a prize.

"She's beautiful. No wonder Midnight is agitated."

Sinclair did not turn around. "Midnight has excellent taste in females."

"We could move him somewhere else for the night," Louisa offered, "though I expect he will settle down once he gets accustomed to the fact she's not here for his own personal use."

"Wouldn't want him to think that, would we?"

Louisa could not think of a suitable rejoinder. The silence between them lengthened, and Sinclair seemed content to let it do so. He had removed his coat, which lay on the straw in a corner. The muslin of his shirt strained over his shoulders as he groomed the gray. It was a new shirt, she realized, undoubtedly sewn by the same London tailor who produced that elegant superfine coat.

"Your new clothes are lovely. Well, not lovely exactly, but handsome. Manly." She cringed as she heard her words. Daisy or Lily could have carried off such a light, flirtatious remark, Louisa knew she didn't have the skill for it.

"I am in your debt for the use of your father's clothes," he said gravely. "I had them laundered in town. You will find them on the table in your foyer." He returned his attention to the gray.

Louisa bit her lip. Small talk was getting her nowhere. She wondered how to broach the subject uppermost in her mind. Finally, she simply blurted it out.

"Alice said there were four other women on that prison ship. I wish to engage you and your boat to rescue them."

Sinclair ran his hands over one of the gray's forelegs, feeling for burrs and bruises. He did not speak.

"I have given the matter some thought," she rushed on. "There would be too many people for a rowboat. And after the last time, the guards are doubtless on the lookout for a small boat."

Silence.

"They wouldn't be looking for a sloop, though. We could sail your new boat right up, big as you please, and—"

"No." He did not even look at her.

"I'd pay you twice your fee for rescuing Alice."

"I'd be twice the fool for taking it."

Louisa's heart sank. "Those women aren't strong like Alice, Sinclair. She says they're often thrown into the hold with the male prisoners—"

"All the more impossible to reach them."

"They're horribly abused," she said desperately, willing him to turn and face her. "They don't trade their bodies for better accommodations as Alice did. They're helpless—virtual slaves."

Sinclair tied a feedbag on the gray. "It would be suicide to attempt a rescue on that scale. You can't save the world, Louisa. When are you going to realize that?"

"When are *you* going to realize you can't live your life apart from the world?" she shot back. "Every person has an obligation to humanity. We're all connected, Sinclair. When are you going to see that?"

"No one is obliged to sail into the teeth of death to rescue four felons whose lives are not worth the risk."

Angry tears welled in her eyes. "Your life's not worth much now, Sinclair. How could death make much difference?"

It was a horrible thing to say. The minute the words were out of her mouth, Louisa regretted them. But she could not, would not, call them back.

His expression was unreadable as he turned to look at her. "Good night, Louisa."

And that, it seemed, was the end of it. He picked up his coat, put it on, and walked toward the door.

"Wait!" Louisa cried. "I'll pay you more, Sinclair. Three times as much."

He strode past her as if he hadn't heard.

"I'll . . . I'll let you make love to me."

It was her trump card. She had thought about nothing else since supper. If money no longer tempted him, *this* would, for Sinclair was a man of base instincts.

He stilled.

"I will," she insisted fiercely. "Whatever you want, Sinclair. On my oath. I'll not object or take sick or complain. Tonight, if you wish. Come to my room. Or I'll come to yours. It doesn't matter."

"No, I can see that it doesn't." His gaze roved over her, inspecting her. " 'Tis unwise to give the goods away beforehand, Louisa. Alice would never approve of such a bargain."

He made no move toward her. Her ultimate sacrifice did not interest him in the least. Louisa felt like a fool. Why had she thought he would agree to risk his life for a night in her bed? It wasn't as though she was an illustrious courtesan known far and wide for her sexual expertise. Her proposition must seem laughable.

But he was not laughing. His eyes were brooding, pensive. As if he was considering her proposal. Dare she think it?

"It would be a bad bargain," he said softly. "A very bad bargain."

"Please, Sinclair. I can't save those women without you." Dear lord, she was begging now, begging him to make love to her, when she didn't even know if she could go through with such a thing.

"As appealing as your offer is," he said with unbearable politeness, "I must decline."

"You cannot!" she protested.

He arched a brow. "I am doing you a favor,

Louisa. I am a scoundrel—remember? You'd never know whether I would live up to my end of the bargain."

"I'm willing to take the chance." She tried to keep the desperation from her voice.

"Allow me to be noble just once." His lips curved in a self-mocking smile. "I promise the opportunity will not come again."

To every appearance, he was quite calm, declining her offer with just the right tone of polite indifference. And yet his mask was not altogether perfect, for his green eyes held flashes of amber. And something else: longing.

Afraid to trust her instincts, Louisa nevertheless reached out and touched his arm. He flinched as if she had struck him.

"Go away, Louisa," he growled. "Take your lofty goals and your valiant sacrifice elsewhere. They are meaningless to me."

"Touch me, Sinclair."

"No."

She caught his hand.

"Louisa—"

"Devil take it!" She tore at the buttons of her frock and shoved his hand inside her bodice. She knew she was doing this badly. But he had sought her breast that night in her chamber, sought it urgently, so perhaps this would move him.

It didn't. He stood motionless, his palm resting on the thin lawn of her chemise, his fingers pressed against her nipple. His gaze was unreadable, save for those amber flecks that seemed to burn and burn. His mouth twisted wryly, as if he had suddenly found himself in the midst of a bizarre and rather distasteful joke.

Tears of shame stung her eyes.

"Damn it, Sinclair." Her voice broke. "Why won't you make love to me?" She closed her eyes, unable to look into his face and see her humiliation reflected there.

"Because I cannot promise you a thing, Louisa."

"You *can*," she said fiercely. "You must have feelings for those women, for their plight. You are no monster."

His laugh was ragged. "I'm no hero, either." Gently, he removed his hand from her chemise. With a murmur of protest, Louisa recaptured it.

"You do not know what you can be." She brought his fingers to her lips and kissed them softly. "You can be more than you are, more than you know—"

"No." He pulled his hand away. "People don't change, Louisa. You won't, and I can't. No miracle would happen if I made love to you. I'd still be on my way in the morning, and you'd still be plotting to save womankind. Only you'd have another man to hate."

Louisa stared at him. "I don't hate you." It was true, she realized. Whatever she felt for him, it wasn't hate.

"Button up, then." He gave her a brooding smile. "Save yourself for someone who deserves you."

And with that, he strode out into the night.

* * *

The mantle of nobility sat comfortably on his shoulders, though it had been a near thing for a while. Gabriel congratulated himself on resisting Louisa's awkward attempt at seduction. That way lay danger, along with a host of murky emotions he had no desire to examine.

I'm no hero, either. That had been a good line. He must remember to trot it out again sometime when confronted with a frighteningly earnest female.

Louisa never ceased to surprise him. Who would have guessed she deemed a night in his arms worth such a sacrifice? That she would deign to touch him, providing he was prepared to risk his life for the privilege?

Anger stirred within him, mixed with the other unsettling emotions she had unleashed in his breast. The woman had no idea how fortunate she was he hadn't accepted her offer. He would have taken his pleasure and left her lying there with only her lofty ideals for comfort. He certainly wouldn't have involved himself in her ridiculous scheme.

The woman was a menace. She looked like any man's notion of perfection, but she was crazy as a loon. She'd put his hand on her breast, let him feel that nipple harden under his fingers like the answer to a prayer. He was crazy for wanting her, for even contemplating such a risk. Sweet Jesus—she didn't want much, only his life. And he was not about to squander that again.

To the brink and back, indeed. He had damned near lost his reason back in London, all because he hadn't seen her for a few days. He had let his imagination go wild, let it draw him back here for one last look at the woman of his dreams. Thank God reality had set in. With any luck, he could be on his way at dawn. He'd never see her again.

"Sinclair." Her voice came from behind him.

With a muttered oath, Gabriel whirled around. Louisa was standing in the stable yard.

Naked.

"Come here, Sinclair." It was a command, delivered with all the authority of one of those mythical Amazon women. But she hadn't quite pulled it off. She didn't look strong and proud, like one of those warrior women. She looked scared, humiliated. And her voice had quavered on his name.

"Where the hell are your clothes?" he demanded.

She lifted her chin defiantly. "In the stable."

"God's blood, Louisa. Get back in there and get dressed. Someone might come out at any moment."

"I don't care."

"I *do*!" With an angry curse, Gabriel ripped off his coat and strode over to her. He wrapped it around her, lifted her into his arms, and carried her into the stable.

At the sight of Gabriel carrying his naked mistress, Midnight snorted loudly. The gray nickered a greeting. In another stall, Mainstay nodded sagely.

"Turn your heads, damn it," Gabriel muttered.

"W-what?" Louisa stammered.

"Nothing." Gabriel dropped her none too gently onto the straw where her clothes lay in a pile. "Get dressed." He turned his back to give her privacy, a notion that seemed ridiculous, since he had now seen every inch of her. But he would not think about that, not now.

She didn't say anything, and he assumed she was getting dressed. The horses had apparently lost interest, for Midnight had resumed his edgy contemplation of the gray. Gabriel almost envied the horses their narrow world, where a newcomer to the stable was as exciting as it got.

He could use a little less excitement. The sight of a naked Louisa standing in the stable yard was too rich for his blood. He wanted only to get a good night's sleep and leave this house full of bedlamites at first light.

"Sinclair?" Her voice, soft and hesitant, drifted out of the shadows behind him.

"What?" he snarled.

"I don't understand. Don't you want me? When you . . . came to my room that night, it seemed that you wanted to . . ." Her voice trailed off.

Gabriel closed his eyes and prayed for grace. "Yes."

"Yes?" She echoed in a puzzled tone. "You

mean that you did—er—do want me?"

"Did. Do. Get dressed, Louisa."

"Then why—"

Gabriel whirled around. "Is this some sort of test of my character so that you can decide whether I am worthy of—" He broke off.

She had not gotten dressed. She sat there on the straw, huddled under his jacket, which did not begin to cover the parts of her that should have been covered.

"Hell," he said. His heart jumped to his throat and stayed there. "Hell and damnation."

Chapter 16

Gabriel knew he had given the game away. As Louisa sat in the straw looking up at him, he couldn't hide the naked desire that rose in him like a fever. He feasted his gaze on her body, devouring with his eyes that which he hungered to possess. She had the basic female parts—he had seen that well enough outside—but on her they flowed together like a wondrously unique work of art.

As he had learned the night of Alice's rescue, her breasts were perfectly shaped, but now he saw the dusky nipples that begged for his touch. Her narrow waist flared to slender, boyish hips. Her legs were lissome and shapely, and he imagined them wrapped around him, urging him on until he spent himself in her.

Gabriel swallowed hard. He felt like an adolescent in the throes of first lust, fixated on the feminine form as if it were the beginning and end of all knowing. But he was no lad. He was a man who knew how to please and to enjoy. He'd seen naked women, yet he was staring at Louisa as if he did not know the first thing about desire.

His predicament was laughable, if he'd felt like laughing.

She stood up, leaving his jacket behind in the straw. "You want me, Sinclair. Here I am."

He ought to flee for his life. He could promise her nothing. And no matter what happened tonight, he meant to leave at first light. He should stop her from wasting herself on a man who didn't know how to take the treasure she offered.

Once, perhaps, he would have enjoyed the seduction. But tonight she'd put the game on a different footing. She had made herself a noble sacrifice, advance payment for rescuing those women. It was a bad bargain for all concerned. He ought to leave and walk away with his own nobility wrapped around him like a banner.

Hell. Nobility was best left to honorable men. Looking at Louisa in all her naked glory, Gabriel knew he was not that.

"Stop it, Louisa," he said hoarsely. But even to his ears, he sounded insincere.

She smiled the fey smile women have owned since Eve. "No."

He would not do this. He would not obligate himself or make a promise he could not keep. He would not let her think he cared for her, because he did not, could not, and the woman was daft to think there was even a chance—

"Sinclair."

Gabriel hated the way she said his name. The way her voice, now strangely husky, wrapped around the word as if it were more than just a name. The way she tried to make him so much more than just a man.

He would not prostitute himself for her foolish ideals. Love didn't last, caring didn't last, and ideals never kept a man from hurting those who most needed him.

Louisa stood on her tiptoes and kissed him. He tried not to move, tried not to show how that simple brush of her lips rendered him utterly helpless. Reason tried to assert itself, but it was no use. Like a doomed fish flopping frantically in the fisherman's net, Gabriel struggled against the inevitable. Desire stabbed him through and through, like the bitter hook that would not be dislodged.

Jesus, he thought. Nets and fishhooks. He had really gone round the bend.

"Louisa." He made one last effort. "I am not worth your sacrifice. Don't you see? I won't help you save those women. I won't be around to see the results of this night. I won't marry you—"

"I don't want marriage." Her blue eyes flashed disdainfully. "And I wouldn't marry *you* if you rescued every wronged woman in England."

"That is very flattering, to be sure."

She tilted her head, studying him. " 'Tis no more than the truth. But enough talk; you want me. I won't make a fuss about it."

No, she wouldn't. He had a pretty good idea

of how it would be. She would lie there and let him take his pleasure, enduring the act as merely the currency in her latest scheme. She wouldn't end all breathless and flushed, slightly embarrassed by her own desire. She wouldn't give him anything; she would withhold herself.

Gabriel knew he could reach her, knew he could make a mockery out of her control, knew he could confound every damned idea she had about sex, for she had no experience beyond the loutish behavior of that stupid husband of hers. She didn't know the first thing about desire, about letting it shoot her to the heavens and back. She didn't know how it could be, and she was too scared to find out. He wanted to wipe that fey smile off her face, to disprove every fearful prejudice she held about desire.

He would be disciplined and cool and masterful. He would play her like a lute and make it good, so very good that she would never again think of him and the dreadful Richard in the same thought.

That is what he would do.

Then she reached for his shirt. Gently, shyly, she pushed the fabric aside. Her fingers slipped under the material and traced the contours of his chest. Her fingertip drew a lazy circle around one of his nipples.

And he was undone—just like his muslin shirt, which she dropped onto the straw with the remnants of his cocky male pride.

*   *   *

Louisa's hands were shaking. As her fingers splayed over his chest, toying hesitantly with one of his nipples, she hoped Sinclair did not realize she had no idea what she was doing.

She had never touched Richard this way. Indeed, the idea of caressing Richard's bare chest—or any of him, for that matter—had made her cringe. She was surprised to discover she liked touching Sinclair. His skin had a rough, masculine feel so different from hers.

He stood stock-still, staring straight ahead as her fingers slid over the musculature of his chest.

Did he desire her? He had said so, but he didn't bear her down to the floor as Richard had done, didn't rip open his trousers to try to thrust himself into any and every opening in her body. Rigid and motionless, he betrayed no hint of his thoughts. She wondered what in heaven's name she was supposed to do next.

She hoped he did not find her repulsive. If he didn't want her, those women on the hulk would be lost. Her sacrifice was nothing to theirs. Sinclair *had* to want her.

She would hate it, of course. She would grit her teeth and accept the pain and degradation, knowing it was for a greater good. Even Sinclair had to have a shred of honor in him somewhere. He wouldn't take her and then go on his way as if she were a whore hired for the evening. He would be obliged to help those women.

Sinclair closed his eyes, as if blocking out

some dreadful image. His mouth contorted in a grimace.

Tears sprang to Louisa's eyes, her humiliation complete. Her body was ugly and unfeminine, her birthmark unsightly, her shoulders bony. Her breasts weren't big and round like Jasmine's. Her hips weren't voluptuous like Daisy's. Sinclair, who'd probably had his pick of women since he reached manhood, was undoubtedly revolted.

Furtively, Louisa wiped her eyes. She would not let him see how his indifference hurt her. She would pick up her clothes and calmly put them on, never letting defeat rule her. She turned away.

His hand touched her shoulder, and she froze.

Wordlessly, he turned her around. For a moment they faced each other, motionless as statues. Then he drew her into his arms.

"Louisa," he murmured, burying his face in her hair. Slowly, he rocked her in his arms. He held her close, so that her breasts rubbed back and forth over his bare chest.

"Yes," he said. "Like that."

He groaned. Then it was as if the floodgates had opened, for he kissed her so passionately she had no choice but to accede to his plundering tongue. Dizziness assaulted her, even as a heavy sensation pooled in her lower body and stirred a great yearning within.

Sinclair's hands roamed over her, caressing her hips, crushing her against him. He didn't seem to notice that her shoulder blades were bony or her hips too slender. He touched her as if she were a priceless treasure.

"Sinclair," she protested weakly, when he bent to kiss the tip of her breast.

"Don't ask me to stop," he rasped. "You wanted this."

Yes, but she had not thought he would stir such unsettling forces within her, or that her breasts would ache so deliciously at his touch. She would *not* enjoy this. She would not grant him the power her enjoyment would bring. Closing her eyes, she willed the heavy yearning within her away.

His hands did not cooperate, however. They wandered wildly, feeding the heaviness, making her head spin and her body reel from the sensations he aroused. Then his hand went between her legs.

Suddenly, the dizziness swept her again, along with a reckless urgency that threatened to swamp her then and there. Weak-kneed, she leaned against him for support. He stroked her with exquisite care.

It was not fair. She was naked and vulnerable and open to him, and he knew so much more about her body than she did.

Now she understood how dangerous Sinclair was—for he meant to turn her body against her, make her lose control. She would lose herself in him and have nothing, absolutely nothing, left.

Louisa tried to steel herself against his touch, but he was skilled in ways she had not dreamed of. Even as desire threatened to overwhelm her, she fought against it. She told herself that Sinclair was a scoundrel and a rake—but even the certainty that he had used dozens of women like this, that she meant nothing to him, did not stop her body's response.

But then she thought of Richard and how he had not considered her pleasure, only his own. She thought of how much she had hated his lechery and the careless disregard of her person. At last, she realized what she could do.

Sending a silent prayer heavenward, Louisa reached for that masculine part of Sinclair that was now so very noticeable under his trousers.

He inhaled sharply. The hand that stroked her went slack. Encouraged, Louisa touched him more boldly, marveling at his hardness, wondering what he was like under that fine kerseymere. Her fingers closed around him.

Sinclair groaned.

Instantly, she released him. "I'm sorry," she said, appalled that she had hurt him. "I did not mean to—"

With a low growl, he bore her down into the straw.

And then he was naked, his body looming over her for the reckoning. He took the bulk of his weight on his arms, but that did not lighten Louisa's horror as their gazes locked and his eyes filled with amber fire.

"Damn," he said. "Damn."

Desire abraded his voice, left it as rough as the calluses on the masculine fingers that entwined with hers. His raw heat and breathtaking vulnerability loosed something deep inside her. Louisa felt herself sinking into the depths of that sensual, swirling chaos in his eyes.

Panic filled her. She had gone too far, unleashed something ungovernable and terrifying in both of them.

He fumbled with his trousers. Blindly, she reached for him again, this time to marvel at the silken smoothness of the part of him that was so proudly and wholly male. Sinclair scowled, but it was a scowl turned inward, not at her. A shudder racked him. It was her doing, that shudder. He was right: She had power.

Marveling at his hardness, Louisa stroked him, urging him on. Now he would submit to her will and spend himself in lust. It was fitting, her woman's revenge. It almost made up for all that Richard had done to her. She had kept herself whole; Sinclair would know that he could never move that innermost part of her, that she had made a mockery of his effort to do so. He hadn't touched her, not really. She was safe from his wiles, his wit, his knowing masculine eyes. *He* was the one who had lost control.

But Sinclair was not Richard—and when he pushed her hands away and thrust himself into her with a hoarse, rapacious cry, Louisa did not feel revulsion or revenge; only a small pain that did not hurt so very much.

She was glad that she had discovered how to beat Sinclair at this game, glad that she had not let him continue stroking her in that disturbing manner. Now there was only this tiny pain and the keening ache deep inside to remind her that she had not enjoyed his lovemaking.

Not one bit.

The gray neighed softly. Midnight answered with a snort and kicked at the door of his stall. Gabriel regarded the stallion with a jaundiced eye.

"Don't let her get to you, man. You're better off in your own stall, believe me."

He stumbled to his feet. He had no idea what time it was, but it had to be well after midnight. Louisa must have slipped away after sleep had overwhelmed him. Unless she hadn't been here at all. Had he dreamed the whole thing?

Gabriel knew he hadn't. The memory was too vivid and humiliating. Besides which, his trousers were off and his shirt lay in the straw where she had tossed it a lifetime ago. Groggily, he struggled into his clothes. Respectable once more. Everything back to normal. No one would guess what had happened in this pile of straw.

Well, almost no one.

A figure entered the stable. Ferguson. He paused, surveyed the horses with a critical eye, and turned his gaze on Gabriel.

The minute their eyes met, Gabriel saw that Ferguson knew. The man's next words confirmed it.

"I don't know whether to consign ye to the

devil or wish you happy," the giant snarled.

Gabriel was in no mood to play David to Ferguson's Goliath. "Go away."

Ferguson's eyes narrowed. He took a step forward. "If ye hurt her, Sinclair—"

"Is this what you do at night—lurk around looking to spy on furtive couplings?" Gabriel demanded. "Your life must be at a sorry pass, man."

Ferguson stiffened. "I was nae spying. I do nae sleep well. Too many ... too many dreams."

"Dreams? Let me tell you about dreams, Ferguson. Dreams are for idiots. I know, because I've had them ever since I laid eyes on that woman, more's the pity." Gabriel crossed his arms and regarded the giant assessingly. The man looked wretched.

Ferguson averted his gaze. "Sometimes I hear voices. In the dreams, I mean. Does that happen to you?"

Gabriel wasn't in the mood to stand around exchanging confidences with Ferguson, trying to figure out which one of them was crazier. Then again, it was not as if Louisa was waiting inside the house, tenderly warming his bed like an eager lover. More likely she was regaling the Flowers with the story of her splendid nocturnal success. "Once in a while," he heard himself confess.

"I hear screams. Slow, agonizing screams."

Gabriel stared at him. Despite Ferguson's enormous size and bulging muscles, the man looked positively haunted. He was covered in sweat. His eyes were reddened and bloodshot. If Gabriel hadn't known better, he would have thought Ferguson was scared to death. "The war?"

Ferguson nodded. "Remember when ye first came here? Ye thought we were going to—"

"Cut off my balls," Gabriel finished succinctly. Oh, yes. He remembered.

"The guards in that French prison were an evil breed. Sometimes they'd butcher one of us for the fun of it. We'd lie awake at night and listen for the poor man's screams. I've heard those screams in my head every night since then."

Gabriel looked at him, comprehension dawning. "You didn't—er—that is, they didn't . . ."

"No. But they might as well have. I haven't had a woman in years, Sinclair. I can nae . . . do it. It's the screams. I can't forget."

"I'm sorry." Ferguson was right. Some things a man doesn't forget. But the voices in Gabriel's head weren't screams of terror. They were the wistful yearnings of a man who had wasted his life. *I was looking forward to that townhouse. Might have made something of my life. . . .*

Like what? Sitting around in the parlor with Louisa, cooking up schemes to rescue womankind from the tribulations meted out by a society that didn't give a damn? Making long-winded speeches before Parliament that no one heard anyway? Siring a brood of revolutionaries, their little minds molded by their mother into thinking that they, too, could change the world?

It's late to make promises. And he wouldn't make them. A life built around fallacious hopes and noble ideals led only to pain. And God knows, there was enough of that in the world already.

Wouldn't have minded one last chance. But Louisa wasn't that chance. She wasn't for him, and if there was anything he'd learned tonight, it was that. There was no future for them together. Dreams and promises and second chances were for people who cared enough to try with their last breath to achieve them.

And damn it, he couldn't do that. He'd wasted his life, and he'd go on wasting it because the alternative was to hang himself out there, like those poor devils in Ferguson's prison who had given their all for their country and gotten their balls chopped off for their trouble.

A long time ago, the boy he had been had given his all, entrusted his heart and soul to a father who rejected them for the glories of revenge and a crown of bayberry leaves.

No, a man didn't forget.

"Don't hurt her, Sinclair."

Gabriel was incredulous. "Hurt her? If you had seen her standing there, naked as the day she was born, issuing commands—"

"I saw."

"The hell you did." Gabriel shot him a murderous glare.

Ferguson shifted awkwardly. "I could nae sleep. I stepped out of my cottage for some fresh air. 'Tis when I saw Louisa. I saw ye carry her in here. I put my head down and took a long walk. I knew ye wouldn't hurt her. I don't know how, but I knew. I've been walking half the night."

"You wanted her for yourself, didn't you?" Gabriel asked softly. "You thought she'd be the woman to cure you."

"No." Ferguson shook his head. "I don't think of Louisa that way. But I worry about her. I worry that some day she'll let down her guard long enough for some bastard to hurt her like that husband of hers did." He gave Gabriel a long, hard look. "I worry that man is you."

Gabriel's laugh was bitter. "Allow me to allay your worries. She hasn't let down her guard. She wanted to persuade me to help free the other women on that ship."

Ferguson swore softly. "That would be suicide."

"Yes."

Ferguson fell silent, which suited Gabriel fine. He was not about to get into a detailed discussion of what had transpired in that pile of straw tonight.

If only he'd had more control. At first he thought only to touch her, to show her a woman's pleasure. But she had turned the tables on him, made a mockery of his control. He had never taken a woman so selfishly, never lost his cool mastery of the sexual act.

He'd had been right about Louisa—yes, indeed. She had lain there and let him take his pleasure because it was part of her scheme. He had spent himself inside her like a damned rutting pig, but she had withheld herself. He hadn't had the woman, only her body.

Hell. He wanted both.

Gabriel didn't look up when Ferguson slipped away. He stared at the straw that had been the site of his undoing. It wasn't the sex but the wanting that had hit him the hardest, for he'd wanted Louisa as he had never wanted anything in his life.

Except love.

Chapter 17

"**E**asy, boy." Louisa kept her voice low and soothing as she examined a scrape on Midnight's foreleg. He must have acquired it yesterday when he covered Starfire. She'd already checked the mare, who had come through the encounter unscathed.

How ironic that the stallion, rather than the mare, had been injured. It was the very opposite for humans.

Deep inside, in a carefully guarded place she tried to ignore, she ached for Sinclair. The ache had nothing to do with the discomfort she'd felt when Sinclair pushed himself inside her in that hasty, fevered joining. What troubled her was not physical.

I won't help you save those women. I won't be around to see the results of this night. She hated him for those truths. Sinclair might be a scoundrel, but he had told the truth last night. She had seen it in his eyes. Her sacrifice was for naught.

She'd waited until late morning to inspect the horses, knowing Sinclair would be gone.

The gray's stall was empty now. Her former stable mates seemed content. To them, it was as if the gray had never existed.

Louisa envied the horses their nonchalance, for Sinclair had haunted her dreams last night. Still haunted her, though the touching hadn't been anything other than a bartering, an exchange of one commodity for another. She'd feared her offer was conceit, that one desperate and inexperienced woman wouldn't possibly affect him.

But she had. She'd seen it in his eyes. The longing, the sudden loss of control. For those few moments, he had wanted her—only her. The ache inside her grew worse every time she remembered the haunted look in Sinclair's eyes—as if he, too, hated the wanting.

It was good that he had gone. In a few hours, when she was stronger, she would go after him. Her commitment to the women on the hulk remained unshaken. Sinclair would see that he could not turn his back on them or her.

And by the time she saw him again, she would no longer remember how it had felt to have him inside her, filling her with his life force and his aching need.

"Oh, there you are, Louisa." Rose popped her head into the stable. "You'd best hurry. We are leaving now."

"Leaving? Where are you going?"

"To Mr. Sinclair's castle. All of us except Violet. Jasmine does not expect the babe for another week or so, but she does not think Violet should travel."

Louisa stared at her, uncomprehending. "Sinclair's castle?"

Rose drew closer. "Did you not hear us last night? We have promised to help the man restore his ancestral home."

"I heard Sinclair say he had no intention of restoring the place—"

"Utter nonsense. It was all decided at breakfast, which you chose not to attend." Rose gave her a curious look. " 'Tis unlike you to miss a meal."

"Did Sinclair change his mind?" Louisa could not imagine him agreeing to such a plan.

"He was not at breakfast, either. He left early this morning. Like most men, Mr. Sinclair doesn't know what's good for him. We mean to surprise him."

Dear lord. This was a disaster in the making. "He will not welcome your interference," Louisa warned.

"*Our* interference," Rose corrected. "You can't deny you are longing to see him again. Face it, Louisa. You've a tendre for him. It's time we set things aright with that man. He needs us."

"I don't think—"

"That's right, dear. Don't think." Rose clamped her hand on Louisa's arm and steered her out of the stable.

*   *   *

"Don't worry," Violet reassured Jasmine as she shifted baby Elizabeth to her other arm. "If I need you, I will send Sam. It is only a few miles."

Jasmine frowned. "Perhaps I should stay."

"Stop your dithering," Rose admonished. "David is here. He will take care of any difficulty."

"You must not exert yourself with the children," Jasmine warned Violet. "Mrs. Hanford has promised to come this afternoon to help."

Violet stroked Elizabeth's cheek. "The children are no trouble. And they adore David. He does not let me lift a finger to help."

"There. You see?" Rose hustled Jasmine into the gig. "She will be fine."

Their expedition made a strange sight. Rose drove the gig, while Daisy and Lily were in the landau, which was open to afford them fresh air and splendid views of the surrounding countryside. The women waved a jaunty good-bye—all but Louisa, who rode Starfire and looked as if she was journeying to her doom.

Violet was not as sure as Rose that Mr. Sinclair would welcome their intrusion. He had sounded quite firm on the subject last night— but then, Violet's mind had been elsewhere. Perhaps he had relented, and she hadn't been paying attention.

As she watched David hitch Mainstay to the dray, she knew exactly where her mind had been wandering. He was tall, taller even than Mr. Sinclair, and his broad back looked to have the strength of ten men. When he removed a barrel from the dray to make room for the children, Violet had the distinct impression he could have lifted the entire cart.

And yet he did not display his strength for all to see or boast about it. He was quiet and respectful, and more than once Violet had heard him reprimand Sam for bragging about his uncle's brawn and might.

There was a sadness in David—perhaps it stemmed from his time in prison during the war. Like those scars, it might always be a part of him. Still, his brown eyes radiated kindness. David was as fine a man as a woman could hope to know. She liked the way he talked, his soft burr and rough accent stirring something soft and rough inside her. If she had met him years ago instead of Will, her life might have been different.

Now she was bloated and fat and ungainly. No man—even a kind one—would look at her twice. She wished she'd never told David about Will's beatings, for the story had caused him to look at her with pity and sorrow, and she did not want those things from him. Just once, she wished, he would look at her as a man looks at a woman he desires.

But she was daydreaming again. Daydreams were for foolish chits who weren't pregnant and penniless.

"Sam and I will take Mary and the twins with us while we bring in the corn," David said, looking down at her from his great height. "They'll enjoy the outing, and ye'll be able to get your rest."

Minutes later he had the children sitting on the cart, squealing delightedly as they drove off toward one of the lower fields. They would be gone all morning and maybe the afternoon, if he decided to bed them down on the dray for their afternoon naps.

As the wagon pulled away, Violet sighed. "Well, Elizabeth," she said, looking down at the babe in her arms, " 'tis just you and me. What shall we do with ourselves?"

Baby Elizabeth yawned. Her eyes closed contentedly. She would probably sleep for several hours.

An ineffable sadness filled Violet. Her gaze followed the wagon as it traveled along the lane in a cloud of dust that got smaller and smaller.

Between her and happiness lay a wide, wide gulf. She was a woman with broken dreams and foolish desires, big as a cow, and about as desirable. No man would want her. Certainly not the man driving that speck of a wagon.

He probably had the children singing by now. He liked to entertain them with nonsensical songs that left them in giggles. It amazed Violet that such a quiet man had such silly songs in him. It was only to the children that he offered this side of himself. Perhaps their laughter swept aside the ocean of pain. With them he could return to a time when life was as simple and rewarding as a child's smile.

In a way, she and David were two of a kind.

Both of them understood that life could be mean, hurtful, unjust. Both received solace from the pure delight of a child's love. But though Violet cared deeply for the children, she craved something else. Loving a child was easy. Loving an adult took courage—especially if the person you had loved had betrayed you.

Though strong in so many ways, David didn't have that kind of courage, Violet decided. She didn't either, at least not now. She had no business daydreaming, when her thoughts should be on the babe growing under her heart.

Elizabeth made a soft, gurgling noise. As Violet stroked the baby's cheek, she prayed that somehow she could protect her child against the travails of life that chipped away at the soul. She prayed for David, prayed that wherever life led him, he would recover his courage.

"Well, well. Mother and babe and another on the way. The picture of maternal bliss. Hello, Bess."

Violet jumped, which made baby Elizabeth grumble in sleepy protest. An unkempt rider sat atop an old, broken-down horse. "Will!"

Her husband glanced around him in appreciation. "You've come up in the world, Bess girl. Shouldn't wonder you'll be reluctant to come away with the likes of me."

"Come away with you?" Violet stared at him in horror.

He grinned, displaying a gap where his two

front teeth had once lodged. "What's the matter, sweets?" He dismounted. "My looks not the same as they used to be? Got your man to thank for that. And that spitfire of a woman that was with him."

"I have no man." Violet edged toward the house.

"No sense in running. You can't get far in your condition. Are you alone, then? Did they leave you in this big old house with no more company than a babe? Now that's a shame. Guess it's good that I'm here."

Violet opened her mouth and screamed.

Baby Elizabeth jerked awake, then began to wail. As the baby's cries joined with Violet's, Will put his hands to his ears in mock terror.

And then he laughed. A great booming laugh that sent shivers down Violet's spine.

His new boat was in fine fettle. Gabriel had dismissed the crew; he desired neither audience nor assistance for his trip. Tomorrow at daybreak he would sail to Sinclair Isle, if the weather held. He studied the horizon. Dark clouds that earlier had been just a speck to the west now lay almost directly overhead. A storm was brewing, but with any luck it would blow itself out by morning.

He had planned to sleep on the boat tonight, but a berth in a storm would be anything but restful. The mooring was as secure as he could make it. There was nothing to do but return to his dilapidated estate and hope the house would have him for the night.

Gabriel had inspected the place briefly this morning. The roof undoubtedly leaked, and most of the windowpanes were broken. Dust lay thick and relentless over the furniture covers, and the pantry had been cleaned out by rats long ago. His mother's large garden had been taken over by the tenacious wisteria she had always regretted planting. A small tree grew through the opening in the privy.

As he rode toward his boyhood home, Gabriel fought back a bittersweet smile. He'd pay his respects at his father's grave, then sail back to London, sell his boat, and be on his way. Daisy's poetic insight notwithstanding, he didn't need a place to set down roots. He certainly didn't need a house full of memories. His own memories were quite enough.

Strangely, though, he was no longer able to visualize his mother. Her portrait had once hung in his father's chamber, and Aloysius had not taken it with them to the island. Gabriel had seen no likeness of his mother since the day he had been packed off to Eton after her death. If the painting still hung in his father's room, he would take it with him or at least have a miniature copy made.

A man didn't need roots or a house. He didn't need a castle, and certainly not a temple to an ancient god. A portrait would suffice, though it was probably faded and dark by now. Gabriel did not want to remember his mother as faded and dark. He wanted to see her as she had been, vivid and engaging and full of laughter. Jollying his father along when his inventions failed, rejoicing when they succeeded.

But alas, life held no permanence. Even madness was silenced by the grave, unless it was visited on succeeding generations, and then a man had to watch for it every step of the way. Sometimes, he had recently discovered, madness masqueraded in the form of soulful musings about a particular woman or as uncontrollable urgings, sexual and otherwise. The overwhelming desire to possess Louisa Peabody against all better judgment was such a madness. And this strange yearning that the Flowers had planted in the barren soil of his soul was another.

He would not rebuild his father's kingdom. In the end it would all vanish, like childish hopes and dreams and the image of his mother. Like Shelley's Ozymandias, who, despite his power, was in death brought low by one great truth: kings and castles, gods and temples, portraits and inventions, love and hate—all destroyed by time.

Even angels and archangels were a notoriously unreliable lot. They popped in and out of the Scriptures with a distressing lack of dependability. Not for the first time, Gabriel wondered why his mother had given him such a name. Had she counted on his working miracles?

The only miracle he had in mind at the moment was reaching the old house without getting soaked. The wind had whipped itself into a fine fury by the time he settled the gray in the old stable. With a faint hope that the structure would hold against the storm, Gabriel wrapped his coat around him and trudged toward the house.

And there, on what had once been his mother's neatly trimmed lawn, were a gig, a landau, and four hobbled horses nibbling the wisteria leaves.

The Flowers seemed to be an exception to the natural law of impermanence. They were everywhere, blossoming like bindweed, tenacious as his mother's wisteria. Girding himself for what was to come, Gabriel stepped through the front door of his boyhood home.

An army had invaded. It had swept the floors, washed the walls, and removed the holland covers. It was apparently reconnoitering in the dining room, for a cacophony of fractious voices floated to him through the dining room door.

"Pink. It must be pink. With gold leaf trim."

"On the moldings? You are quite mad, dear. Nothing but good stout oak will do. 'Tis a man's house, remember."

"Just because he is a man, he needn't have the esthetic sense of a moose. No, it must be gold leaf. If Mr. Adam used it, you can be sure it is acceptable."

"Did you notice the marble fireplace? Italian, I'll wager. *Pink* Italian."

"All the more reason for gold leaf."

"No man wants pink and gold in his study."

"Since when did you become an expert on such matters?"

"I have had three husbands, and if that doesn't qualify me to judge what a man wants, I don't know what does."

"But you *killed* them, Rose, dear."

"They were pigs."

"My point exactly. We can't trust *their* tastes, now can we?"

Gabriel pushed open the door. The Flowers were seated around the enormous dining room table, poring over sketches. They took no notice of him.

Sitting alone in a chair, one foot drawn up under her riding skirt, the other swinging aimlessly, was a glum-looking Louisa. Gabriel was riveted. He'd thought he preferred her in breeches, but the riding skirt afforded him a glimpse of bare leg above her boots.

Their gazes met and held.

"Now that we see what must be done," Rose said, "we can return tomorrow to hire men from that village up the road."

Jasmine shook her head. "Violet is near her time. I'll not leave her again."

"She'll need help with the children," Lily agreed. "We can't leave her to manage all alone."

Rose signaled for quiet. "We will return home tonight. Sam can fetch Mrs. Hanford in the morning. Those who can, will come back tomorrow. I don't trust those men to do a proper job without us."

"I am afraid you won't be going anywhere

tonight, ladies," Gabriel drawled, feeling the heavy hand of fate. "Apollo has made a hasty journey across the sky, and Zeus has seen fit to send us a storm. Chaos, it seems, has come to rule."

Startled, the Flowers stared at him. And then as one, they broke into smiles.

"Mr. Sinclair!" Rose exclaimed. "You do know how to give a body pause. Come, sit and look at our plans. What's this nonsense about a storm?"

A great boom resounded from the heavens, providing answer enough.

"Oh, dear," Jasmine said. "Violet will be worried."

"David will look after her and the children," Louisa assured her.

"There. It is all settled." Rose grinned. "As you can see, Mr. Sinclair, we have taken the liberty of conducting a thorough cleaning and inspection. Your house is in dreadful shape, I don't mind saying. You ought to raze the thing. But for now, a few improvements will make it habitable. Would you care to hear my ideas?"

Gabriel opened his mouth to reply.

"You do not need to thank us," Rose rushed on, before he could speak. "We think of you as one of us. You may consider us your family from now on."

A family. Sweet Jesus. Inadvertently, his gaze traveled to Louisa, just as a great clap of thunder boomed overhead. A bolt of lightning crackled unnervingly close to the house.

Gabriel wondered whether the gods had at last decided to speak to him. And if so, why the devil they had to be so noisy about it.

Chapter 18

Violet could smell the gathering storm. It mingled with the scent of fear. *Her* fear. The air was heavy and thick, acrid with foreboding.

Baby Elizabeth had cried herself to sleep. The tears had dried on her cheeks, leaving little trails of sorrow on her smooth, delicate skin. She slept on the daybed in Louisa's parlor, because Will had refused to let Violet take the child upstairs to the nursery.

"Did you think I would let you out of my sight again?" Will gave a rough laugh. "Not bloody likely, wife."

Wife. On Will's lips, the word was a curse. She had changed her name, her home, her friends, but nothing could change the fact that she was his wife. She had no right to dream about another man. She would always belong to this one.

"What about Helen?" Violet asked quietly.

He shrugged. "She is old. I tired of her."

Violet's gaze narrowed. "She is but two years older than me. I'd wager she found someone better. How easy that must have been. Newton is filled with men better than you."

Will reddened. The anger that was never far from the surface exploded. He jerked her to him, nearly wrenching her arm out of its socket. "Watch that tongue of yours, Bess," he snarled, "or I'll cut it out."

"My name," Violet said through gritted teeth, "is Violet."

Will guffawed. "Violet! Now *that's* rich. Got yerself a fancy name, a fancy house, and a fancy man to go with them." He bent closer, and his foul breath nearly suffocated her. "Where is he? Where is the man who rode into town and stole you away from me?"

"No one stole me away." Violet tried to slow her breathing, to keep panic at bay. "You forfeited your claim to me the minute you took up with Helen."

His big, filthy hand closed over her breast. "I didn't forfeit anything," he growled. "You belong to me and you always will. We had something once, didn't we, Bess?"

"No." Violet closed her eyes, denying the truth of his words, hating his touch. Perhaps she had loved him once, but that was long ago. She'd been weaker then. More helpless. Three months of living with Louisa and the others had shown her a woman's strength. And though fear rose within her, threatening to shut out reason, Violet would not cower before this man. For the sake of baby Elizabeth and her unborn child, she would keep her wits about her.

Violet shrugged off his hand. "How did you find me?" she asked, buying time, knowing he loved to boast about his cleverness.

Will laughed. "The stallion. Everyone who's ever seen him remembers that one. A tooth drawer at the Chatham fair had heard of a woman with yellow hair who kept a big black stud. 'Twas easy to find you."

"Helen threw you out, didn't she?" Violet taunted softly. If she made him angry, all the better. Will never thought clearly in the throes of rage. "What happened, Will? Did you seduce one of her friends?"

He struck her full across her face. Violet reeled with the force of the blow, and tasted blood.

"Don't say I didn't warn you about that mouth of yours, Bess." Suddenly, a knife glinted in his hand. "Helen was a stupid woman. Told the constable I was the one poisoned her oaf of a husband, not you. I had to kill her, you know. I'll kill you, too, Bess, if you don't come along nice like."

"Temper always was your worst feature," she said calmly, letting her gaze wander about the room, searching for anything to use as a weapon. But the fireplace tools were too far away, and she didn't think she could lift the heavy vase on the side table.

Will took the decision out of her hands.

"Enough of this," he growled. "You're my

wife, and you're coming with me." He jerked her toward the door.

"I can't leave baby Elizabeth," Violet protested.

Will shook his head. "I don't need another mouth to feed."

"Then you don't want me," Violet replied quietly. "My babe is due soon. There'll be two of us then."

"I'll not have another man's get slowing me down."

Violet was incredulous. "The babe is yours. Don't you remember how you raped me? Night and day. To put me in my place, you said."

"Rape? Not bloody likely." He scoffed. "A husband has rights. As for that babe in you, it can be disposed of easy enough."

"How could I ever have loved you?" Violet stared at him. "You are a monster!"

Will laughed. "Because I knew how to kiss you without rushing my fences. Stirred you up, didn't I, Bess? You were ready for it."

Yes, she had been ready. For love, for a husband, for children. So ready that she had not opened her eyes to the truth about Will's character. He had been handsome, clever, brash. And yes, he had known how to kiss her, how to stir up a heat she had never dreamed existed. She'd gone to him breathless and full of longing, mistaking that for love. But he had taken her roughly, never fanning the flames of the fire he had stirred within her. Then came the beatings, the humiliation, the other women. Too late, she realized that he hadn't cared for her at all.

She hadn't loved Will. She'd loved the man she wanted him to be. The man of her dreams.

Foolish woman. She'd been dreaming those same dreams about David, imagining herself in love with him, as she had once imagined herself in love with Will.

"Come, gel," Will barked. "The law's after me. This broken-down nag won't last as far as the next town. But I'm thinking that big stud will do just fine."

Of course. He'd come for the horse, not her. But he would take her, too, as payment for the humiliation he'd suffered the day David and Louisa rescued her. Helen was gone; he needed a woman. Will always needed a woman.

Violet cast one last, worried look at the sleeping Elizabeth before he pulled her out of the house. She scanned the horizon, searching for any sign of David and the children, though they weren't due back for hours.

Unless that bit of dust on the far side of the hill was the dray, which meant David had sensed the coming storm and decided to bring the children back early. He wouldn't expect to find a dangerous madman with a knife. He and the children would be as vulnerable as babes.

"Midnight's in the last stall." Violet's mind raced as they neared the stable. Somehow she had to protect them. "He's not easy to handle. Even Louisa sometimes has trouble with him."

"The day I can't handle a woman's mount is the day I have one foot in the grave."

Midnight neighed a greeting as they entered. "See, Bess?" Will gloated. "A horse knows the measure of a man."

"My name," she said evenly, "is Violet."

Ignoring her, Will studied the stallion. "That's a rare blood there. He's up to both of us, even with your extra weight."

Violet sank into the straw and prayed that Will's skills were up to his boasting. He'd always claimed to have a touch with animals, but she had never seen him handle any horse as spirited as Midnight. The thought of riding the stallion with him scared her to death. What if they were thrown and she lost the babe?

Will opened the stall door. The horse snorted loudly but allowed himself to be led out. But when Will offered the bit, Midnight tossed his head defiantly.

Violet thought of that speck of dust on the lane growing larger and nearer. She thought of the children coming to find her as Sam and David unhitched the dray. She imagined them all, relaxed and unwary, running into the stable, and Will's knife.

"Please hurry," she pleaded.

"A moment ago you were too good for the likes of me," Will snarled as Midnight shuffled backward. He yanked the horse's mane, trying to force the stallion to the bit. Nostrils flaring, Midnight tossed his head angrily. Then he bared his teeth and sank them into Will's hand.

"Damned cur!" he roared, trying to pull his hand free. But the horse wasn't about to let go. Will fumbled for his knife, but the weapon clattered harmlessly to the floor.

Blood oozed from Will's hand as his other one strained to reach a whip on the wall near the stall. At last his fingers closed around it, and he brought the whip down hard on Midnight's face.

With an enraged cry, the stallion reared. His powerful hooves slashed within inches of Will. Then Midnight thundered from the stable just as a bolt of lightning lit up the sky like a torch.

His face pale, Will examined the mangled flesh of his hand. Violet knew he would blame her for this, just as he'd blamed her for every disagreeable thing that occurred during their marriage. He never saw that it was his quick temper that got him into trouble.

Sure enough, his gaze was murderous as it met hers. Violet stared at the man who had given her this babe she carried and who now regarded her with such vicious rage. His only virtue was this one unintended treasure, which she loved as much as she hated the man who had begotten it.

Will groped on the floor for his knife, found it, and came at her with a roar.

Violet rolled away, trying to protect her belly against the punishment to come. She wished she had Midnight's strength and courage. And that the flashing heavens would strike her husband dead before he killed her only treasure.

*   *   *

Thunder roared around them like cannon fire. The wind whipped up so fiercely that Louisa couldn't make herself heard over its insistent whine. An angry swirl of low, black clouds obliterated the horizon. Lightning knifed from the skies, infusing the air with its acrid heat.

The heavens hadn't loosed a deluge yet, but the air was heavy with promise. Eyes wide and tails swishing, the horses snorted uneasily as she and Sinclair struggled to get them into the dilapidated stable before the storm unleashed its fury. Louisa was thankful she had left Midnight at home to nurse his injury. Storms unsettled him.

An uneasy kinship surged between her and Sinclair, as if the race against the storm bound them together in some elemental way. They had not spoken of last night, of the intimacy they had shared, more unsettling than any storm. But the brooding intensity glittering in Sinclair's eyes told her he had not forgotten. The silence between them stood in stark contrast to the rumbling of the elements, but it was just as portentous.

Louisa did not want to look at him. She did not want to see how effortlessly he lifted the saddle from Starfire's back and how the wind ruffled that thick red hair into a tousled halo that was anything but angelic, especially when he glanced at her from eyes as turbulent as any storm.

She did not want to think of the sensual

sparks that lurked within that brooding gaze or of the wildness in him that made a mockery of her carefully ordered world. Sinclair threatened everything she had become since Midnight sent Richard to his just reward three years ago.

But Sinclair was not Richard. And she wasn't the person she had been three years ago. When had she changed? How had her loathing of Sinclair transformed into this heavy awareness that suffused the air like the gathering storm?

Louisa forced herself to concentrate on the horses, which were none too pleased at finding themselves in a rotted stable with a storm raging outside. When at last she settled Starfire in a stall, Louisa sighed in relief. She turned and found Sinclair, his foot propped on Starfire's saddle, studying her.

"Shall we wait out the storm here or make a run for it?" he asked. The electricity that jolted Louisa as their gazes met had nothing to do with the lightning outside.

Only a fool would stay another minute in a stable with Sinclair.

"Run," she said grimly.

Without waiting for his reply, she stepped outside just as a few large raindrops hit the dirt. The keening wind had whipped itself into a rare frenzy. The deluge was only seconds away, but Louisa didn't care. The danger behind was far worse than the danger ahead.

Mocking her cowardice, the wind whipped her hair into her face and caught at her riding skirt until it was an impossible tangle. She stumbled, tried to regain her footing, and failed.

Just as she went sprawling, the heavens opened.

Louisa burst into tears. Sinclair had done this to her. She'd been content before he came into her life, bringing chaos and longing and doubtless the rain, too.

Her tears mingled with the stinging drops on her face. If only the storm would cleanse her of this strange fascination for him.

Sinclair extended a hand to help her up. Louisa batted it away.

"Go away, wretched man!" She sat in the dirt, which was fast turning to mud, and crossed her arms over her chest. She'd rather catch her death than let him help her.

With a muttered oath, Sinclair yanked her to her feet. Then he lifted her into his arms and carried her through the downpour toward the house.

"Put me down!" she demanded. Rivulets of rain ran down her face and neck, mingling with the salt of her tears. She felt sodden, ugly, and miserable.

"You don't want rescuing, do you?" he shouted over the tempest. "Well, I've no taste for playing rescuer. I'd sooner leave you in the mud."

"Why don't you, then?" she dared him. Horrid man, he looked magnificent in the rain. Gold-flecked lashes caught the rain, giving his eyes a shimmer of lush, primeval magic. He wore the water on his skin with perfect aplomb. He might have been Adam, carrying Eve through a waterfall. Or the snake.

Sinclair did not take the bait. He did not dump her in the mud. For this unexpected kindness, Louisa wanted to consign him to the devil. Instead, she huddled against his chest, feeling foolish. Neither of them would have gotten soaked if she'd had the courage to wait out the storm in the stable. Sinclair was furious with her—but no, that wasn't it exactly. His mouth was grim, but his brooding gaze still held an unsettling sensuality.

A strange exhilaration filled her—the taste of battle joined and rejoined. When they gained the house and he set her on her feet, Louisa felt suddenly bereft.

Rose greeted them at the door. "Tsk-tsk. You look terrible."

"Best get out of those wet things," Jasmine warned.

"Trapped by the elements," Daisy murmured happily. "Forced into each other's arms by the wild thundering of true hearts."

Sinclair made an unintelligible sound.

Louisa closed her eyes in mortification. "Daisy—"

"I am afraid of storms," Lily said suddenly. "They give me nightmares. I wake up screaming and can't sleep a wink afterward."

" 'Tis the tumult of the spirits that brings them," Jasmine explained. "Pity we have no incense to keep them away."

"Incense?" Sinclair slipped off his wet

jacket. Louisa couldn't help but stare at the way his shirt clung to the corded muscles of his shoulders and arms.

"To appease the—" A bolt of jagged lightning lit up the skies as thunder drowned out Jasmine's words.

"Spirits," Rose finished for her. "Not that I believe in such nonsense, but I've seen storms do strange things to people. My second husband—quite a tippler, he was—drank himself silly one night and climbed on a broken tree limb, thinking it was his horse. Lightning came right down that limb and struck him. He was scared to death of horses ever after."

Lily frowned. "Why not of the lightning?"

"Fools see what they want to see, dear," Rose replied. "And Oscar was more foolish than most. I should know—lived with the man for ten years." She paused. "Or was that James?"

Sinclair met Louisa's gaze. And despite the simmering anger and unsettling currents between them, despite the fact they were both wet to the bone, he grinned.

That slightly crooked smile encompassed absurdities big and small, from Rose's hard-luck husbands and Lily's fears to Daisy's dreams and her own heart's foolish thundering. It was reckless and daring, that smile. It said this night was rare and precious and worth the storm to come.

It scared her out of her wits.

"I suppose we ought to see whether any of

the chambers are habitable," Lily said. "This storm won't end soon."

"We'll search the house," Rose decided. She found some candles in the pantry, and the group fanned out in search of dry clothes and bed linens.

As it turned out, most of the bedding was rotted and the few garments they found unusable, but Sinclair discovered some old blankets that had survived. He offered one to Louisa, then wrapped another around himself.

After the Flowers' inspection, three beds were deemed serviceable. The rest had long since succumbed to the ravages of rats and mold.

"The four of us will share two beds," Rose announced, when everyone gathered in the dining room to report their findings.

"That leaves the third for Louisa," Lily said, "and—"

"Mr. Sinclair." Daisy finished, giggling. The women burst into laughter.

Louisa was about to say that they were quite mad to think she would spend a moment alone with Sinclair, much less share a bed with him, when he took a candle and put a hand under her elbow.

"Come." He steered her to the stairs. "A conspiracy is afoot. It wouldn't surprise me if the Flowers overlooked a serviceable bed or two. We'll see for ourselves."

"I wouldn't dream of sleeping alone," Daisy called after them. "There isn't a window in the house that isn't broken. Think of all the bats and owls that must fly in at night. I shouldn't like to face them."

"Stop it!" Louisa said crossly.

Sinclair placed a finger against her mouth to quiet her. "They only want your happiness."

"My happiness doesn't include sharing a bed with you."

"You prefer straw, then?" he asked politely. When she didn't answer, he merely turned and started up the stairs.

Louisa glared at him. With as much dignity as she could muster with her skirts dripping puddles around her, Louisa followed him.

At the top of the stairs, Sinclair started down a dark hall, leaving her no choice but to follow the flickering light of his candle. Louisa could make out few details of her surroundings, other than the paneled walls and sconces that at one time must have looked cheerful and welcoming.

A musty smell permeated the air, and the sense of decay was overwhelming. As Sinclair took them farther down the dank hall, Louisa felt increasingly uneasy. He hadn't stopped at any of the rooms, which was curious, since they were supposed to be checking the beds.

At last, he paused before a door. Almost reluctantly, he pushed it open. Louisa followed him into a large chamber with a bed almost hidden by the heavy, worn hangings. A portrait hung above the mantel.

Sinclair held the candle up high, illuminating the portrait, until all of it was visible. Though faded, it was still possible to see the woman's easy smile and the compassion in her sparkling green eyes. She looked full of life and impossibly young. Sinclair drew closer. Gingerly, he reached out and touched the woman's face. Louisa read sorrow in the slant of his shoulders.

"I had almost forgotten," he whispered.

A clap of thunder sounded directly overhead, and he turned toward her. He held the candle up, subjecting her to the same intent inspection he had given the painting.

"Louisa." Low and intense, his voice wrapped around her name like a sigh. He set the candle on a table. "So fierce and proud. Did I hurt you?"

She lifted her chin. She wouldn't pretend to misunderstand. She knew he referred to last night.

"Only a little." Her voice sounded dry and harsh. " 'Twas nothing of import."

"Nothing of import," he repeated slowly. His probing eyes seemed strangely vulnerable. "I didn't mean to hurt you. I wanted to please you, but you took the decision out of my hands and into yours. So to speak." His half-smile held no mirth. "Are you so afraid of me?"

"I fear no man." But the words had a hollow ring.

Sinclair held the ends of his blanket and extended his arms so that he enveloped her in its folds. "You are trembling."

"No." She tried to remain aloof, but his

warmth beckoned her. She nestled closer, seeking his heat.

"I won't lie to you, Louisa. I have known other women. No one has ever made me lose control like that." Dark, tortured fires burned deep within his eyes.

She lifted her chin a notch. "Am I due a medal, then?"

He put his finger under her chin, tilting her face to his. "I *have* hurt you."

"Not at all," she flung at him. "You think you know everything, but you know nothing of me. I don't want to be cajoled. And your stupid jokes are worth nothing. *Nothing!* Do you hear?"

"I couldn't agree with you more."

Louisa's heart lurched. Something wild and dangerous spiraled through her. "Don't," she said. "Don't pretend that you are special. Or that I am. Don't pretend you want nothing more than to forsake all others and spend the rest of your life with me. I won't believe it." She ripped her gaze from his.

"No, I won't pretend." He toyed with a lock of her hair, wet and matted, hanging limply over her shoulders. "I want to make love to you, Louisa." He pulled the ends of the blanket, enfolding her more tightly in his warmth. "I want to do it right. I want to please you."

Louisa pulled away. "Why do men think their animal urge is a gift they are privileged to give and women honored to receive? The only way you can please me, Sinclair, is to rescue those women."

He absorbed her words in silence. "No," he said at last, "that is not the only way."

But it was. If he couldn't do that for her, then she never wanted to see him again. Because nothing else mattered. Not him or his wit or his mesmerizing touch. Certainly not his touch.

His fingers brushed her elbow. With no more pressure than that, he brought her back into his arms. It was as if he were a puppeteer and she a marionette, doing his bidding at the slightest touch of the cross sticks.

But she was not a puppet. She would not compromise her principles for him, even if he applied his considerable skills to the task of winning her over.

"Go to hell, Sinclair."

His smile was slow, dangerous. And despite her anger, despite her hands balled in fists at her sides, despite the fact that she wanted to loathe him more even than Richard—despite all this, Sinclair bent down and took her mouth in a kiss that was as sweet and winsome as an angel's song.

David found her in the stable, curled up in a ball. Her hands gripped her belly protectively. A great gulp of air constricted the center of his chest as he felt for her pulse. Strong and steady. He nearly died of relief.

He brushed the hair back from her face. A bruise the size of a man's fist swallowed one eye. Her hands bore cuts from the struggle. But the bleeding had stopped, and he saw that the wounds were not life-threatening.

As he lifted Violet into his arms and held her still form against his heart, the rain came. Thunder boomed like the guns he had once dodged on the Peninsula. But the nightmare of battle was nothing like the terror he felt carrying Violet and her unborn child into the house.

Laying her on the bed in her room, he carefully pulled off her half-boots. She bore no other obvious injuries, but perhaps there was some grave internal wound. Her arms were cold and mottled and strewn with goose bumps, her wet clothes matted against her skin. She risked a fever if they did not come off. Still, he hesitated. Removing the clothes of a pregnant woman seemed a sacrilege somehow.

"David?" Sam stood at the doorway.

David nearly jumped. How long had he been standing here, staring at her? "How are the children?" His voice did not sound like his own.

"The twins and Mary went right to sleep. I gave baby Elizabeth a bit of watered porridge. She's sleeping, too."

David stared at the motherless boy who suddenly looked so tall and manly. He had grown up almost overnight, it seemed. So many responsibilities rested on his young shoulders.

"Is Midnight settled in?"

"Went right into his stall, docile as you please," Sam responded. "I guess he didn't have any more fight in him after stomping Violet's husband." He hesitated. "Should I go for the doctor?"

David shook his head. "I'll nae send you out in the storm, lad. Midnight's too dangerous to ride now, and the dray horse won't lift a foot in this weather." The man in the stable would either live or he wouldn't. In his condition, a doctor wouldn't make much difference.

He had known the moment he'd seen Midnight, foaming and breathing hard out in the yard, that something beyond the gathering storm had caused the stallion to flee the stable. Inside, David had instantly recognized Violet's husband, or what was left of him. The man lay senseless in the straw, his features frozen in rage, the same expression he had worn that day in the village when they freed Violet. The knife clutched in his hand, along with the imprint of Midnight's hooves on his back, told the terrible story.

Violet lay a few yards away, her eyes closed in a deep, unnatural sleep. How and why Midnight had saved Violet's life David couldn't begin to guess. He had spared only a thought for the horse and none at all for Violet's husband as he carried her into the house. Sam had taken care of everything else.

"Is Miss Violet all right?" The boy's question brought David back to the present.

"I think so. That bruise looks bad, but her color's good. The cuts need cleaning." David didn't voice his fears about internal injuries. A doctor was beyond their reach tonight. Tomorrow, when the storm cleared, he'd send Sam for Miss Jasmine, whose judgment he trusted a damned sight more than any quack's. For now, the storm held them hostage.

Violet's fate was in his hands. And while he had tended men felled in battle, this was very, very different. This was Violet lying on that bed with her unborn babe, and he could not bear to think of failing her.

He met Sam's searching gaze. "Go to sleep, boy," he said. "I will call if I need you."

Sam nodded. And then David was alone, with nothing to stand between him and fear.

Gabriel meant to please her this time. There was something different about her tonight, something soft and yielding—despite her curse and her fists and her rage—that bespoke a crack in her iron resolve.

He saw it in her eyes, felt it in the way she parted her lips for his kiss. There was a yearning in her. Perhaps it even matched the yearning in him.

With a low growl, he pulled her close and kissed her again. A little gasp escaped her lips. She wanted him. Maybe not in the light of day or in a stable in the straw, but here, with the storm raging around them, a thunderous accompaniment to lust. His hands roved over her in a burning need to kindle her desire.

Suddenly, she jerked away. "I hate your kiss."

Gabriel stilled.

"It is practiced and perfect and just what I would expect of a man like you." Anger and frustration glinted in her eyes. "You don't give anything, do you Sinclair? You just take."

He let his hands fall away from her.

"I hate you for what you are trying to do to me," she said.

"And that would be what, exactly?" Gabriel fought the urge to strangle her. Why did she always paint everything in black and white? Why didn't she see the delicious grays, the space where a man could escape his destiny, if only for a time. Why must she fight him at every turn?

Back and forth she paced across the musty chamber that had been his father's. She paused to face him, to let him feel the full force of her fury.

"You want to make me want you. I don't. You want to prove you can seduce me. You can't. Face it, Sinclair: you've made love to scores of women, but you don't know how to make love to me. Because I won't let you. I'll have you on my terms or not at all."

She crossed her arms, a picture of righteous indignation. A veritable Joan of Arc, facing down her persecutors. *Scores of women.* Jesus. Did she think him an utter profligate?

"You are right, of course," he said calmly.

Puzzlement swept her features. She eyed him with suspicion.

"I don't know how to make love to a coward," he growled. "And that is what you are,

Louisa. Too scared of yourself to risk losing
control."

"That is an outrageous lie!" she sputtered.

Gabriel scowled. "Let me put it this way: I
am standing in my father's bedchamber, ready
to commit the unpardonable sin of making
love to a woman in front of a portrait of my
dear deceased mother, and you are scared of
your damned shadow. Jesus Christ—I must be
insane to want you."

They stared at each other. The silence
stretched between them like an enormous
question mark. At that moment, Gabriel
wouldn't have touched her on a bet.

But he looked. God, how he looked. He
looked his fill at those wide blue eyes and pale
cheeks and even that tiny birthmark above her
trembling lips. His eyes devoured her hair,
and he imagined losing himself in its golden
glory. His gaze slid lower to the slender, boyish form outlined by the wet riding outfit that
begged to be dispensed with.

He wanted Louisa more than he had ever
wanted any woman. And he thought that perhaps she was right, that he didn't know how
to do it properly—not with her, not with a
woman who guarded herself so closely and
had let that despicable husband ruin something priceless.

But he sure as hell was going to learn.

"Louisa."

She looked at him, not saying a word.

"Come here." Gabriel knew he should be
cajoling, beguiling, reassuring. "Come," he

barked again, his control teetering on the edge of some dark, bottomless abyss.

She didn't laugh or curse or spit accusations. Her eyes filled with a yearning that shot right to his gut.

And then she walked into his arms.

Chapter 19

Coward. Louisa hated that word. She'd match her courage against any man's. No one had ever accused her of letting fear rule her.

Except her father. That ugly scene in his study came rushing back. *What's the matter, Louisa? Are you a coward? 'Tis your duty. You can't shirk it."*

She had not shirked her duty. She had married Richard, and from that one night of degradation she'd won her independence and the freedom never to be touched again. She'd been lucky. Most women never had such freedom. But as much as she told herself that last night had been just a bartering, that Sinclair hadn't really touched her, not in any way that mattered, she didn't quite believe it.

"Come here."

Fear made her mouth dry. Her hands trembled. She could not get enough air. Perhaps she was a coward after all, because it had been easier to stand at the altar with Richard than to take the few steps into Sinclair's arms.

I'll have you on my own terms or not at all. She went to him anyway, making a mockery of her defiance. And when his arms closed around her, Louisa knew what Sinclair had doubtless known all along: she could not resist him. Not now, not ever.

"I hate you." She buried her face in his chest.

"I know." He stroked her hair. "It's all right."

But it wasn't. They were wrong for each other. All that had gone before told her he cared for nothing and no one.

People don't change, Louisa. You won't, and I can't. No miracle would happen if I made love to you. I'd still be on my way in the morning, and you'd still be plotting to save womankind. Only you'd have another man to hate.

What she felt for Sinclair wasn't hate, though. It was violent and savage and frightening.

He bent his face to hers. Louisa braced herself for his practiced kiss, but instead his lips ground brutally into hers, as if he meant to claim her for all time.

But nothing was for all time. One day she would have nothing left of Sinclair or Richard but memories that had lost their sting. One day, this sudden, shuddering passion within her would be no more. Even the brightest stars burned themselves out, and the storm that raged tonight would be gone by morning.

But for now, the ache within her kindled a flame nothing could extinguish, and she could not stop herself from being consumed in its fire. Tonight would not be a repeat of last night. Tonight she would get burned.

Every place his mouth touched blazed white-hot. Her lips, her ear, the hollow of her neck. Soon would come the dizziness and queasy stomach. If she was lucky, they would save her. Louisa was not sure she wanted to be saved.

Abruptly, Sinclair released her. His mouth thinned into a grim line. "You were a virgin. Before last night." He paused, waiting for her confirmation.

"Yes." She wondered why it mattered, why he made it sound like a crime.

"You should have told me. I could have made it . . . better."

"I didn't want that," she said.

"But you'd learned enough from your husband's piggishness to make sure I didn't spare a thought for your virginal sensibilities." Anger darkened his eyes to stormy seas.

"If you didn't, then I expect that's your fault." Why couldn't he just hold her, without asking questions that were bound to put them at odds?

His gaze narrowed. "Tell me, Louisa, do you always insist on being in control?"

Louisa didn't want to quarrel. She wanted his arms around her. Shyly, she touched his shirt.

He stepped adroitly out of her reach. "No, you don't," he growled. "I'll not have you turn the tables again."

"I don't understand."

"I think you do. Suppose we take this slowly." His brooding gaze held hers. "Tell me what you want."

Louisa looked away. "I don't want anything, exactly."

"Coward," he said again, softly.

When she did not speak, he shook his head in exasperation. "We'll start with the dizziness. Suppose you tell me when you feel ill. Can you do that?"

She nodded.

For almost a minute he made no move to touch her. They stood there at arm's length, their blankets wrapped around them, facing each other like wooden soldiers. He did not seem to notice that she yearned for his touch. Louisa felt utterly humiliated.

"Is this a game?" she demanded in a shaky voice.

A provocative light came into his eyes. "If it helps you to look at it that way, I don't mind. May I touch your breasts?"

Her eyes widened. "I—"

"Too intimate? Very well. What, then?"

"A k-kiss might be acceptable," she stammered.

"Done."

Louisa saw the beginnings of a smile as his lips brushed her mouth. "You are making sport of me," she cried. "This is all a great joke to you, isn't it, Sinclair? You think it such a lark that I want you—"

"Do you?" His smile vanished. "Want me, that is?"

Louisa clamped her mouth shut.

"Ah." He arched a brow. "It's as I said. You are scared."

She crossed her arms over her chest. "I'm no coward."

"Nonsense. We're all cowards at something. Take me, for example. Right now, I am scared to death."

Louisa eyed him dubiously. Sinclair looked anything but frightened. His hair had dried into an undisciplined mane that looked vaguely leonine. Even his soggy clothes did not diminish the cool, masculine authority with which he studied her from hooded eyes. He towered over her, a portrait of manly power and grace.

"It's true." He leveled a gaze at her. "I'm scared you'll turn and run out that door before I have a chance to make love to you. I'm scared you won't like it when I touch you. I'm scared that I'll like it too much, that I'll never get you out of my mind and my heart. Does that scare you too, Louisa? It ought to. It sure as hell scares me."

Louisa could not think of a thing to say. "I like it when you kiss me," she blurted out.

"And that's all you'll admit to, isn't it?" he said grimly. "I suppose it's a start. Now, where were we?" Amusement gleamed briefly in his eyes, then was gone.

"A kiss," she volunteered hesitantly. "Just . . . a kiss."

His lips brushed her mouth, touching but only just. Louisa gave a little cry of dismay.

"Not much of a kiss, was it?"

"It was—" Louisa broke off in consternation as his mouth again descended to hers.

"I can do better," he murmured.

Odious man, she thought, even as her lips parted in anticipation. His tongue flirted with hers, but he did not press his advantage. Instead, he withdrew again.

"Sinclair," she moaned in frustration, putting her arms around his neck and pulling him back to her.

He kissed her again, this time with bald, undisguised need. She lost herself in the sudden, fierce mating of their tongues. It was as if her entire world was wrapped up in that kiss, and when he once more set her at arm's length, she whimpered in protest. Sinclair regarded her warily.

"Do you feel sick yet?" His voice was ragged.

Louisa shook her head. "Just ... overwhelmed."

He seemed to like that answer. His mouth curved upward in an expression that was neither mirth nor disdain. "And if I touch you here," he asked softly, "how does it feel?"

The back of his knuckles grazed her breasts.

"I thought you were going to ask permission first," she whispered hoarsely.

"You were wrong." His smoldering gaze bored into her. And though her breasts were not wondrously large like Jasmine's or full and pendulous like Violet's, he caressed them through the damp fabric as if they were rare treasures.

"And this, Louisa. Does this make you ill?" His fingers traced lazy circles around her nipples. A delicious tingling went through her, and before she quite realized what he was about, he had worked the top buttons of her riding habit free. As his searching hand touched her bare skin, a reckless longing threatened to consume her. It was wild and daring, like Sinclair himself.

Sinclair did not seem to expect an answer. Louisa leaned into his touch, like a cat nuzzling its master at dinnertime. She felt his arousal and was filled with wonder that she had affected him so. When she reached out to touch him there, however, he drew away.

"No." His sharp tone jarred her. "Not now. Not yet."

"But I want to," she protested.

"You don't know what you want," he growled.

"I *do*. Don't give me orders, Sinclair."

"I wouldn't dream of it. Walk over to the bed, Louisa."

She stared at him, uncomprehending.

"Do it," he rasped. "*Now*."

Louisa couldn't move. The naked promise in his eyes took her breath away.

He swore, then picked her up, blanket and all. "It's good you have that blanket, Louisa, because it's too late to back out now. There is dust and dry rot all over this bed, and at the moment, I don't give a damn."

She didn't, either, as he deposited her there and covered her body with his. He had stolen her reason until all she wanted was to wallow in the glory of this wild desire.

His knee went between her legs, letting her feel the pressure at the juncture of her thighs. Moaning shamelessly, she arched toward him. Suddenly things were moving fast, mindlessly fast, and yet not fast enough.

Sinclair gave her no time to turn back. He fumbled with her riding skirt, nearly ripping the fabric in his haste. Then he touched her *there*, that spot that seemed to ache for him, and Louisa thought she would die of pleasure. He stroked her slowly at first. Then his fingers found new places, deeper pleasures, faster rhythms. They urged her on toward some unseen goal.

"No," she groaned, unwilling to grant him this mastery over her. She would never be the same if she gave him this.

But the ache deep in her soul merged with the more distinct one between her legs, and she cried out his name as the storm of desire built to urgent release.

First you dare. Then you soar. It went on and on, this fierce pleasure, and the minute one wave ebbed, another took its place. Louisa cried out in joy and despair at the loss of this piece of her to his skill and cunning. And she knew then that he was right: the other side of fear was desire; the other side of hate, love.

Just as the final wave of pleasure ebbed, a savage roll of thunder boomed overhead and a jagged streak of lightning lit up the room like the devil's own torch.

Sweet, hateful love. It would always be mixed up in her mind with the acrid scent of fire.

David's hands trembled as he gently turned Violet on her side to get to the buttons on her back. Her frock was soaked through; it would have to come off. He wished to hell there was another woman in the house.

His large fingers were not suited to the tiny buttons that ran from her neck to her hips. As he fumbled with them, David prayed that Violet would not awaken just yet. He didn't think he could make her understand that his intentions were honorable, that even strong men weakened by combat had been known to die of exposure as rain and cold seeped through their clothes.

Already, thousands of goose bumps dotted her skin. He saw them as soon as he slipped one shoulder of her dress off her arm. Sam had built a fire in the hearth, but its cheerful blaze would not banish this kind of chill.

With renewed determination, David eased the dress off her other shoulder. As he slipped the bodice down, he realized she was not wearing anything underneath. He didn't know what he had expected—a chemise, perhaps—but Violet wore nothing except this sodden frock.

David couldn't help but stare at her breasts. They were full and lovely, ready for the babe that would soon claim them. He swallowed hard as he slipped the dress over her abdomen. Her belly was smooth and firm and filled with new life. The man who begat the babe was a monster, but the child would be innocent of that stain. David had seen the sorrow in Violet and knew her husband had caused it. He prayed she could set it aside once the babe came.

Some sorrows, he knew, never went away. Their pain could suck the joy out of life, deny the soul its nourishment. It had happened to Louisa, and though he hoped Sinclair would free her from her misery, David knew better than to bet on the future. The present was all a man had.

As he eased the dress over Violet's hips, David saw the scars. They ran the length of her back, and though months had passed since Violet had stood in that village square, the scars were all too visible. David would gladly have killed the man who had given her those marks, but Midnight, it seemed, had beaten him to it.

He tossed the dress on the floor and placed a blanket over her, tucking it under her chin as one might tuck in a child. Violet lay on her side, her hands pillowed under her head, her legs curled slightly. Her face was pale but unlined, as if in sleep she had finally found peace.

She still looked cold. Her skin was mottled,

and her lips had a bluish tint. David sat on the bed and began to rub Violet's arm, willing her blood to rouse itself and warm her. His hands moved to her shoulders, back, and hips, massaging her briskly but gently through the blanket. He tried not to think about the fact that she was naked underneath, but everywhere his hands rubbed, he imagined it was her skin he touched, not the soft wool of the blanket.

Touching her, even through the blanket, made him feel strong in a way that had nothing to do with might. It was as if she was giving him strength, rather than the other way around. He had a sudden, vivid image of Violet in his cottage, nursing her babe while he massaged her feet.

David's shoulders slumped. He knew better than to put faith in dreams. Who was he to think Violet could come to care for the likes of him? He wasn't even a man, not in the way a woman had a right to expect. He had the strength to slay dragons, but he couldn't begin to measure up as a man.

"Don't stop."

He nearly leaped off the bed, so startled was he to hear Violet's soft voice. "You are awake," he stammered.

Her gaze clouded, and he could almost see the memories of her ordeal come flooding back. She touched her abdomen, as if to reassure herself the babe was still there. Then her fingers went to the bruise on her face. She winced.

"Where is Will?"

"In the stable. He'll nae trouble you again." He wished she had not asked about her husband so soon. Despite the man's cruelties, she'd obviously kept a place for him in her heart.

Violet regarded him with somber brown eyes. "I remember Midnight," she said slowly. "Lightning was flashing something fierce. He raced into the storm, then galloped back into the stable and—" Her eyes widened. "Is he dead?"

"The horse is unharmed," David said gruffly, deliberately misunderstanding her. "He pummeled your husband to a fare-thee-well. If he is nae dead by now, he deserves to be." He searched her eyes, wondering how she would take the news.

Violet said nothing.

"How do ye feel, lass?" he asked, because he could not think of anything else to say.

"Cold." She gave him a rueful smile. "And fat. Enormously fat."

"You are beautiful." The moment he said the words, David wanted to call them back.

Violet stared at him.

"I only meant—" He eyed her helplessly. She adjusted the blanket, and he saw the instant she realized she was naked under the covers.

"Where are my clothes?"

He sprang to his feet. "On the floor. The dress was wet through, and I—"

"You took it off."

David could not meet her gaze. "I did nae

want you to get a fever. I tried not to look, if that means anything."

"You were repulsed." She sighed. " 'Tis all right, David. I know I look like a cow."

"No. You and the child—'tis beautiful. I wanted to touch the babe, but—" He broke off, horrified that he had confessed so much.

Violet captured his hand between hers, leaving him no choice but to perch awkwardly on the edge of the bed, trying to look anywhere but at her. He stared hard at the intricately carved mantelpiece.

"Touch the babe, David."

He froze.

"Go ahead," she said softly.

He could not move.

She lifted the blanket and placed his hand on the fullest part of her abdomen. Then she pulled the covers over her, patting his hand through the blanket as she met his terrified gaze. " 'Tis all right, David."

Under his callused palm, her skin was smooth and satiny. He had no right to such an intimacy, but she'd granted it, and so he sat awestruck with his hand on her under the covers, wondering what he was supposed to do next.

To his dismay, tears filled her eyes. "Violet," he rasped, shamed. "I'm sorry about looking at you, lass. I didna' mean to—"

"I'm cold, so very cold. Lie with me, David."

His heart leapt to his throat.

"Just for a little while," she whispered, and

there was a world of sorrow in her tone, and he knew he would do anything to make it go away.

He eased himself down on the bed on top of the blanket. He tried to keep a respectable distance, but she turned on her side again, still holding his hand securely on her abdomen. He had to nestle against her backside, the curve of his body mirroring hers. He had never felt so awkward in his life.

"Thank you." It broke his heart to hear the gratitude in her voice. Warming her with his body was such a little thing. He didn't want to be thanked for it.

Beneath his hand, he felt a sudden twitch. "What was that?"

"The babe."

The babe. A wee person under that skin, ready to pop out into the world. "Does it— he—do that often?" he ventured.

"More and more these days." Though she was not facing him, he heard the smile in her voice. "He is eager to meet us."

Us? David swallowed hard. He forced himself to banish that image of Violet and her babe in his cottage. She couldn't have known about his daydream. He wouldn't take her words to heart.

"David?"

"What?" He scarcely recognized his own voice.

"I have wanted you for so long."

David stared at the back of Violet's head

and wondered whether his hearing had gone bad.

She turned toward him, and he saw tears on her cheeks.

"You don't need to say it. I know you can't possibly care for someone so huge and unattractive. I've been lonely, that's all."

"Damn it, Violet. Stop saying that. You're beautiful."

Violet smiled. "Thank you, but I know the truth. I'm afraid I've been feeling sorry for myself again. I seem to be all mixed up these days. Please forget I spoke."

And pigs would fly. "Did you mean it?" he croaked. "About . . . wanting me?"

Violet nodded.

"I'll always stand as your friend, lass," he said carefully.

She shook her head. "That is not what I meant."

David took a deep breath. "You want us to be—"

"Lovers," she said quietly.

Everything a man could want was contained in that word, but David knew she didn't mean it. Pregnant women were said to have strange yearnings. This had to be one of them.

"I can nae," he said gently.

Her expression crumbled. She turned her head away.

"Violet." He hated himself for hurting her. "It's not that I do nae want . . . It's that . . . I can't. The war left me . . ." He took a deep breath. "I haven't had a woman in years. I can't."

Her startled gaze found his. "Were you injured?"

"Not in that way." David couldn't believe he was telling her this. "They did horrid things to us in prison, Violet. I can nae get beyond it. And even if I could—" He broke off.

She waited. He plunged ahead. "Your babe is almost ready to be born. You canna' be serious about—"

"Making love? Yes, David, I am." She closed her eyes, as if in pain. David cursed his awkward tongue. He had to make her understand.

"I would nae know what to do. Even if a miracle occurred, and I could manage to . . . What I mean is that I'd be afraid of hurting you and the baby. You're a pregnant woman, for God's sake—"

"I'm still a woman. With a woman's wants and needs." She paused. "I don't think the baby would mind."

David eyed her helplessly. She had no idea what she was asking. "I'd give my right arm to please you, Violet."

"I'll take it." She patted his hand—his right hand, as it happened—resting on her abdomen. She turned back on her side, away from him, securing his hand with hers. "And if that is all I can have, that's enough. For now."

She fell silent. For a long time David stared at the curve of her shoulder, wondering whether he should say something. But she did not seem to expect it, and when she stretched like a lazy cat and yawned, he began to relax. Eventually he heard her steady, even breathing and knew she had fallen asleep. He nestled against her backside, warming her with his body all night long, his hand still on the place where the babe grew. And every time the baby kicked, he smiled in silent wonder.

He had no nightmares that night.

Chapter 20

⌒◯◯⌒

From the shelter of the stable, Gabriel watched his boyhood home burn to the ground.

The steady rain kept the fire from spreading to the outbuildings, and finally, about dawn, the blaze burned itself out. Nothing remained of the manor house except its stone foundation. All else had been reduced to rubble.

Including his mother's portrait, Rose's drawings for the renovation, and the musty bed in which he had brought Louisa pleasure.

At first, Gabriel hadn't noticed the scent of fire. He'd been consumed with Louisa, about to take her to the peak again, damn near unhinged from wanting her. The sudden, acrid explosion that reverberated above the noise of the storm might as well have been miles away.

The Flowers' screams had finally penetrated the haze of his desire. Gabriel and Louisa had stumbled out with the others to huddle under a blanket in the stables and watch the conflagration wrought by a vengeful bolt of lightning.

He wished his mother's portrait had been spared.

"Such a shame." Daisy dabbed at her eyes with a handkerchief.

"A pity." Jasmine nodded somberly.

"A disaster." Rose gave a heartfelt sigh.

Gabriel shrugged. "It is best this way. Saves everyone a lot of trouble."

They gazed at him in disapproval—not that he cared. He wanted nothing more than to be on his way. The house meant nothing to him now. It was just a pile of rubble, and at last he was free of it. In his mind's eye, he saw Sinclair Isle as vividly as that burned shell of a house before him. He'd sail there this morning, make London by nightfall. Soon he'd catch one of the East India ships to the far corners of the world. By tomorrow, England—and the past—would be behind him.

He couldn't wait to be away from the treacherous memories that brought this unexpected moisture to his eyes. So seductive, this place. It smacked of permanence and longing, things that were only illusions, no more than a trick of the mind. It wasn't real anymore—not the portrait or the bed or . . . Louisa. How fitting that her keening cries of fulfillment were eclipsed by the fire. How swift was the revenge on mortals who tampered with the flames of desire.

Gabriel had not looked at her in a very long time. An hour or more, though it seemed longer. He had stood here all night, his gaze fixed on the flames, and watched the past shoot heavenward in formless plumes of smoke, as if it had never existed.

Making love to Louisa in his father's bed was part of that past. Now it, too, was gone.

"Stop it." Her voice was low, fierce.

Gabriel turned, feigning surprise at her nearness. "I beg your pardon," he said stiffly, as if she was a stranger, not the woman he'd held in his arms a few hours ago.

"Stop telling yourself that it doesn't matter. You know it does."

He should have known she would make things difficult. The crusader in her wouldn't let him be. "Leave it alone, Louisa. I'm not one of your desperate causes."

"Your family is dead, Sinclair. Everything they touched—the beds they slept in, the table they ate upon—has just gone up in smoke. All of it, gone. And you want me to believe you don't care?" She stared at him, incredulous.

"It was just a house. The past is over and dead. I buried it a long time ago."

"No," she said softly. "That is the problem, isn't it? You've never buried it. You've carried it around with you like a stone. You've run to the ends of the earth to rid yourself of its weight. Now you're pretending it doesn't matter, just as you pretend not to care about anything."

Behind them, the Flowers had fallen silent. Every ear was attuned to her accusations.

"Be quiet," he growled.

Her brilliant blue eyes glinted angrily—the fire hadn't changed those, at least. "Tell me,

Sinclair," she said, biting off each word, making his name a curse, "are you also pretending that you didn't make love to me last night? Because if you are, I'm going to hate you for a long, long time."

There came a collective gasp behind them.

"Louisa," he growled.

"Don't," she snapped. "Don't remind me that you didn't make promises, that you have to be on your way, that what happened between us doesn't change things. I know that. I also know that you're so dead inside you wouldn't recognize a scintilla of real feeling if it struck you like that lightning bolt."

"Oh, dear," murmured Daisy.

Louisa stood there like a hellion, eyes snapping, daring him to fight her. But the fight had gone out of him. He was tired of crossing swords with a woman who wouldn't let anything rest. Anyway, the rain had finally stopped.

Gabriel turned to the Flowers. "Good-bye, ladies. I appreciate your kindnesses, individual and collective. I regret the inconvenience this night has brought. I will hitch up your horses and see you on your way. If we never meet again, I will count it as my loss."

Daisy sniffed loudly. The others looked as if they would turn into watering pots as well. Only Rose gazed at him with clear, assessing eyes. And Louisa. Always Louisa.

The horses were uneasy after such a night, so it took Gabriel a while to harness them to the two carriages. He was about to saddle

Starfire when Louisa marched over and, without a word, took over the task. Gabriel shrugged and turned his attention to the gray.

Silently, the Flowers climbed into their conveyances. Daisy and Jasmine dabbed at their eyes, Lily managed a tearful smile, and Rose merely shook her head. Gabriel turned to help Louisa onto Starfire, but she was already there.

He mounted the gray. He had always detested sentiment, but an unfamiliar lump in his throat made him stumble over the round of good-byes. Perhaps they *were* a family of sorts. Thank God he would never see them again.

Jasmine flicked the reins of the landau. Rose maneuvered the gig onto the lane. Atop Starfire, Louisa was still and silent. Courtesy dictated that he remain until the ladies had departed, but Louisa was, as usual, making things difficult. He forced himself to look at her.

The storm had turned her hair into an impossible mass of golden tangles. Her clothes were no longer wet, but the fabric of her riding skirt was limp, formless. He waited for her to signal to the horse. She did not move.

"What the hell is wrong now?" he demanded.

"Nothing. Everything. I am going with you."

Out of the corner of his eye, Gabriel saw that Rose had slowed the gig, doubtless so she could hear every word.

"You will take me to Sinclair Isle," Louisa

said. A cold fury warmed her blue eyes. "You will show me your kingdom. And mayhap I shall pretend to be your queen, and we will make love in the sand, and you can show me how little you care."

She was mad, Gabriel decided, thoroughly mad. And he was something of an expert on the subject. "Leave me be, Louisa. I am in no need of rescue, and I have no intention of letting you on that island."

"Which of us is the coward now?" she asked softly.

Death on the gallows might have been preferable to being rescued by Louisa Peabody. Gabriel spurred the gray. She brought her horse alongside.

"What is wrong, Sinclair?" she taunted. "Did you like touching me? Did you like it too much? I'm sorry for you, then. You were right to be scared. But I was scared, too. And now I'm not. Because I learned something last night."

"Always glad to oblige," he muttered darkly.

"You don't want to hear it, do you? But here it is. We fit together, Sinclair. You and your refusal to care about anything, and me caring too much. We complete each other."

Gabriel stared at a fixed point on the horizon, where he knew his boat stood ready.

"I do care for you," she continued in a subdued tone. "You don't mind, do you? No one has ever made me feel as you did last night."

Gabriel willed himself not to look at her.

"Forgive me for pointing out the obvious, which is that your only standard of comparison was that disaster of a husband."

"Go ahead and joke about it," she bit out. "But last night—"

"Don't say it," he snarled, desperately afraid that she would. "Don't confuse pleasure with love."

"Of course not," she rejoined. "Only an idiot would confuse the two."

Gabriel eyed her suspiciously, then turned his attention to the road. It did not surprise him in the least that she kept pace with him or that when he stepped onto the deck of the sloop, she was at his side.

He shot a quick prayer heavenward that this trip would be mercifully short. And he prayed, but not quite as fervently, that he would not feel compelled to make love to Louisa ever again.

The wind ruffled her hair as they sailed. The sun bathed her upturned face in its warming light. The sea spray kicked up all around her, its salty essence making her senses tingle. Louisa had never felt so free, so full of wonder.

She watched Sinclair closely, as if relentless scrutiny would reveal the source of his magical connection to these waters. On deck, he walked like a cat, his weight perfectly balanced on the balls of his feet. He did not lurch as she had, or shriek when a powerful swell splashed them or when a gust of wind caused the boat to lean precariously. He handled the craft as if he had been born to test his mettle against life's unpredictable seas.

Sinclair was perfectly at home on the ocean, and it struck her that this might be the only place where that was true. Endless and churning, never the same from one day to the next, the sea reflected Sinclair's mercurial nature, offering a vast canvas upon which to write—and rewrite—each day's truth.

Regrettably, one truth she had recently learned was that Sinclair had captured her heart. How awful that it was so—that a man with such an empty soul had ensnared hers with no effort at all. There could be no hope for anyone who cared for a man whose moral compass was dangerously askew, who asked only to be left alone so that he could partake of pleasure without cost to himself.

But then, hopeless causes were her specialty.

Louisa had never dreamed she could respond to any man's touch. But Sinclair was not any man. In him lurked a fire so wild and elemental that her heart thrilled to the danger.

You want to make me want you. I don't. You want to prove that you can seduce me. You can't. Mere bravado, hurled at him as the net closed around her. Now something wonderful and new threatened to burst in her. It was fragile and uncertain, but growing stronger by the minute.

Sinclair would not be bound by promises or pleasure, or even love. Still, he had given her something as sweet and fierce as any love.

Love. Was that the name for this strange yearning? Oddly, it was not the yearning in her that had brought her here, but the yearning in him. The longing in his eyes, the vulnerability he could not completely hide. She wondered if beneath the sardonic facade was a man who wanted desperately to love but did not know how.

What had he said? *People don't change, Louisa. You won't, and I can't. No miracle would happen if I made love to you.* Ah, but one had. He just didn't know it yet.

Louisa knew she was a fool to believe in miracles. And more the fool not to.

Gabriel brought the sloop into the little cove he knew as well as his own name. The boathouse was still there, though part of its foundation had washed away. The empty beach fanned out on either side in a perfect half-circle.

Exotic shells dotted the fine, white sand.

His father had chosen the island because it was a perfect vantage point from which to see any invader approaching from the east. Here, a man could see for miles in any direction. A boy could point his spyglass at that fierce, lonely sea and wonder whether the world out there was as desperate and empty as this island paradise.

"It's lovely."

Gabriel tore his gaze from the dilapidated boathouse and the ribbon of sand that framed it. He didn't look at Louisa for fear she would see the desolation in his eyes.

"I want to see everything," she said.

Gabriel scowled. "Let us be clear, Louisa. I'd give anything to be elsewhere. Failing that, I'd rather be here alone. Do not expect me to fall over myself showing you the sights."

Her mouth tightened, and Gabriel waited for her biting retort. She had been strangely silent during the trip. He preferred the sharp-tongued revolutionary to the woman who looked at him from eyes as calm as the lapping waves that masked a treacherous riptide.

"No," she said quietly. "I don't expect that."

He slanted her a gaze. "Meekness does not suit you."

She didn't reply, which unsettled him further. Louisa was not herself. She cared for him, did she? He hadn't wanted to believe her. But now he was beginning to, and it alarmed him no small amount. He didn't need that complication, not today.

Feeling like a man about to be sucked into deadly waters, Gabriel trudged up the rocky path from the cove. He didn't bother to see whether she followed, knowing that she would. They hiked a half-mile through sawgrass that clung to their limp clothes and dragonflies that darted about with reckless abandon. Gulls flew overhead, and now and then a hawk rode a downdraft with deceptive ease. The sea breeze blew steadily, pulling him inexorably into the past.

The grave was there, just as he had envi-

sioned it every day for the last ten years. Aloysius's resting place lay atop the island's
highest hill, where east wind met west and
where a ghost could spend eternity staring at
the far horizon and plotting his revenge. This
beautiful spot, Gabriel's favorite perch as a
boy, had been his final gift to his father and
perhaps the only lasting one.

He had carved the stone himself. It bore
only Aloysius's name and the date of death.
His father had made him promise to carve a
likeness of the bayberry crown he'd worn until
the day he died, but Gabriel had not done so.

It was a betrayal, of course. The last wishes
of the dying ought to be honored. But Gabriel
had not been able to bring himself to inscribe
that crown on his father's tombstone. If it
meant that he would be haunted by a vengeful
ghost for the rest of his days, so be it.

Looking at that stark, spare stone, Gabriel
waited, expecting grief or regret or anger to
assail him.

He felt nothing.

His gaze spanned the horizon. The sea that
had beckoned him when he was a virtual prisoner on this land looked exactly the same.
White frothy seacaps rolled onward, splashing
and frolicking under that wide expanse of sky,
as if they possessed some profound but fleeting secret to happiness. Gulls swooped down,
gloating as they plucked a meal from the
churning waters.

The sea teemed with life, with vibrancy. It
was the same as it had been—and not, for the

man who looked upon it now was not the boy who had done so years ago.

Still he felt nothing, only the presence of the woman who stood in silence behind him.

At last, Gabriel started toward the cabin that lay just through the copse of trees. After that, he might go to the cave, but he wouldn't tarry. Tonight, in some London hellhole, he'd drown the memories in a bottle of brandy.

Louisa tucked her hand into his, offering silent comfort.

Suddenly, he knew that the worst of this day wasn't over. After his father's grave, after that cabin and the cave, after this empty pilgrimage was said and done, he would still have to reckon with Louisa.

God save him from a woman who cared.

Chapter 21

❧

"What is this?" Louisa stared at the round-bodied object that seemed the size of a small whale. She'd followed Sinclair all over the island, which was much smaller than she had envisioned. Almost as an afterthought, he'd brought her to this cave, which opened onto the far end of the cove and ran deep into the rocky cliffs. Though they were only a few yards from where Sinclair's boat bobbed serenely, the watery cavern was so secluded it might have been the other end of the earth.

Sinclair shrugged. "My father's last invention."

Louisa had never seen anything like it. The exterior looked to be of copper, banded with iron stays. One end tapered to a snub nose; the other held a propeller. A large frame that spanned the cave's width kept the craft just above the reach of the water.

And then she knew.

"The underwater boat," she whispered, awed. " 'Tis the submersible, isn't it?"

"Yes." His voice was flat, lifeless.

The craft rested on the enormous frame just as Sinclair's father must have left it. The iron was rusty, the copper tarnished, the propeller blades chipped and worn, but the submersible itself was magnificent. Frozen in time, it presided over the damp shadows of the cave like a creature from another world.

"How does it work?" she asked.

Sinclair's eyes glittered strangely. " 'Tis fairly simple. It has a single mast and sails on the water like an ordinary boat, albeit a cumbersome one. When the pilot wishes to descend, he folds the mast and collapses the sail. A hatch seals the interior, and a propeller moves the ship underwater. Two rudders, horizontal and vertical, control depth and direction."

"How does one breathe?" From here the boat seemed large, but it must be horribly confining inside.

"There's enough air inside for a short trip, as well as a tank of compressed air for longer ones. The craft can support three men for about six hours, as long as no candles are lit."

"Candles?"

His gaze, which until now had been riveted on the boat, met hers. "The deeper one descends, the darker it gets. Without light, you might as well be steering from inside a coffin."

A shiver rippled her spine, whether from Sinclair's words or his bleak eyes she didn't know. "You have sailed it?"

"Yes. My father rigged a series of pulleys to

raise and lower the frame so he could launch and operate the craft alone. But I was his helper more often than not."

"What is that spike on the top?"

" 'Tis meant to hold the boat under the enemy's hull long enough for an explosive charge to be delivered. I believed he called it a torpedo."

"It's brilliant," she said softly. "Your father was a genius."

"Every inventor in Europe had a submersible. Fulton, Johnstone—I've forgotten them all."

"You hate it, don't you?"

Sinclair said nothing for a moment. Then, carefully: "I hate what it represented. Which is to say everything that took my father from me."

"But he was trying to save lives—to win the war. He would have destroyed that underwater channel if Napoleon had tried to build it."

"Don't paint him in hero's colors, Louisa. He wanted revenge on the French for my brother's death. He was a sad, embittered man who let grief rob him of whatever rational mind he had."

"As you've let anger destroy your love for him."

A muscle clenched in his jaw, visible even in the shadows of the cave. "Damn it, Louisa. Stop this nonsense. I am not one of your desperate causes."

"No, you're beyond rescue," she flung at

him. "You're full of pain and you wallow in it so you don't risk getting hurt again."

His face contorted in anger. His hands went around her upper arms, as if he wanted to shake her. It was the first time he had touched her since the storm.

"This is about last night, isn't it?" he growled. "You're just like all the other women I've known. You want to dress it up and call it love when it's only sex. Rollicking, lust-driven sex. That's all we had, Louisa. Nothing more."

Louisa balled her hand into a fist. And though he must have seen it coming, and could have stopped her in time, she slammed it into his gut as hard as she could. He stared at her with a stunned expression. "I know about lust," she said fiercely. "Richard showed me lust. It didn't look anything like what I saw last night."

"Louisa . . ."

"You don't get to talk, Sinclair. You only get to listen. I know about selfish fathers, too. Mine traded me to Richard to satisfy his gaming debts. I wanted to hate him for making me no better than a whore. I did hate him some. But I loved him, too. Children do, you know."

She took a deep breath. "Love hurts, but you can't let the pain make you turn your back on the world." She glared at him. "Though if I had it to do over again," she said softly, "I'd let them hang you."

Louisa turned and fled toward the entrance of the cave. Tears seared her eyes as she stepped into the late afternoon sun that bathed the beach in forgiving amber.

"By the way," she shouted over her shoulder. Her voice echoed deep inside the cave. "I am not like the other women you've known, Sinclair. Not by a long shot."

With that, she fled blindly toward the sun, away from the shadows of Sinclair's bitterness.

Gabriel found her near the boathouse. She sat on the beach, staring at the horizon, her arms wrapped around her knees, not bothering to hide the tears that fell from her cheeks onto the sand. He slowed his pace, wary of intruding. She didn't look at him, not even when he sat down beside her.

"You're right," he said with a heavy sigh. "You're not like the others. Damn it all, Louisa, you're worse."

She looked at him then, her blue eyes deeper than the sea as she searched his face. Gabriel did not flinch from her scrutiny, though he knew it was bound to leave her unsatisfied.

"I can't change, Louisa," he said. "If my father taught me anything, it's the insanity of living one's life for others. I'm no hero. I'm not the man you deserve."

She shook her head. "You're wrong."

"No." He felt bereft, as if acknowledging that simple truth marked the death of something precious between them. "Your head is full of illusions. About me, anyway."

"Touch me, Sinclair. Then tell me what is illusion."

He looked away from that sudden, challenging sensuality in her eyes. "You're like my father. You fit the world to your view, regardless of the truth."

"The truth is that I love you," she said defiantly. "I don't care whether that scares you or not."

Gabriel stared at her, wanting to pretend he hadn't heard, unable to think of a single thing to say. Louisa put her arms around his neck and drew him down with her into the sand. "Last night you showed me a woman's pleasure," she murmured. "You forgot about your own."

"I didn't forget," he growled. "The damned house burned down around us. See what I mean, Louisa? You twist the world to fit your own truth."

She laughed, a teasing sound that said he was wrong, that he *had* placed her pleasure above his, that she would make it up to him now—whether he wanted her or not.

Gabriel wanted her. He had never wanted anyone or anything so much—not his father's love or the moon or the stars or even life itself. Even if it meant he'd have to go back to that gallows tomorrow, he would do so gladly if he could only spend the next few hours in her arms.

Well, not gladly, perhaps. But he would go, and his last words would be for her alone, and they would be something like—

"I love you," she said as her lips took his in a demanding kiss.

Gabriel held her as if she was a lifeline in storm-tossed seas. He kissed her as if he'd suddenly been given his last, best wish. Then he made love to her on the beach and, for the first time in his life, held nothing back.

Louisa. Her name was on his lips and in his heart when he drove himself into her and filled her with his desperate need.

Louisa felt a curious numbness.

She allowed Sinclair to help her mount Starfire, though she could have managed it on her own. The ostler he had hired to look after the horses while they sailed to Sinclair Isle had done his job well. Starfire and the gray had looked quite contented in the little paddock behind the nameless inn that overlooked the bay.

The world was the same as it had been yesterday, before she'd lost herself in the walking maze of contradictions that was Gabriel Sinclair. But she had changed—not necessarily for the better.

Almost, it didn't matter that he would not take up the gauntlet she'd thrown down. Almost, she could imagine him as a man of principle, who burned as she did to right society's wrongs. Almost, she was willing to forget who she was, who he was, why they had to part.

After the loving, after she had contemplated the wonder of the passion they'd shared, her world had started to spin again. She'd gazed on the sand, the waves, the sun setting at a place far beyond Sinclair Isle, and one word had come to her. Not anything as profound and mysterious as love, but a single word, quite miraculous in its own way.

Submersible. It was as if the loving had opened a wealth of possibilities, for her mind was suddenly spinning with plans for Aloysius Sinclair's invention.

"It's perfect," she told him. "We would catch the guards unawares. We'd pop out of the water and spirit the women away before anyone was the wiser."

"No." He'd let the word hang there, hovering ominously over the joy between them. "I can't."

"*Won't*, you mean."

Sinclair shook his head. "You're a dreamer, Louisa. I'm not. You want someone I will never be."

"I want *you*," she had protested, but he'd only smiled and taken her in his arms again, deliberately misunderstanding her words.

They had moved to the boat, to the tiny cabin little bigger than a man but large enough for a night of love she would carry with her forever. And too soon, they were back in Kent and forever had begun.

Sinclair escorted her as far as the lane that led to Peabody Manor. "Do not attempt it, Louisa." His eyes mirrored the loss she felt. "It will only end in disaster."

She had given him a shaky smile, but they both knew that she would do what she had to do and that he was forfeiting, now and for all time, the right to prevent her.

And that was that. Dry-eyed, she sat atop Starfire and watched Sinclair until the curve of the road took him out of sight. He would go to London and then to the ends of the earth. She would never see him again.

Perhaps she wasn't numb, just stunned.

Somehow, in the barren soil of her heart, love had taken root. Sinclair had banished the poisonous nettles Richard had planted there. He was rash and wild and free, and no woman would ever change that. But within that unpredictable spirit was a soul capable of great love. If only he could see what she saw, if only he would try—

"And beggars would ride," Louisa muttered as she settled the mare into her stall. A few minutes later, she knocked at the door to David's cottage.

It opened slowly. David stood at the threshold, filling the door frame, blocking her view of the inside. He did not look especially glad to see her.

"Louisa!" To her surprise, Violet's voice floated out to her. The door opened further as Violet gently nudged David aside. "I have been worried about you! Rose and the others have been so tight-lipped about what happened. Come and have some tea. Is Mr. Sinclair with you?"

Violet walked to the fire and reached for the kettle. She had a bruise over one eye but otherwise looked perfectly well.

"No," Louisa replied. "He has gone."

"I am sorry. I heard about the fire. He must

be terribly upset. Rose has already begun work on the new plans."

"Plans?"

"To rebuild the house. Rose is not a woman who admits defeat."

"Forgive me for asking, Violet, but have you, that is, did you—" Louisa broke off in confusion. She looked from Violet to David and back.

"Move in with David? Yes, two days ago. It is shocking, I know. I hope you are not offended. Sam does not mind. He is in sore need of a mother, I'm afraid. Oh, dear. I can see you are confused. David and I have become very close since Will's unfortunate visit—"

"Your husband was *here*?" Louisa was horrified. "Oh, Violet, I should have been here. Did he hurt you?"

"Only a little. The bruise on my face is rather noticeable, I'm afraid, but it will go away. David has taken wonderful care of me. We have decided to marry."

Louisa's gaze shot to David, who had not said a word. His expression darkened. " 'Tis not right to speak so, Violet. That mongrel hasna' kicked the bucket yet, though he came near enough. There's a trial to go through—"

"After which they will hang him." Violet looked unruffled. "That is why we cannot marry yet," she explained to Louisa.

"That is nae the only reason," David said darkly.

"There is another inconvenience," Violet

said cheerfully, "but I have every confidence that with time, all will be well."

David stared at Violet with such longing that Louisa felt she was intruding on something extremely private. She rose. "I am glad for you both," she said, and meant it. She had never seen Violet look so happy. And David's eyes held such a tremulous hope that it was almost painful to see.

"I'll leave you now," Louisa told them. "David and I need to discuss the plans for the prison hulk rescue, but I can see this is not the time."

"Prison hulk?" Violet frowned. "Oh, I see. You intend to rescue those women Alice mentioned."

"Yes. Sinclair refused to help, and in any case, he is gone." Louisa felt a stab of jealousy at what David and Violet had, what she would never have. "It is up to David and me, I'm afraid."

David tore his gaze from Violet. "I can nae help ye, lass," he told Louisa. "Not this time."

"David!" Violet looked dismayed. "Think of what those women must endure. Think of what Louisa has done for all of us. Think of what might have happened to me. You must help."

David shook his head. "I have too much to lose now. I mean to take care of you, Violet, for the rest of my days."

Violet touched his arm. "And you will," she said gently, "but first we will help Louisa."

"We?" He glowered. "Not you. I will nae hear of such a thing."

"My mind is made up," Violet said firmly. "We owe Louisa a great debt. It must be paid."

"Nay. You must think of the babe," he protested.

"I do think of her, or him—every day. Do not worry. I shall do nothing to jeopardize this precious life growing inside me. But there comes a time when one must take a stand, else life is not worth living."

" 'Tis worth it to me," he insisted. "It has never been so precious—"

"It will be all right, David. You will see."

"Violet," he growled. "Come here."

Neither of them noticed when Louisa slipped out of the cottage and carefully closed the door.

"What plan?" Rose demanded.

Sam shuffled awkwardly. The roomful of ladies made him uncomfortable, but he had known the minute he heard Violet and David arguing that something had to be done. He barely remembered his mother anymore; he didn't know what had caused Violet to move into their cottage to take care of them, but he wasn't about to lose her.

"To save those women on the prison ship," he said. "David doesn't want to, but Violet says they owe it to Louisa."

Rose frowned. "So that is why Louisa is being so closed-mouthed. And here I thought she was moping over Mr. Sinclair, when it was only another rescue. Why she insists on keeping these things from us is a mystery."

"You know that she wants to protect us," Daisy put in.

Rose's gaze roamed around the room. "Ladies, I say it is time to stop letting Louisa do all the work."

"Then you'll do something?" Sam ventured hopefully. "Violet doesn't have to risk her life?"

"Don't be silly, boy," Rose said. "Nobody will risk anything. *I* have matters firmly in hand."

Daisy rolled her eyes, but Rose merely smiled and returned to her drawings of Mr. Sinclair's new house. It was going to be even better than the one that burned.

Chapter 22

Time had dimmed Gabriel's memory of Mother Dolores's daunting red nightcap— a curious excess for one whose mission was to mold virtuous minds, not inflame them.

Tonight, Gabriel did not waste his time on those virginal young ladies. Mother Dolores and her enormous red cap with its wide fringe of white lace compelled all of his attention. The woman slept the sleep of the dead, emitting mooselike snores that made her room sound like a zooful of bellowing animals. The covers were pulled up to her bulbous nose. He caught a whiff of spirits and wondered whether the good mother had tippled her way into sleep.

He could not take the chance that her well-lubricated voice would summon that army of virgins. He covered her mouth with his hand-kerchief, gagging her as she came awake on a scream. Swiftly, he bound her hands and legs.

She was trussed up like a turkey at Mich-aelmas, which suited him perfectly. Her red-rimmed eyes blinked, trying to discern what demon had invaded her sanctuary, then widened in alarm. Gabriel waited until recognition set in before sitting in a chair at her bedside.

"I am prepared," he said solemnly, "to donate a generous sum of money to your convent."

He could almost see her brain struggling through the layers of sleep and whiskey to make sense of it all.

"Yes, I know that's a bit queer, but I am afraid you have been mistaken about my character." He paused to let that sink in. "Gravely mistaken."

Her gaze shot to the door, which Gabriel had made certain was firmly closed and locked. "No help there, unfortunately. Everyone is abed but us." He might have felt sorry for the woman but for the memory of her testimony at his trial.

"You embellished, you know," he said reproachfully. "I never touched your girls. I only wanted a lock of hair. It was a bet, you see. A drunken one—most unwise, but perhaps you understand what spirits can do to a desperate soul."

She looked away, and Gabriel knew he had correctly surmised her secret weakness. "Do not worry. I won't tell anyone that you are given to a nip here and there. Actually, I'd like to tell you a tale, a sad one. I warn you, it gets ugly in spots, but life outside the convent is like that. My story is about some women. Four, to be precise, who have been given over to a bunch of vile criminals for their base amusement.''

Her startled gaze met his.

"I see that I have your attention." Gabriel stretched out his legs. "What I want you to see, madam, is that while my crimes exist primarily in your well-developed imagination, there are many crimes against humanity toward which you could better direct your efforts."

He paused to allow his message to sink in, then leaned forward in his chair. "How long has it been, Mother Dolores, since you reevaluated your mission on this earth?"

She frowned.

"Oh, I know what you are thinking," Gabriel said. "But I am no proselytizer, nor insane. Well, perhaps I shouldn't go *that* far. I only suggest that you could do a great deal of good in this world."

He rose. "Now, as to the specifics: I shall require that you go to the Old Bailey and swear an oath as to grievous errors contained in your account of the night I so unwisely made your acquaintance. At the time this statement is entered into the court records, a copy of which is to be sent to my solicitors, the sum of four thousand pounds will be delivered to Our Lady of Mercy convent. I would offer you more, but it is all the money I can lay my hands on at the moment. This you may use in any way you choose, but I imagine it will be no great sin if you decide to use a shilling or two to purchase a new nightcap."

Gabriel pulled an envelope from his pocket. "You will wonder at my sincerity, of course. It is one thing to make promises, quite another to deliver on them. And our previous encounter was not the sort upon which trust is built. So here is five hundred pounds in advance. I hope it may begin to alter your opinion of me."

Mother Dolores stared at the bank notes.

"Words fail you, do they?" Gabriel arched a brow. "I quite understand. And now I shall do a very risky thing. I shall release your gag and bindings, and then perhaps we can begin to discuss my proposition in earnest. There are one or two other items I have neglected to mention."

"I don't see why it has to be tonight," grumbled Lily, sitting in the landau with Rose and Daisy. "Besides, there is not enough room for us in this contraption. I should have stayed back with the children."

"Nonsense," barked Rose. "Mrs. Hanford has everything under control."

"You know that we have to act tonight because of the full moon," Daisy said. "Otherwise, it would be too dark to see. Louisa said—"

"I do not wish to hear any more about what Louisa said," Lily grumped.

Daisy gave her a long-suffering look. "Louisa has done this plenty of times, dear. We must trust in her judgment."

"I trust *her*, but I don't like that wild look

in Rose's eye. Any woman who did away with three husbands—"

"Is the woman you want on your side at a moment like this," Rose snapped. "Do be quiet, ladies. I believe that is the ship ahead."

Sam, who had been riding postilion on the lead horse, slid off and ran to take Midnight from Louisa.

"That boy has no business being involved in this," Lily said, quite out of sorts now. "He should have stayed behind with the other children."

Rose arched a brow. "He is no child, as you would have noticed if you had eyes for anyone other than yourself."

"You know, Rose, you are not as clever as you think," Lily retorted. "Sometimes, in fact, you are positively witless."

"Why, I never—"

As Louisa studied the spectral hulk that lurked ahead in the river, she could only hope that the wind prevented the guards from hearing the women's bickering. Lily and Rose usually rubbed along tolerably. But tonight, the tension had infected all of them. Louisa watched uneasily as David eased the traveling coach containing Jasmine and Violet into the shadows.

Though she rejoiced in David and Violet's happiness, she knew it meant the end of her missions. The Flowers were obviously not suited for clandestine activities. She would never have involved them tonight had Rose not ambushed her in the parlor and argued with unassailable logic that Louisa had no alternative plan.

If only Sinclair—but it was no use going down that road. He had made his choice, and who could blame him? After so narrow an escape from the hangman's noose, he could not afford to involve himself in such ventures.

Louisa tried to tamp down the sorrow that threatened to overwhelm her. She had no heart for this venture, nor for anything now that she and Sinclair had parted. Moreover, David had had another of his premonitions. This night had all the marks of a disaster in the making.

With five horses, two vehicles, and eight people in all, their little band of rescuers was about as subtle as an army. Already, there were ominous signs. They couldn't risk lanterns, so they had to rely on the moon to light their way. But the wind had whipped up, and a cloud was headed right for that full moon. Louisa prayed they wouldn't face another catastrophe like Alice's rescue. She was wearing breeches in case they had to make a run for it; she planned to use Midnight to distract the guards while the others fled to safety.

They gathered around to go over final instructions. Louisa tried to sound confident, but a sense of foreboding gripped her.

"When Jasmine and I lure the guard onto the gangway, Rose will pop him with the skillet. Lily and Daisy will tie him up. When the other guards come to check on him, we'll dispose of them in a similar fashion. But we must

be quiet. We don't wish to bring them down
on us all at once. After we've taken care of the
guards, Jasmine and I will search the ship for
the women."

It was a lame plan, but the best she could
devise when faced with so many willing vol-
unteers. Rose wielded an iron skillet with
magnificent effect, having learned the talent
while defending herself from her various husbands. Jasmine, with her full figure and doe
eyes, was an ideal decoy. They were to pretend to have lost their way and stumbled on
the hulk while looking for assistance.

Louisa had no illusions about the sort of assistance the guards might envision. By Alice's
account, they were an unsavory lot. But presumably they'd all had mothers. That was her
trump card.

"Any questions?" Louisa asked. "Remember: if we are not out in ten minutes, Daisy is
to come in, then Lily and Rose. As a last resort,
Violet will create her diversion." If a woman
giving birth at the end of the gangway didn't
move them, nothing would.

"What about me?" Sam asked, withdrawing
a small knife from his shoe. "I could sneak up
on those guards and—"

"You are to stay with the horses," Louisa
said. " 'Tis an important job," she added, seeing his crestfallen face. "Our getaway must be
swift."

Reluctantly, Sam put away his knife. Louisa
knew, if Sam did not, that there would be no
missions for him after tonight. From now on,

his duties would be limited to the stable.

Louisa caught David's eye. Though Violet had every expectation of appearing on the gangway on cue, Louisa and David had privately agreed she would have no part in the rescue and would remain in the carriage under his watchful eye. David himself would be a liability for now; his appearance in the midst of a group of seemingly helpless women would only alert the guards to the ruse. He was to stand ready at the carriage to drive Violet and the four prisoners to safety.

They were ready. Louisa tried to summon a mental image of the notes she'd hastily scribbled at Peabody Manor. She'd drawn a diagram of the ship from her memory of Alice's rescue, but her mind was so filled with images of Sinclair from that night she could scarcely concentrate.

With a sigh, Louisa moved toward the gangway.

"Wish I was back at Coldbath Fields." Captain Josiah Selby gave a bored yawn and took a swig of rum. He hated the hulk, hated the river's damp, hated that he spent his days and nights in charge of the dregs of society and a group of sodden guards vastly beneath him in every way. Sometimes he relieved his boredom by taking his pleasure with the female inmates—a whining lot, to be sure—though that lowered him to the level of the other guards, some of whom possessed notoriously unsavory tastes.

"That hellhole?" A guard spat on the floor. "Wretched place. Lost my arm in the aught-hundred riot."

The other guard nodded. "Prison's no place for politics. Look what happened at Newgate. Quaker reformers nearly turned it into a damned church. I hear the Duke of Gloucester attends Sunday services in the chapel."

Derisive guffaws followed this statement. The three men each took a swig from the bottle—though Selby was careful to wipe the rim before drinking after Tom and Bill. The trio turned their attention to the cards on the table.

Selby grunted. He had an inferior hand, which didn't matter much, since besting these louts was no great challenge, even with such a handicap.

"We're due a dozen more prisoners by the end of the week," he offered by way of an opening gambit. He had found that conversation distracted the others from their cards as well as covered the raucous sounds below deck that always made Selby feel slightly unclean.

"Hope there's women among them," said Tom. "Ain't a one of the wenches here can compare with Alice."

Privately, Selby agreed, but he kept silent. One of the fictions that made the tedious days and nights endurable was that he presided over a harem of women, each craving his masterful touch. That his underlings had ready access to the same women, he preferred not to acknowledge.

"To Alice, gents." Bill raised his glass. "A woman who understood her proper place."

"Deserves to be whipped for running off like that," groused Tom, whose well-known taste for punishment made him the only one among them truly happy with his assignment.

A silence followed, during which each man indulged in fond and considerably varied memories of the departed Alice. Just as Selby returned his attention to his cards, another guard entered the cabin. He was escorting two women.

"Found these two on the gangway, Captain," he said, his mouth curling in a sneer. "Claim to be damsels in distress or some such."

Selby studied the intruders. One wore a simple cotton frock and a brown shawl over what looked to be ripe, full breasts. Her dark hair fell gracefully over her shoulders, and her brown eyes looked calm and wise. The second woman was more slender of build and wore breeches that outlined a pair of lissome legs. Her golden hair was tied back at the nape of her neck. Her blue eyes radiated authority, and it was to her that Selby addressed his question.

"What is the trouble, ma'am?"

"We have lost our way," she said fretfully. "Our carriage struck a rock, and the wheel is damaged. We must get home. My sister is increasing and very near her time. I warned her against coming out tonight, but she was ever one for adventure. I do not wish to impose, sir, but we are in grave need of assistance."

Selby was intrigued. He'd never seen a woman in breeches and rather liked the view.

"Please excuse my odd appearance," she said, correctly reading his thoughts. "Our coachman is ailing. I thought to act the part myself, as I am a fair hand with the horses. But it seems I only got us lost."

There were not many people—females or otherwise—who would venture aboard a notorious prison hulk. The women were either wildly ignorant or possessed of uncommon daring. Either way, Selby decided, it could work to his advantage.

"And remiss we would be," he said gallantly, "if we failed to rise to the occasion. How many of you are there?"

"Four, including our poor sister who was so unwise as to leave her confinement."

"Ought to whip her," Tom said pleasantly.

"Pay him no mind." Selby shot Tom a stern look. "We have so little to keep us occupied at night I'm afraid our minds tend to wander."

The woman eyed him anxiously. "Would it trouble you so very much, sirs, to examine our carriage? There are no men among us to perform that service."

Selby's gaze narrowed. "I do not allow my guards off the ship at night. Every man is needed to safeguard the ship, for we harbor heinous criminals."

The woman looked startled. "Criminals? Oh, dear. I had not realized—"

"You need not worry," Selby quickly assured her. "They are under lock and key." He gestured to the wall peg, which held a large ring of keys.

"Perhaps you could spare just one man to come and inspect our carriage?" This came from the other woman, the one with the large breasts.

"Do sit for a moment, ladies, and tell me a bit more about your situation," Selby replied. Something about these two was not quite right. "May I pour you some wine?"

"There is no time," persisted the golden-haired woman. "My sister may be giving birth even now. Please. You must send someone."

Perhaps, Selby thought, they were prostitutes trying to make up for an evening that had been less than profitable. Or those gypsies that were notorious for haunting the docks. Or perhaps they truly had a broken wheel and a sister laboring to give birth, in which case they would be completely at his mercy. Whatever their motives, a seasoned captain of the guards could easily turn the situation to his advantage.

Suddenly, the night ahead looked much more interesting. Mayhap he would have them all—not the pregnant one, though. He had no taste for screaming women. That was in Tom's bailiwick.

The wine glasses Selby found in the table drawer looked filthy, but he doubted the women would be too particular. Just as he set them out, however, there came a great clamoring outside. The two women exchanged puzzled looks.

Selby reached for his carbine and dashed out onto the deck, followed by the other guards. At the strange apparition before them, they pulled up short.

More than two dozen women attired in flowing white robes stood in formation behind a larger, similarly attired woman with an imposing headdress.

"Sweet Jesus," Tom muttered. "It's a bunch of angels."

"Not angels, you idiot," Selby corrected. "Nuns."

The woman with the headdress regarded Tom with cold fury. "You, sir, ought to be whipped for taking the Lord's name in vain," she thundered.

When Tom gave a happy sigh, Selby knew it was time to regain control of the situation. "What is this about, Sister?" he demanded.

She drew herself up and regarded him over the tip of her bulbous nose. "We have heard," she said in a damning tone, "about the foul sins you foster and permit upon this vessel."

"Aw, hell," said Bill, rolling his eyes. "It's another reformer."

The woman eyed him contemptuously. "Now is your chance to redeem yourselves, to turn your backs on sin and release the martyred women upon whom you have visited the vilest of deeds."

"Release the women?" Selby scoffed. "You are mad, Sister. Take your flock and get off my ship. I have other business tonight."

She raked him with a condemning gaze. She did not budge, nor did the women behind her.

"If you do not leave, Sister—"

"Mother," she corrected disdainfully.

"—I shall have to shoot you." Selby waved his carbine in their direction, then turned away with a smirk. He wouldn't really shoot them—the reformers would have had a field day with that one—but he didn't mind scaring the wits out of them. The sooner they were gone, the sooner he could turn his attention to the women in his cabin. He'd have the flaxen-haired one first. She looked a bit more spirited, and he liked gumption in a woman. Tom and Bill would have to wait their turn—no more leavings for him.

As Selby was contemplating exactly how he would remove the woman's breeches, he heard the nun issue a strangely ominous command.

"Sit on them, girls!"

Damn, it was dark down here.

How he needed that full, fickle moon. The glass scuttle that served as a porthole picked up what little moonlight penetrated the surface of the murky river, but even so, Gabriel could barely see where he was going. He couldn't even find the controls without the candle, which was using precious air. No more than an hour of air was left. Far less, if he took on passengers, which—like a fool—he meant to.

How a month changed things.

On the scaffold that day at Newgate, he'd felt only the numbness acquired from a lifetime of tamping down the waves of fear and sorrow that had threatened to swamp him as a child. But Louisa had pushed and pushed until his world spun off its axis and split into relentless black and white with nothing of gray in between.

Louisa loved him. For her there was no middle ground. She made him want to be the man she loved.

He'd spent the last week working on the submersible, scrubbing and tinkering and oiling and praying he could make the craft seaworthy again. When he locked the sail into place and set his course, he'd not known whether the submersible would turn on him, repaying his years of neglect and scorn with a sudden fatal descent to the bottom of the sea.

But he'd made it from Sinclair Isle to the mouth of the Thames, deferring the tricky submersion until the last moment, because his skills were as rusty as the iron bolts reinforcing that copper skin. When at last he had slipped under the water with only the moon and the candle and the darkness as guides, a reckless joy filled him. What more could a man want?

Only a chance to go down as a hero, even if it was all a sham, maybe the biggest sham of all. Only a chance to discover whether it was possible to escape that all-consuming numbness.

Save yerself, angel. He'd written off the jeers and mockery as the scorn of jackals. Now he saw how perfectly the sentiment captured his goal: to save himself, and maybe win a piece of heaven in the process.

Disaster loomed on so many fronts. Perhaps he wouldn't be able to surface again. Perhaps he'd be blown to bits by a carefully aimed carbine. Perhaps someone who'd seen him before he submerged was even now sounding the alarm that England was being invaded by a madman riding a whale. Perhaps Mother Dolores's black heart had already betrayed him.

Suddenly, the spike came up against something hard and hung there like a pesky fly on a cow's underbelly. If his calculations were correct, he had reached his destination.

Working the rudders, Gabriel eased the submersible down and slightly away from the hulk's keel. His arm already ached from operating the propeller, which did not bode well for a speedy escape.

He was twenty feet deep, preparing to risk his life to rescue four felons he'd never met. All for Louisa's love. In the dank gloom of the craft that might be his tomb before the night was done, Gabriel grinned.

Was there a better reason?

Chapter 23

"There is an odd-looking group of women on that ship." Violet peered out the carriage window. "Why, I do believe they are nuns! Look, David. They are talking to the guards."

David frowned in consternation as he took in the scene on the deck of the hulk. He had parked the carriage close enough to see all that occurred but far enough so as not to be noticed by anyone on board. "Must be nigh thirty of them."

"I do not see Louisa and Jasmine, do you?"

"Nay."

Violet shifted awkwardly on the seat and reached for the door. "I believe I will just stretch my legs a bit."

David's hand clamped down on hers. "None of that," he warned. "If the guards insist on seeing Louisa's pregnant sister, then we'll give them a look at you. For now, you'll stay here." His arm curved protectively around her shoulders.

"But Rose and the others—"

"Are staying out of sight, like us. We can do naught as long as those nuns are there."

"What about Jasmine and Louisa—"

"They will be making the best of things. No harm can come to them while the nuns are there. You could nae ask for a better distraction." He shook his head. "I should never have allowed you to come tonight."

"I am my own person, David Ferguson." She glared at him. " 'Twas my decision to come and mine alone."

"Aye." He eyed her darkly. "What am I going to do with ye, lass?"

Impulsively, Violet reached up and stroked his cheek. She loved the feel of those coarse whiskers that defied even the sharpest razor. "As to that," she said, nestling against his chest, "I've a few ideas."

David reddened and looked away. "I can nae be a man to you, Violet. I'm content with what we have. 'Tis more than I ever dreamed of. Holding you at night—"

"Is a start," she agreed. "And if it is all we ever have, 'tis more kindness than I've known in a lifetime. But I think there is more for us, David. Much more."

"Nay, lass. Do not tempt the heavens by asking for more than we've a right to claim."

Violet ran her fingertip along the long, jagged scar that disappeared into his shirt. " 'Tis no sin to wish to share the pleasures of the flesh with a loved one."

"Wishing is one thing—"

"And doing is another. Yes, I know." Violet

toyed with the edges of his shirt. "May I touch you, David, the way I have wanted to touch you all these nights?"

The longing in his eyes almost broke her heart. " 'Tis no use, Violet. I am only half a man."

"Touch the babe, David." Violet caught his hand and placed it on the fullest part of her belly.

" 'Tis a privilege to feel that life within you." Emotion suffused his voice as he stared at his hand, then sorrowfully removed it from her abdomen.

"Don't pull away," she pleaded. "You have good, strong hands. They were made for a woman's body."

He glowered. " 'Tis a cruel jest, lass."

"I was not joking," Violet said softly. "I love your hands. I love them touching me." Again he looked away, and she sighed. " 'Tis not your fault that you survived that horrible prison while other men were maimed. You must shed this guilt, David. 'Tis robbing you of every pleasure."

His tormented gaze held hers. "When my strength was most needed, I was helpless as a lamb. Every night I'd hear the screams, and stare at those bars on my cell, and know that I could have stopped them if I'd been man enough."

"Even you can't rip apart steel bars. What happened to those men was horrible, but it was not your fault. This guilt you bear has deprived you of the happiness you deserve."

He said nothing. Hot anger filled Violet, anger for what he had suffered, for what they had both endured. "Bloody hell, David," she said furiously. "You might as well have stayed in prison."

His eyes widened in shock.

She leveled a gaze at him. "I'll never forget what Will did to me, never. But for every time he hit or betrayed me, I'm going to kiss you, David. And you'll see. 'Twill be all right."

"I wish I had your faith," he said bleakly.

"You have more than you think." Violet unbuttoned the top of her loose-fitting bodice. "Look at me, David. My breasts are great with the milk that will nourish the babe."

"Good God. What are you doing, Violet?" He stared at her as if she had lost her wits. And perhaps she had, for her insides burned with need, robbing her of all rational thought.

"Feel how they swell with love for the babe." Violet caught his hand and brought it to her breast. "Here, David. Touch me here."

His trembling fingers grazed the swell of one breast. He closed his eyes, as if in pain. "Do nae do this," he groaned. "It can only make us yearn for what is impossible."

Violet placed his fingers over one nipple, which immediately puckered into a hard, round nub. She sighed in longing. "Perhaps you could touch the other one, too. I fear it is a bit jealous."

David's stark gaze slammed into hers. "They are beautiful, Violet."

"They won't always be this big," she murmured apologetically. "I'm told that after one nurses, they shrink and shrivel in the worst way. Do you think you would still care to touch them when they are small and shriveled?"

David stared at his hands, which, seemingly of their own accord, continued to caress her breasts, weighing them, measuring them as if they were priceless treasures. Slowly he ran his thumbs over Violet's nipples, teasing them until they were proud, erect, and weeping with pleasure.

"Aye," he said roughly. "I should still care to touch them. God, Violet, have you any notion what you are doing to me? We must stop this."

"No. Not yet. Maybe never." She kissed the tips of his fingers, letting her tongue linger over them as if they were a rare delicacy.

David groaned. *"Violet."*

"Are . . . are the nuns still there?"

David ripped his gaze from her and looked out the window. "Aye. It looks like they've damned near taken over the ship." His low, animal growl thrilled her.

"We have time, then." She moved his hand to her abdomen, but when he would have lingered there, she slipped his hand under her skirts so that it rested on her bare thigh. Slowly, she guided his hand upward.

His eyes closed in tortured pleasure. "You are soft and smooth, like nothing I've touched before," he said hoarsely. "You are . . . perfection."

"That is how you feel to me," she murmured. "You are rough in the places I am smooth. I love that roughness and the tenderness underneath. I love you, David. Forever and always."

"Violet." He whispered her name like a prayer.

"I am yours," she whispered. "I shall die if you do not touch me."

David held her gaze and dared to hope.

And when at last his hand moved of its own accord to the place that burned for him, Violet gave herself over to his ministrations. It did not surprise her in the least to discover that he knew precisely what he was doing.

As she moaned in pleasure, Violet groped blindly for that most masculine part of him and found that it, too, was swollen with precious new life.

Clutching the ring of keys she had plucked from the guard cabin, Louisa crept toward the hatch that led down to the lower decks. Jasmine followed silently.

Louisa couldn't begin to guess why those nuns had come to the hulk. The distraction they caused had provided the perfect opportunity she and Jasmine needed to search the ship, but they had to move quickly. Any guards elsewhere on the ship would soon hear the commotion.

The next deck down was dark and forbidding. A few lanterns hung on pegs, but they merely kept the shadows at bay without dispelling the oppressive sense of gloom and decay. A whiff of briny air wafted through a square, partially covered opening in the ship's side.

Square. The holes are square.

Of course. These were the gun ports Sinclair had spoken of that day in her drawing room. The same ports he had breached the very next night.

How little she had known then of him then. A rootless renegade, she had thought, and time had proven that so. She had given herself to a man unable to commit himself to anything lasting.

People don't change, he had told her. But that hadn't stopped her from wishing that her love could spark a desire in him to claim her for all time.

A small voice inside her made a disapproving sound. *Most unfair to expect him to change when you aren't willing to do so yourself.*

Louisa frowned. A woman didn't abandon every principle she held dear just because a man made her heart sing in a way she had never dreamed possible.

Quite the lofty one, aren't you? Shouldn't wonder if the weight of all that self-righteousness is too much to bear.

She looked around. It was almost as if someone else was here on this ship, taking her to task. And that insistent inner voice bore Sinclair's insolent irony.

"Is everything all right?" Jasmine, calm as always, placed a hand on her shoulder.

"Yes." Louisa forced herself to concentrate on the matter at hand. "Sinclair thought the women might be on the gun deck near the guards' cabins. 'Tis where he found Alice."

"But Alice was willing," Jasmine pointed out. "The other women might not have received such privileged accommodations." She tilted her head, listening. "I suppose we will find them down there." She pointed to the sturdy planking beneath their feet.

Now Louisa knew why she had been concentrating so hard on that imaginary voice in her head. She had not wanted to hear the real voices, the sounds that emanated from the bowels of the ship and which were beyond imagining. Cries of anger, scorn, and helpless torment floated upward, muffled by that thick oak planking.

Beneath them, on one of those stifling lower decks, perhaps even in the hold, the inmates lived in the closest thing to hell on earth.

Trembling, Louisa walked to the hatch that would take them into that abysmal pit. A flat iron bar lay across the opening. It would take both of them to lift it. Not for the first time, she wished that Sinclair were here.

A bit late for that, isn't it? that inner voice chided.

Louisa gritted her teeth and reached for the bar.

Gabriel perched on the top of the submersible, now floating on the surface. From down here, where the river lapped gently at the submersible's rusty iron stays, it looked as though the hulk's gun ports were nailed shut. Evidently, the guards had not forgotten his last visit.

Still, a deck without air could be stifling, and since several of the guards undoubtedly had cabins on the gun deck, it was likely that some of the ports were open. He couldn't be sure in the darkness; he'd have to start at the bow and work his way back. He checked to make sure the iron scraper was tied securely to his waist and that his knife was at hand.

Gabriel shinnied up the anchor cable easily enough, but the rake over the port flanges looked as if it had been nibbled by a horde of seafaring termites. Edging carefully over each port, he used his scraper to confirm his suspicion: the covers had been nailed shut.

He looked down. The submersible rode low in the water, hitched to the hulk's anchor cable by a piece of hemp he'd found in the cave. Up here, balanced precariously a dozen yards above the Thames, Gabriel suddenly realized he no longer felt numb.

There was fear, for this night might end in his death, and loss—acute loss—because Louisa had left him. The loss was far worse than the fear. It burned like a wound inside him, festering and aching for surcease. But there was something else, too: exhilaration.

Damned if he didn't have it in him to be a hero after all. Damned if he wouldn't win her back by a stunning exhibition of his bravery.

His feet slipped.

Just as he pitched forward, Gabriel caught the flange of the next gun port. One of his feet caught the port lip. For a precarious moment, he hung there, suspended in space, his fingers clutching the flange as his foot tried to stake a claim on the narrow lip. Beneath him, the river yawned invitingly.

Gabriel pulled himself up slowly, testing every balance point to maintain the delicate harmony between disaster and salvation. At last he stood on the port lip and wedged his scraper into a gap—the smallest of gaps, but an opening, nevertheless. And then, though he still clung to the rotted ship by the slenderest of threads, the fear left him.

When a man stares death in the face, he has to ask himself exactly what he is dying for. Gabriel already knew. He had made his choice, made it some time ago, in fact. Faced with risking his life or losing Louisa, it had been no choice at all.

Louisa loved him. And if the only thing heroic about him was her love, that was more than any other man possessed. She had given him a priceless treasure. He had failed to recognize it in time and deserved to be whipped for his stupidity, but not, surely, tonight.

Tonight he would send his prayers heavenward and trust in love to make him what he had never, ever been: a man strong enough to embrace love, even if it hurt like hell, and who could, with love at his back, dare the impossible.

He pried the cover loose, and elation filled

him. If this night didn't bring Louisa back to him, there was no justice in the world.

His feet hit the deck. He stepped into the relentless gloom of the stinking hulk. And, cruel irony, there was Louisa.

Running for her life.

Five women were with her, only one of them fully clothed. He recognized her as Jasmine, but it was a fleeting impression, lost in the horror of the realization that they were being chased by two guards and a frantic mob of naked convicts clawing at the women in a wild frenzy.

One of the guards lifted a carbine and drew a bead on Louisa.

Gabriel pulled out his knife and with a hoarse cry threw it straight and true at the knave who dared harm her.

The knife hit the guard in the throat. The carbine fell to the floor. The women began to scramble up the ladder to the upper deck. As each woman gained the hatch opening, white-draped arms reached down and pulled them to safety. Mother Dolores had never seemed so heaven-sent.

Jasmine followed, then Louisa. The hatch slammed shut, and the bar locked in place, cutting off those shrieking, desperate souls from the upper deck.

But no, Louisa hadn't followed. She stood on the bottom rung of the ladder, staring at him as if he were a ghost. Then, as the mob closed around her, she broke away from the clawing hands and ran full tilt into his arms.

"Oh, Gabriel! It was horrid!" she sobbed. "They'd been stripped—all of them, all the prisoners—and the guards were laughing as if it were a great lark."

"Louisa—"

"They didn't notice Jasmine and me until I opened the women's cell and dropped the keys. I couldn't help it—my hands were shaking so—and one of the prisoners reached through the bars and got the keys. Then they were all rushing at us and grabbing. It was awful!"

Gabriel held her roughly, fleetingly treasuring the feel of her against his chest, for it was almost too late to save themselves. Hands tore at their clothes, and bony fingers grabbed Louisa's arm. Just as the hands closed around her, Gabriel shoved Louisa through the gun port to the darkness and water below. He kicked out at his assailant, who bared his teeth like a crazed animal, and leapt into the river after her.

A rush of air, the welcoming shock of cold water, and he was free, blessedly free, of the hulk.

He fought his way to the surface and looked up to see that none of their pursuers had been crazy enough to follow them into the river. In another minute, he and Louisa would be in the submersible, where no one could track them. Mother Dolores's flock had things well in hand up above; his mission was complete.

Euphoria filled him. He had done it—*they* had done it. Against all odds, they had risked everything and emerged victorious.

Then he remembered: Louisa did not swim.

And the dark depths of the Thames were notoriously unfriendly. Especially at night.

Louisa fought her panic. She let herself go limp and tried not to flail about. Surely Sinclair would find her. But the water was deep and cold and so very, very black.

Her lungs burned; she could not hold her breath much longer. She moved her hands ineffectually, trying to remember how Sinclair had used his when he plucked her from the river a lifetime ago. She was cold, horribly cold. Desperately, she tried to propel herself upward, but the river's icy fingers sucked her down.

How do you like your principles now? A bit soggy, eh?

That inner voice again, taunting her even in death. *He came through for you, didn't he? You ought to have had faith. Not to mention a few swimming lessons.*

Blackness overwhelmed her, and Louisa knew this was her last moment of awareness before final oblivion. Her heart filled with love for Sinclair, and she wished with her final breath that she could tell him so.

And though that was to be denied her, Sinclair was in her heart and in that insistent inner voice that chided and prodded her. Though she would never see him again, she had never felt closer to him. She prayed that somehow he would know she died with love for him in her heart.

Coming it a bit too brown, dear. Get those feet and arms moving before you turn into a bloated piece of flotsam. Up! That's the ticket. Push!

Slowly, sluggishly, she tried again to move her arms and legs as she had seen Sinclair do. But she was tired, so very tired. She couldn't do it. She couldn't.

Louisa broke the surface at the precise moment that her strength ran out. She had just enough time to gulp in air before the water closed over her again.

This time she didn't sink. This time two strong arms gathered her in, and when Louisa opened her eyes, she was plummeting head first into the mouth of something that looked like an enormous fish.

The submersible.

Sinclair tumbled in after her, but he didn't even glance at her. She heard a loud clang as he sealed the hatch, then a whirring sound. He worked some levers with one hand, the propeller with the other. The submersible gave a great shudder . . . and began to move.

They were safe. Her prayers had been answered. The future, whatever it might be, lay before them like a blossom ready to come into full flower.

Longing and happiness filled her. She was glad Sinclair hadn't yet spoken, for there was so much she wanted to say first. For now, though, she was content to recover the soggy remnants of her strength.

An abrupt grating sound reverberated through the craft. Her heart lurched. "What is that?"

"The horizontal rudder is not working." Sinclair stared savagely at the lever under his hand. "We are sinking."

"That's all right, isn't it?" she ventured. "It's what the submersible is designed to do."

"No. And yes."

Louisa waited, hardly daring to breathe. He pulled violently at one of the levers, but it did not budge. He turned to her, his expression grim.

"The craft is designed for a depth of twenty-five feet. By the time we reach the mouth of the river, we'll be in water almost four times that. If we descend that far, we'll be crushed."

"I don't understand."

"We'll implode. The pressure outside the craft will become so great that it will crush us."

"Can't we get out?"

"No. The pressure outside now is too great."

Louisa stilled. Other than that loud grating sound, the submersible seemed to be operating normally. It moved smoothly through the water, slipping steadily deeper—

"Exactly." Sinclair read her thoughts. "We're already at thirty feet."

"My God."

"Or mine." He shot her a ragged smile. "It doesn't seem to make much difference, does it?"

Chapter 24

So a man couldn't count on anything really, not in this world. The payback for all his cocky daring was to learn once again that nothing is permanent, that the people you love can be ripped from you without notice. Reason enough for a man to turn his back on the world, to flee to the ends of the earth to avoid the losses sure to come.

Gabriel stared at the levers, rusty and rotted as that damned prison hulk. He had dared to think the impossible was possible, and he had almost made it, save for that broken horizontal rudder. Now they were sinking and sinking fast.

Faith. How did a man get it? And what was he supposed to do once he realized that even if he braved the fires of hell and the wrath of an angry mob, the victory might be meaningless? There were no guarantees in life or in love. A man couldn't be sure that something wouldn't come around to destroy what he had worked so hard to win.

How was he supposed to accept that truth?

"Gabriel." Louisa's voice, soft and sure, drew him from the abyss. Gabriel pulled her into his arms.

"I am sorry, Louisa," he rasped. "So very sorry."

"Can nothing be done?"

"I wish to hell I knew."

She wrapped her arms around him and was silent.

Gabriel kissed the top of her head. "I love you. Whatever else, there is that."

"That is everything," she murmured.

"No, it's not, damn it all!" His hands balled in fists. "It's *not* enough. Don't you see? We are sinking to our doom. I want a lifetime of you, Louisa. Even that would be too short, but I never expected it would end here, now."

"Kiss me, Gabriel. I don't care about the rest."

Kissing her was the sweetest pain he had ever known. The knowledge that soon there would be no air to sustain them and that they would be crushed, their lives snuffed out like insignificant creatures in a meaningless sea of existence, was almost too much to bear.

But he *would* bear it, because she deserved that from him. He would be strong, because he had promised himself he would be strong enough to embrace her love, to stand with it at his back and slay dragons. Even if it hurt, he would claim her love and give it back a thousand times more.

He covered her with kisses. He wrapped her in his arms, as if they could keep her safe for all time. And though he was just a mere mortal flinging his helpless rage at the heavens, he had this love and her. What was between them would last for all time—all the time that mattered, anyway. Not even death could change that.

Got a bit of your own back, didn't you?

Gabriel went still.

Thought you could slip by without paying the piper, but no one does that. And now you think you can thumb your nose at death, just like you've been thumbing your nose at everything these last ten years.

"Shut up," he muttered.

Louisa looked at him. "What?"

"Sometimes I talk to myself." He tried to smile. "I suppose I inherited my father's madness after all."

"What if you did? Who's to say what is sane and what is not? Sometimes I think we're all a bit mad."

"Some more than others," he said grimly.

"Gabriel." Louisa clutched the drenched fabric of his shirt. "Do you believe in second chances?"

"No." But even as he rejected the notion, that gallows scene came hurtling at him across the days and nights and love that had passed between them since.

Might have made something of my life. . . . It's late to make promises. . . . No, I don't mean a word of them. . . . Wouldn't have minded one last chance.

One last chance. To get it right. But he'd been given that. And squandered it.

"I believe," she said fiercely. "I believe in grace."

"Grace?"

"A reprieve. A pardon. A lucky roll of the dice—only you wonder whether it's luck or part of some larger scheme."

"Louisa—"

"That day on the scaffold. What made them put your execution ahead of Alice's? What brought us together that day, Gabriel? Have you ever wondered?"

He stared at her.

"We're meant to be. And if it means that this is the last moment we'll ever know, at least we have each other."

"Yes, well, I'd like to have a little more air, a rudder that works, and about ninety-nine more years to think about it."

She smiled. "I love you, Gabriel."

I'd take up my seat in Parliament, turn all those lords against slavery. Even rebuild the manor, though not that god-awful temple. I'd do it all, if I could have Louisa. Otherwise, life's not worth living.

He cradled her in his arms and wondered whether he was due a miracle. Because they were going to need one to get out of this fix.

No deals, Sinclair.

He swore softly.

"Gabriel?"

But he wasn't listening. He had just thought of something. Maybe it would work and maybe it wouldn't, but it was worth a try. A man had to try. Even if it seemed that the heavens were against him.

"I can't change the descent, but I *can* change our direction." Gabriel eyed the vertical rudder, which, as far as he knew, still worked. "If I can steer us close enough to one of those big ships in the harbor, we might just clip it on the way down."

Louisa shook her head. "I don't understand."

"A collision might open a hole. If enough water seeped in, it would equalize the pressure. We'd have to wait until the cabin filled so I could open the hatch and—if we weren't killed on the spot—swim us to safety. It's a gamble. Hell, we'd need a miracle."

"What would happen as we took on water?"

"We'd sink even faster. The trick would be to get the hatch open before we sank too deep."

"I see." She smiled tremulously. "We have nothing to lose, do we?"

"Hell, no."

"Then roll the dice, Sinclair."

They locked gazes, and in that heart-stopping moment, Gabriel knew that his entire world was contained in her eyes. Even if he failed to save them, which was likely, he would die with her name on his lips and her love in his soul. It was worth his life to know that one simple truth.

He had no idea how far downriver they had drifted. The big ships that unloaded their cargo at the East End docks might be near or miles away. The odds of ramming one of them were terrible. On the other hand, they were better than nothing.

Feverishly, he worked the vertical rudder. Their air supply was almost gone. Louisa leaned against the bulkhead, her face pale and her limpid blue eyes fading into a glassy emptiness. Gabriel hated what this had done to her. What *he* had done to her. If they ever got out of this mess, he'd insist that she spend the rest of her life with servants at her beck and call. He'd never allow her out of his sight.

They had to ride the currents, because the effort required to crank the propeller used up precious air. Gabriel gave a silent prayer of thanks for his father's steering compass and the permanently magnetized needle that worked as well now as it had ten years ago.

At first, he tried to work them north, toward the docks, but the current was strong and carried them east too fast. At this rate, they'd end up in France, he thought grimly. So he tried to work them southeast, hoping to make Sheerness or thereabout before his strength evaporated.

The crash knocked him off his feet.

Then came the tearing of metal, the snap of the iron stays, and the sudden whooshing of water. It rushed in faster than he wanted, fast enough to drown them like rats caught in a rain-soaked stream that suddenly turns ugly.

Whatever they had hit peeled the submersible's copper skin like a paring knife. Within seconds, the water lapped greedily around his knees, seeking to consume them as it rose. Gabriel pulled Louisa to her feet and prayed she would not panic as the water moved higher, fast turning the little craft into a waterlogged coffin.

As the water buoyed them upward, Gabriel put his hands around Louisa's waist and held her securely against him. She gave him a weak smile, but the strength had gone out of her. She looked tired, fearful, and resigned.

"I'm going to try to open the hatch now," he said gently. "Put your arms around me and don't let go."

Her eyes widened with fear, but she nodded and locked her arms around his neck.

"That's it," he murmured approvingly. "You're a fighter. A little longer, and I'll have you safe." Their chances of survival were slim to none, but her eyes held trust and a faith that awed him.

Suddenly, it didn't matter about the odds. A man who believed in love had the most precious gift of all. Nothing else mattered—not the future, not the past; only the loving.

Gabriel pulled the hatch lever with every ounce of his strength. It didn't budge. "Not enough pressure inside yet." He tried to sound reassuring. "It should open in another minute."

Which was about all they had. The last pocket of air occupied a few precious inches around their heads.

"Breathe in as much as you can, then hold

your breath," he told her. "I'll try to surface quickly."

She nodded. His hand closed over the hatch lever. It moved ever so slightly.

"This is it," he warned. "Hold on tight." As the water edged relentlessly toward their last pocket of air, he locked one arm around Louisa and thrust the hatch open.

They shot out of the submersible like cannonballs. Up and up he swam them toward the life-giving air. His lungs burned like the fires of hell, and he could only imagine what Louisa was feeling. Cold, dark, treacherous, the river wrapped its deadly arms around them, seeking one last embrace that would hold them forever in its thrall.

At the last moment, as he was certain they were lost, they cleared the surface. They clung to each other and swallowed air in great hungry gulps. But it wasn't over yet. He still had to get his bearings and swim them to safety before fatigue swamped him.

Night covered them like a shroud. Other than the stars, there was precious little to guide them. They might be a few yards out or many miles. He saw no sign of a boat, so the submersible had probably struck rocks, not another vessel. That meant the odds were better than even that they were near a coastline, but it was impossible to tell.

Gabriel shot Louisa a crooked smile as he shifted her around onto his back. "Best odds we've had all night. Put your arms around my neck and hold on."

"Tired," she said weakly. "So tired."

"Hold on, dammit," he growled. "I want a lifetime with you, Louisa, and by God, I'm going to have it."

Louisa clung to his neck, and he swam. Into the night, headed for the invisible shore that had to be there beyond lethal tides and murderous rocks. A safe harbor where he and his love could lie.

He was beyond fatigue, beyond feeling the aching muscles that had been called upon to do so much. But though his strength should have long since reached its limit, his body tapped reserves he hadn't known existed. His lungs and muscles worked smoothly, rhythmically, effortlessly—as if he were carrying only his weight instead of Louisa's, too.

A strange calm enveloped him.

If there were riptides, he didn't find them. If there were perilous sharks and devil rays, he didn't find those, either. He knew then that he'd been given one more chance. Grace, faith, a miracle—whatever it was, he would hold it close and never let it go.

He swam endlessly, not knowing if a night or a day or an hour had passed. When at last his feet touched the smooth, sandy beach, he knew he was home.

Stumbling out of the water, Gabriel let the brackish Kent air fill his soul. As he placed Louisa gently on the sand, he felt like the king of the world.

Damned if he didn't believe that love had saved them.

*   *   *

Dawn crept quietly over the beach, painting the sky in shades of blush and rose. Louisa opened her eyes and drank in the start of a new day.

Sinclair was staring at the horizon, seeing things she couldn't. The past. His father. Perhaps even the ghost of that old submersible. Louisa studied him, marveling how all this time he had hidden his exquisite strength, kept it to himself, leaving her to learn for herself the dint of his will and stamina. That biting wit, that careless air, that effortless charm—they had hidden a man of such courage and grit that she wouldn't have believed it had she not witnessed it herself.

She had loved him before, when he had shown her the worst of himself and been brave enough to trust her with his pain. Now she could only stare in awe. He had saved her life many times over, but that was the least of what Gabriel Sinclair had accomplished this day.

With breathtaking daring, he had given himself completely—to death, to love, embracing them both—and in doing so, lowered the walls he had so diligently erected around his soul. She wondered if he felt this strange new wholeness that engulfed them. The night and the sea had cleansed them of all but their love for each other. In speechless wonder, Louisa watched the dawn slip across that wide expanse of sky. She had never felt more alive.

He looked over and saw she was awake.

"Breakfast is fresh seaweed," he said softly. "It tastes just like Daisy's cooking, so you will feel at home."

The waves lapped lazily at her feet. Louisa stretched her legs and wiggled her toes in the sand. "As long as I'm with you, anywhere is home."

His expression clouded, and he looked away. "I'd never be a proper husband."

"I'd never be a proper wife."

"Damn it all." He buried his fist in the sand. "I'll take up my seat in Parliament, do my civic duty and all that. But not the rest, not the meddling. I'm too selfish." His jaw clenched. "I don't want to share you with anyone—not even the Flowers or the women from that miserable hulk. I can't take the risk you'll be harmed."

He took a deep breath and leveled a dark, swirling gaze at her. "You'll have to stop meddling, Louisa. That is all I'll ever ask of you, but I will ask it."

Louisa was silent. "And what will you give me in return?" she asked softly.

His fierce gaze impaled her. "My love. My devotion. My loyalty. All those things I never dreamed I could give." He hesitated. "Maybe a family, though I don't know what kind of father I'd—"

"A wonderful one."

Again he looked away, toward something on the horizon only he could see. "I might rebuild the submersible," he said at last. "There are a few design flaws, but it has potential. My father always wondered how to manage the increased water pressure at greater depths. Perhaps I'll find a way."

She held her breath. "The house—would you want to rebuild that, too?"

"Perhaps. But not that damned temple." He turned to her. "I don't want to recreate the past, Louisa, just come to terms with it."

"I think you have."

"Hell. You'll marry me, won't you?"

To spend the rest of her life with Sinclair— it was almost too much to absorb. They had been so close to disaster, and now this—a new dawn, rich with possibilities. Still, she hesitated. "I've always been a meddler. I don't know if I can stop."

"Yes or no?" he demanded in a ragged voice. "Will you marry me?"

"Yes."

He pulled her into his arms, surrounding her with his strength, murmuring his love like a prayer. For a long while they did not speak. But at last he ended the embrace and regarded her with a rueful expression.

"About the meddling; righting wrongs doesn't have to mean dodging bullets or a watery grave. We could work in Parliament, in political gatherings."

"You would turn yourself into a reformer?" She eyed him skeptically.

He grinned. She had always loved his lopsided grin. Reckless and wild, it held a self-mocking amusement, as if he was laughing at some wry joke on himself only he understood.

"No," he said, nuzzling her ear. "But *you* might turn me into one. I'd follow you anywhere."

A sudden shaft of desire shot through her. Exhaling slowly, she tried to rein in her longing as she searched for the words to make him understand. "Then follow me, Sinclair. Follow me home."

"For a day or two, perhaps." He ran his fingers along the length of her arm. "I need to go to London, to settle things with my father's solicitors and make certain Mother Dolores has cleared my name."

"Mother Dolores?" Louisa frowned. "Does she have something to do with those nuns last night?"

"Perhaps I'll also pay a visit to Lord Upton, so that he doesn't drag his feet on the settlements."

"He wouldn't dare." She closed her eyes and savored the feel and scent of him here in the sun and the sand. "You aren't going to tell me, are you? About the nuns."

"It can wait," he murmured, nibbling at her ear. "I figure we're just opposite Sheerness, at the mouth of the Medway. We'll make Peabody Manor by afternoon." He planted a kiss in the sensitive hollow of her neck. "Let's tarry a while. I want to make love to you. And celebrate everything that we came so close to losing."

"No."

He stilled. "*No?*"

"I don't want to go to Peabody Manor. Take

me *home*, Gabriel. To Sinclair Castle."

She threw her arms around his neck.

"Give me your love, Sinclair," she said fiercely. "Give me your devotion and loyalty. Give me a strange ship that sails under the water and a cave to put it in. And your dreams—I want those too. All of them. Give me a home. A family. That most of all."

He arched a brow. A slow grin spread over his features. "You want the world, it seems."

"I *have* the world," she corrected. "It's you, Sinclair. Only you."

Tenderly, he laid her back in the sand. "It's *you*, Louisa. And a miracle or two thrown in for good measure."

As he kissed her, the wind whispered a sweet melody that swirled around them like a benediction. Something brilliant and wonderful filled her heart with its song. It might have been only a seagull heralding the new day.

Or the angels, rejoicing.

Epilogue

To no one's surprise, the name Sinclair became synonymous with meddling. Gabriel took his seat in Parliament and worked to end slavery and improve prison conditions. Louisa founded a ladies' society devoted to achieving equitable treatment for women. Both were frequently called upon to advise King George IV and later Queen Victoria on social issues of the day.

With the money from the sale of Sinclair Isle, Gabriel restored the family estate in Kent, except for the temple, which he turned into a playhouse for their children. Before he put hammer to nail, however, Gabriel insisted on teaching Louisa to swim—a skill she eventually mastered, though not without a great deal of trepidation.

Violet and David adopted baby Elizabeth and built a new house to accommodate their growing brood. Their firstborn, Bonnie Hyacinth Ferguson, arrived in the world the morning after the hulk rescue.

Louisa deeded Peabody Manor over to Rose and the other Flowers. The rescues of downtrodden women continued under Rose's capable direction. Two of the women from the hulk joined the group, taking the names Camellia and Marigold. A third elected to join Mother Dolores and her band of novitiates, who were frequently seen at the Old Bailey, testifying in glowing terms to the character of various female defendants, or at Our Lady of Mercy School, which Mother Dolores founded to educate poor young women.

Alice was eventually transported to Australia, as was the fourth woman from the hulk (whose name, unfortunately, escaped this record), in lieu of being hanged for yet another crime. Lord Upton died of a malady acquired during too-frequent congress with the ladies of the Covent Garden set.

Three summers after the restoration of Sinclair Manor, Gabriel completed work on a twenty-seven-foot-long submersible that could descend to a depth of eighty feet. He called it the Aloysius Sinclair Submersible Marine Vessel, later known simply as Sinclair's Sub-Marine.

After his family, it was his pride and joy.

Author's Note

We think of the submarine as a modern invention, but it was hundreds of years in the making. Today's subs owe their existence to the remarkable inventors who looked at the impossible and saw the future.

The concept of a diving bell dates to the late fifteenth century, but it is to a sixteenth-century Englishman, William Bourne, that we owe the notion of a vessel that could submerge to evade or fight an enemy. Cornelius Drebbel, a Dutchman, made the first submersible boat to Bourne's design. It looked like two conventional boats, one inverted on top of the other, with holes cut out for twelve oars and fitted glass windows for the oarsmen. In 1620, Drebbel staged a public demonstration of the boat in the Thames. Some accounts claim that Drebbel's patron, King James I, took a trial run in the craft, but this is probably a tale grown taller with the telling.

In the 1770s, American David Bushnell invented a tiny, egg-shaped ship, the *Turtle*, that was propelled by hand-operated screws. Valves let in water for the descent; a pump forced water out for the ascent. In 1776, the *Turtle* tried to blow up a British ship in New York Harbor; the British spotted it, and the attack failed.

Robert Fulton, another American, brought the submarine nearer to something the modern world might recognize. His *Nautilus,* completed in 1801, used a folding mast and collapsible sail for propulsion on the surface, a hand-cranked propeller underwater. A vertical spike held the submersible in place under an enemy ship long enough to deliver an explosive charge, known as a torpedo (named after an electric stingray). Fulton used bottled compressed air to enable his ship to stay underwater for hours. In 1810 Fulton persuaded Congress to put up $5,000 for a steam-powered submarine, but he died before technical difficulties with the craft could be resolved.

Over the years, privateers, spies, and adventurers flirted with variations on the submarine—often with disastrous results. One crew, on a bet, descended to a depth of twenty-two fathoms (132 feet) and was crushed by the pressure. It was left to Wilhelm Bauer, a Bavarian, to discover how to escape from a sunken submarine in 1851. When he hit bottom at sixty feet, his craft sprang a leak. He forced his crew to wait for six hours as water seeped in until the pressure inside the craft matched the external water pressure—whereupon the hatches could be opened. The crew shot to the surface in their own air bubble.

Semisubmersibles like the ironclad *Monitor* and the *David,* and the submersible *H.L. Hunley* were used in the American Civil War. From there it is a short jump to Robert Whitehead, an Englishman who developed the modern torpedo.

In 1870 the British purchased the rights to manufacture Whitehead's designs, which were tested, as it happens, off the coast of Sheerness in Kent.

Dear Reader,

Karen Ranney's love stories are so filled with passion and emotion, that once you open one of her Avon books I can't imagine you'll want to put it down. In next month's MY BELOVED, Karen spins an unforgettable love story between the convent-bred Juliana and Sebastian, a man haunted by the demons of his past. Wed when they were mere children, Sebastian refuses to share a bed with his wife. Can she break down the walls that keep them from surrendering to a passion neither can deny?

Readers of contemporary romance won't want to miss Patti Berg's delicious WIFE FOR A DAY. Samantha Jones needs money desperately, so when she meets millionaire Jack Remington she agrees to his wild proposal—pretend to be his fiancee for one night...no hanky-panky allowed. But when the night is over Samantha finds it nearly impossible to say goodbye...

THE MACKENZIES are one of Avon's most beloved series, and now Ana Leigh brings you another one of these wild-western men: JAKE. Jake Carrington is determined to win pert Beth MacKenzie any way he can...even luring her into marriage with a proposition she cannot refuse.

A dashing rogue, a young Duchess, and a Regency setting all add up to another fresh, exciting love story by Malia Martin, THE DUKE'S RETURN. Sara Whitney has no desire to marry again, especially not to rakish Trevor Phillips...but she has no choice but to surrender herself to him.

I know you're going to love each of these unforgettable Avon romances. And, until next month, I wish you happy reading!

Lucia Macro

Lucia Macro
Senior Editor

ael 0799